Readers Love K.L. HIERS

Acsquidentally in Love

"Hiers rolls worldbuilding mythology, delicious flirting, erotic scenes, and detective work into a breezy and sensual LGBTQ paranormal romance."
—Library Journal

Kraken My Heart

"This is a really good series. It is one that is worth reading over again, just for the fun of it."
—Love Bytes Book Reviews

Nautilus Than Perfect

"If you're new to the series - WHAT the hell are you waiting for, go and read the first book!"
—Reading Under the Rainbow

Just Calamarried

"Sloane and Loch are so crazy in love that you can feel it."
—Virginia Lee Book Reviews

Our Shellfish Desires

"It's a really lovely use of the romantic triad idea...four stars."
—Paranormal Romance Guild

By K.L. Hiers

SUCKER FOR LOVE MYSTERIES
Acsquidentally In Love
Kraken My Heart
Head Over Tentacles
Nautilus Than Perfect
Just Calamarried
Our Shell ish Desires
Insquidious Devotion
An Inkredible Love
Love You Always, Suckers and All
Ollie's Octrageously Official Omnibus

Published by DREAMSPINNER PRESS
www.dreamspinnerpress.com

Love You Always, Suckers and All

K.L. Hiers

Published by
DREAMSPINNER PRESS

5032 Capital Circle SW, Suite 2, PMB# 279, Tallahassee, FL 32305-7886 USA
www.dreamspinnerpress.com

Love You Always, Suckers And All
© 2023 K.L. Hiers

Cover Art
© 2023 Tiferet Design
http://www.tiferetdesign.com

ISBN: 978-1-64108-584-7
Digital ISBN: 978-1-64108-583-0
Trade Paperback published July 2023
v. 1.0

Printed in the United States of America
∞
This paper meets the requirements of
ANSI/NISO Z39.48-1992 (Permanence of Paper).

CHAPTER 1.

ELLIAM STURM was the Kindress.

The firstborn son of Great Azaethoth, a child of starlight trapped in an endless cycle of rebirth and death whom stories said would destroy the universe if Great Azaethoth did not drown him in his tears; the being that ancient Sages revered out of fear and modern witches considered a myth; a god whose incredible power was only rivaled by the Creator of All, Great Azaethoth himself.

And he'd just fled King Thiazi Grell and Tedward Sturm's wedding in a really, *really* bad mood.

Sloane Beaumont had battled against old gods and madmen, solved many heinous crimes as a private investigator, but this was going to be his first time dealing with a literal legend.

"Can you track him?" Sloane asked Loch urgently.

"No." Loch shook his head, and his brow scrunched. "There's... *nothing.*"

Loch was Sloane's husband, a gorgeous redhead, and also Azaethoth the Lesser, the ancient Sagittarian god of thieves, tricksters, and divine retribution.

Fred Wilder, a ghoul and Ell's boyfriend, was especially distraught. He punched the closest wall, shattering the brick and howling in rage. He was a huge man, and ghouls were very strong. No one dared approach him.

Lochlain Fields, a thief and Loch's twin, tried to comfort Fred in spite of the clear danger. He was also Fred's best friend. "Hey, hey, stop that. Come on."

"No." Fred pushed Lochlain away with a snarl, his eyes dark with anger. "This is because of *you.*" His gaze traveled across the other occupants of the room with equal fury. "All of you. You did this to him. You pushed him! You all acted like he's some kind of a fuckin' *monster!*"

Lochlain stumbled back into Robert Edwards, his husband, and he argued, "Hey, no! We didn't—"

"Shut the fuck up!"

"Fred!" Sloane hurried over, though he stayed out of swinging range. "Hey, please listen to me. We didn't know! Okay? No one knew. We didn't mean for this to happen."

"The important thing now is to stay calm," Grell said quietly. He was in his true form of an Asra, a black cat monster with a mane of thick tentacles and more sprouting from the tip of his tail.

He'd been the one to identify Ell as the Kindress by his scent, and he had transformed to defend Ted and the other guests.

Not that it would have mattered.

Even the King of the Asra would not have been able to do anything against the Kindress.

"Stay calm?" Fred snarled. "Says the asshole who flipped out and turned into a giant fuckin' cat—"

"We need a plan," Grell continued, ignoring Fred's cursing, "or life as we know it is going to become very unpleasant for all of us. We have to stop him."

"Stop him?" Ted echoed.

Ted was human, Ell's older brother, and his large size suggested a former career in professional wrestling. It was said he had a rare gift of starsight that allowed him to speak to the dead. It would probably come in handy fairly soon because he looked ready to murder Grell.

"I'm sorry, is there an echo in here?" Grell rolled his eyes. "Yes, stop him."

"You mean fuckin' kill him," Ted seethed.

"That's usually the general idea involved with *stopping* someone. It sounds nicer than saying let's go plot to viciously murder him—"

"He's my baby brother!" Ted roared. "No fuckin' way! You don't even fuckin' know he's gonna do nothin'!"

Sloane retreated into Loch's arms for comfort, and he gazed up at him helplessly. He tried to ignore Ted and Grell fighting, asking quietly, "What the hell do we do now?"

"I don't know yet," Loch said, forcing a smile, "but we're going to do it together."

"All of this time, he's been right here with us. The whole damn time!"

"As Grell said, gods can hide themselves very well." Loch frowned. "If Ell truly believed himself to be human or the descendant of an everlasting race, then that is what he would appear to be even to other gods."

"He didn't know." Sloane's stomach twisted. "By all the gods, he *didn't know*."

"Well." Loch grimaced at the putrefied state of the wooden floor where Ell had been standing before he vanished. "He certainly does now."

Jay Tintenfisch came stumbling out of the bathroom with Prince Asta right behind him. Jay was an IT tech at the Archersville Police Department where Sloane had worked years ago. Asta, Grell's son and another Asra, was Jay's boyfriend.

The pair had been decidedly absent, though it didn't take a private investigator like Sloane to deduce what they'd been up to—especially since Jay had a fresh hickey on his neck.

"Whoa, buzzkill." Asta stared owlishly at them all through a pair of small round sunglasses. "What the fuck did we miss?"

"Ell is the Kindress," Sloane said, still having trouble believing it. "He, uh, just left."

"Very displeased," Loch added. "Did not want to stay for cake."

"Wait, what?" Asta actually laughed.

Jay paled. "Elliam Sturm is the Kindress?"

"And there isn't any damn cake," muttered Grell.

"No cake?" Loch gasped.

"No, no bloody damn cake." Grell sighed heavily as he transformed back into his human form. He was wearing a black-on-black suit, surprisingly drab for what Sloane had seen him wear before.

He grimly thought it looked like Grell was heading to a funeral—for the whole universe in fact, if the legends about the Kindress were true.

Sloane's thoughts ran wild, and he took a deep breath to sort them out.

The stories said that the Kindress was the first child of Great Azaethoth, but he sadly died before taking his first breath. Great Azaethoth cried so hard and for so long that a fountain had to be built to hold his tears. Great Azaethoth brought the child back to life, but his lingering pain was corruptive and drove the Kindress mad. The Kindress then tried to destroy the universe, and to save it, Great Azaethoth drowned his own child in the fountain of his tears only to resurrect him later once more and start the cycle all over.

Birth.

Impending destruction of the entire universe.

Death.

Again and again.

Something had to have changed. *Something* broke the cycle.

But what?

They knew that there was more to the story thanks to Oleander Logue's translation skills and that the Kindress's own tears might be involved. That was important somehow, that was—

"Hey, Asta!" Ted shouted angrily. "Know anything about Asran divorce? Because I think I'm gonna fuckin' need one!"

Sloane blinked, the thought lost for now.

"Nope, nope, nope." Asta shook his head. "Don't drag me into your gross domestic situation, step-kitty kicker. I don't want nada fuck all to do with it."

"Don't be dramatic," Grell scolded Ted. "We're going to—"

"Going to what?" Ted barked. "Talk about killing my brother some more? You bastard! You fucking scared the shit out of him! No wonder he took the fuck off!"

"He is literally capable of destroying this world with an errant *fart*, and he was scared of me?" Grell scoffed. "Do you hear yourself right now, my love?"

"I was trying to talk to him, and you were too busy being a giant asshole!"

"And by giant asshole, you mean a loving husband who was trying to protect you—"

"Ell would never hurt anyone!"

"Are we so sure about that? What of this Jeff?"

Sloane cringed at the mere mention of the name, and a funny voice in his head said Je-*fahfah*.

Jeff Martin was a cultist who'd tried various schemes to awaken Salgumel, Loch's father, the god of dreams who had gone mad in his divine slumber. He and likeminded followers wanted Salgumel to remake the world where Sages were ruling once more. Although the old religion was having something of a revival due to the many strange events of the last few months, it was still widely regarded as an antiquated joke.

"He's dead." Sloane grimaced. "Jeff had a magical artifact that somehow kept the rot from taking him. Rot that he claimed was from being touched by the Kindress. Well, he took it out, and then...." He waved vaguely. "It wasn't very pretty."

"It was soupy," Loch recalled.

"Ugh."

"Well, it *was*."

"What you saw is what will happen to each and every one of us if we touch him," Grell said firmly. "Even gods."

Ted opened his mouth to speak, but he paused. "That's why he wouldn't touch nothin'? I thought he didn't know... I...." His brow wrinkled.

"Even if Ell didn't know he was the Kindress, he knew his touch was deadly," Robert said. He glanced to Lochlain for encouragement to keep going, and he said, "I almost touched him once, and he completely freaked out. I never knew why."

"We do now." Lochlain rubbed Robert's back.

"That's how he was healing ghouls," Jay said suddenly.

Everyone turned to stare at him, and he shrank back.

"Go on, babycakes," Asta urged. "Flash that big sexy brain of yours."

"Well, uh...." Jay fidgeted with his glasses and cleared his throat. "The Kindress brings death to where there's life, yes, but he also brings life where there's death. I'm not sure how he figured it out, but he had to know—"

"Of course he fuckin' knew." Fred growled. "He thought he had a gift from bein' part fuckin' Eldress. He used it to fuckin' help people! People like me! He is the best man I've ever known, and I'll be damned if I let any of you assholes touch a hair on his fuckin' head!"

Jay cowered behind Asta as much of Fred's wrath seemed aimed at him.

"Calm the fuck down, zombie boy," Asta warned, flashing his sharp teeth at Fred. "I will not hesitate to double tap your bitch ass."

Fred rose to his full height and stalked toward Asta. "Who are you callin' a bitch, *bitch*?"

"The bitch ass bitch walkin' this way!" Asta grinned.

Though Asta appeared to be a tall young man with the lean build of a scarecrow, hiding inside was another monster as formidable as his father's.

Sloane's heart ached for Fred, and he quickly left Loch to intervene. He pushed Fred back, soothing, "Hey, hey! I know you're hurting, but that is not the fight you want right now!"

"Fuck you!" Fred growled.

"We'll find Ell, I swear it! Okay? We will find a way to help him!" Sloane said earnestly. "He's my friend too!"

"But you… you don't…." Fred's rage wilted in a wave of grief, and his voice cracked. "I'm… I have to go find him. I have to tell him…." He hissed, fighting back a sob, and he suddenly wrapped Sloane up in a rib-crushing hug.

Loch was there next, his grayish-blue tentacles unfurling to wrap around them both. "We're here, my child," he said to Fred. "All will be well."

Fred looked at Loch, and his eyes were damp. "You told me that after Lochlain was murdered, and now he's standin' right there. I… I really wanna fuckin' believe you."

"Believe it," Ted said firmly. "We're getting Ell back, okay?" He cut his eyes at Grell. "*Alive.*"

"What?" Grell pouted. "Oh, *sure*, suggest one little tiny murder and everyone thinks you're a monster."

"We'll find him," Sloane reaffirmed. "He was able to live this long without hurting anyone—"

"Except Jeff, who was a dillweed and absolutely deserved it," Loch chimed in.

"We can figure it out." Sloane smiled with what he hoped was confidence. "He probably didn't go far, all right? We should start checking familiar spots first. Your place, wherever you guys liked to hang out, okay?"

"Home," Fred grunted. "He probably went home. We…." He sighed. "We didn't go nowhere else."

"I'll go with Fred," Ted said immediately. "Probably best to see some friendly fuckin' faces, and not assholes who wanna kill 'em."

Grell huffed.

Loch withdrew his tentacles, and Fred nodded slowly, much calmer now. The touch of a god could be quite comforting, and Fred appeared focused, but not about to break anyone's arm anymore.

"I'll drive," Fred said.

"I'm going too," Grell announced as he fell into step behind Fred and Ted.

"The fuck you are!" Ted snapped. "Ell will flip the second he sees you!"

"So I'll make sure he doesn't." Grell narrowed his eyes. "Allow me to illuminate that thick shadowy skull of yours, darling. I love you. You're a strong queen, you have an ass that won't quit, and I adore every moment I have the honor of spending in your delightful company. I know you're angry with me right now, but if you think I'm going to let you waltz off to go poke at one of the most powerful beings in all of creation, brother or not, with only a ghoul to defend you, you clearly have underestimated my affection for you."

Ted smiled as if deeply touched, but then he scowled. "Wait, did you just call me stupid?"

Asta snorted out a laugh.

"I would never." Grell quickly turned to Sloane and Loch. "Summon any other gods who are awake. Let them know what's happened. We need to gather our allies."

"Why?" Sloane frowned. "If Fred and Ted can calm Ell down—"

"Mighty big *if* to hang the fate of the universe on." Grell's bright eyes glittered. "We must be ready for the worst. We need the old gods to help us, as many as we can."

Sloane's stomach turned harder, but he nodded. "Okay. Well, as luck would have it, one of them is watching our daughter right now. We'll start there."

"May Great Azaethoth watch over us all."

"Good luck, guys." Sloane waved to Fred and Ted as they departed with Grell in tow.

"Be careful!" Asta called out after Grell. "I'll be real pissed off if you get turned into soup!"

"Love you too, my precious spawn." Grell winked, and then he vanished.

Sloane didn't know if Grell portaled or had gone invisible or what, but he now had much bigger problems to worry about. Everyone left in the room was looking to him for what to do next, and the resulting pressure weighed a ton.

"So." Sloane took a deep breath, grateful for Loch's lingering tentacle around his arm. "We let them go see if they can find Ell and reason with him. A small group is probably best for now since Ell's already upset, and his boyfriend and brother are our best shot at getting him to get himself under control."

"Then what?" Lochlain asked. "We have a welcoming party for the Kindress?"

"The Kindress is still Ell," Sloane said firmly. "We can talk to him. We can find a way to make this work. He lived his whole life without hurting anyone, but then...."

But then something changed.

"What is it, my love?" Loch asked. "Your nose is doing the wrinkle thing."

"We need to see Ollie. Right now."

"Would you like me to go fetch him?" Loch fidgeted. "It would certainly piss off Alexander, and oh, I would very much like to do it even more now."

"Can you go tell your uncle what's going on and bring Pandora here?" Sloane took Loch's hand. "I'd feel much better having her with us."

"Of course, my sweet husband." Loch kissed Sloane's brow. "I'll speak to my mother and sister as well, see who else we can rouse from their slumber in Zebulon."

"You know, we should probably call Stoker too."

Loch retched dramatically.

Sullivan Stoker was a local gangster who also happened to be Jake the Gladsome, the son of Zunnerath and the legendary Abigail, the first Starkiller—the first mortal to ever slay a god.

Sloane was the second.

"He's half-god and very powerful," Sloane drawled. "I know you two don't get along, but we may need his help. He might even be able to help us find Ell."

"Anything that pinstriped slimeball can do, I can do better." Loch turned his nose up.

"He can hold a sword of starlight."

"I can make *macarons*."

"Yes, and they're delicious, but if Ell does something bad, well...." Sloane didn't want to think about it, but he knew Grell was right.

They had to prepare for the worst.

Ell had always been such a sweet young man, and it was hard to imagine him being a danger to anyone....

The Kindress, however, was the very antithesis of life itself, and there was no telling what he might do. The vivid image of Jeff's face decomposing in seconds flashed in the front of Sloane's mind, sending a shiver down his spine.

He had fought and defeated vile murderers, deranged cultists, and old gods, but the Kindress was in a completely different league. He was a being of pure starlight, the most powerful magic known in the universe, and Sloane had no idea if the sword Great Azaethoth had given him would even be able to hurt Ell should the need arise.

After all, one touch from Ell would turn any one of them—even a god—into soup.

Shit.

Loch must have seen the worry painted all over Sloane's face because he said, "For you, my love, I will subject myself to his loathsome presence."

"Thank y—"

"Though I am reserving the right to decide how I deliver the message."

Sloane sighed, and he couldn't help but smile. "Thank you." He tilted his head to catch Loch's lips in a kiss. "I love you. So much."

"And I love you, my beautiful Starkiller." Loch's eyes turned black, filling with a quick flash of stars before he disappeared.

Sloane didn't miss a beat, addressing Asta, "Hey! Can I get a favor?"

"Yeah?" Asta peered over his sunglasses. "But if it involves whipped cream, I'm sorry but I will have to decline. I'm spoken for now, you know."

"Can you portal over and bring Oleander Logue here? Tell him that it's urgent. Oh, and that it's for me. If a guy named Alexander is there—"

"Yeah, yeah. I'll tell him you wanna make out with him again real bad." Asta grinned. "Consider it done, Starkiller."

"No, Asta—"

Asta was already gone, the portal popping so quick it sounded like a snap.

"Does he even know where Ollie lives?" Jay wondered out loud.

"I'm sure he'll figure it out." Sloane grinned sheepishly.

"What can we do to help?" Robert asked. "There has to be something."

"If you need something stolen, I'm happy to oblige." Lochlain offered a sly smile that didn't seem to have its usual charm. "Otherwise, it seems that we might just be in the way. I'd rather not die again, I'll be honest."

"It's okay." Sloane patted Lochlain's shoulder. "Look, let your sister and Milo know what's going on. I want all the members of the Super Secret Sages' Club to be on alert. While I hope this is an easy fix, well…."

"Best to be prepared for anything," Robert finished. "We know. I'll see if I have any leads on artifacts that may help us. Jeff had one, after all. So there's gotta be more out there."

"Thank you, guys. Seriously. We'll keep you updated."

Robert and Lochlain left, and Jay found his way back to the table he'd been sitting at with Asta. He had a glass of wine that was still full, and he grabbed it and chugged.

Sloane sat down across from Jay with a heavy sigh. Someone's wineglass had been left behind there, and he picked it up to steal a sip.

Fuck.

"What now?" Jay asked worriedly.

"We wait," Sloane replied with a wry smile. "Loch will bring Pandora, plus his uncle, Merrick, and Chase. Asta will pop back up with Ollie, hopefully soon, and I'm betting with Alexander and Rota following right behind once they realize we borrowed Ollie."

"How are you so calm?"

"I…." Sloane laughed. "I don't know. Practice?" He fidgeted with his glass. "Not my first crisis, you know."

"Right." Jay chuckled nervously. "I kinda slept through my first one."

"Yeah." Sloane thought over the question again, and he had a better answer now, adding, "I think part of why I'm so calm is because I know I don't have to do this alone. I have Loch, his family, and all my friends like you and Asta. Together we're powerful, and we're a force to be reckoned with." He held his head high. "Ell is one of us too. Kindress or not, we can help him."

Jay tipped his glass back. "I really, *really* hope you're right."

Asta popped back through a portal, and he had a very startled Ollie with him. "Found him!"

"Sloane?" Ollie's eyes were wide. He was a tall, muscular redhead known for his odd malapropisms and unusual stutter. "Why did the cat monster kittennap me? I'm pretty sure this is real and not a dream."

"Hey, Ollie!" Sloane grinned. "I'm really sorry, but it was the fastest way to get you here." He rose from the table to greet him and give him a hug. "We really, really need your help."

"Uh, sure. Nothing weird about this at all." Ollie purposefully turned away so he wouldn't have to look at Asta. "What's up?"

Ollie had a blessing of starsight like Ted did. Ollie's particular gift allowed him to see all that was hidden, so he could see what Asta truly was beneath his human form.

Asta didn't seem to notice, and he probably assumed Ollie was trying to avoid staring at him because he was naked now.

"Short version, uh, is that Elliam Sturm is the Kindress," Sloane said quickly, also averting his eyes from Asta's bare ass. "He just took off out of here pretty upset. Apparently, he didn't know who he was, and we need to find him fast before anything bad happens."

"Kindress?" Ollie blinked slowly. "The… the firstborn of—"

"Yes, that one."

"Fuck, fuck, fuck." Ollie headed right for the nearest table to grab an abandoned drink. He chugged it. "Fuck, fuck, fuck—"

Sloane cringed. "Yeah, it's a little concerning. More than a little, I guess."

Asta sat back beside Jay and stretched his legs over Jay's lap. He nodded toward Ollie and magically refilled the glass he was trying to reach the bottom of. "There ya go, Red. Enjoy."

Ollie paused long enough to say, "Thanks."

All at once, Loch, Pandora, Merrick, and Chase appeared. Merrick and Chase were shouting at Loch, Loch was shouting at them, and Pandora was giggling.

Pandora was Loch and Sloane's infant daughter, although, being a demi-goddess, she was prone to growth spurts. She was the size of a one-year-old child, though she had just turned four months. She had a big mop of curly red hair like Loch, Sloane's thick arched brows, and eight teeth that she enjoyed using frequently almost as much as she liked setting things on fire.

Merrick was a handsome black man in a sharp suit, and Chase was an older pale ginger in a slightly less sharp ensemble. Merrick was Gordoth, the Sagittarian god of justice, and he and Chase were both detectives at the Archersville Police Department as well as partners off the clock. They were also both uncles, Merrick to Loch and Chase to Ollie.

Chase had his ever-present fedora on, and it appeared to be smoking.

"—certain words that make her very excited!" Loch was saying. "You can't announce that you're going to B-U-R-N rubber!"

"It's a common expression!" Chase argued. "You know, hey, let's go! We're in a hurry! Let's burn some rub—"

"Don't say it!"

Pandora squealed excitedly and clapped her hands, and the tablecloths all ignited.

"Bad girl, bad!" Loch tutted. "No more fire!"

Merrick pinched the bridge of his nose, and the flames were quickly extinguished, including the last bit of smoke from Chase's hat. "If I am understanding what my very excitable nephew told us, the Kindress is here on Aeon and just left in a very poor mood?"

"You got it," Sloane confirmed, walking over to smooch Pandora's cheeks. "Hey, Panda Bear. We've talked about fires, young lady."

"Firahhh!" Pandora's eyes gleamed.

"*No*. No more fires."

"Hey, Daddy Ginger," Asta purred toward Chase. "Never did get a chance to thank you for the hookup. The dicking down has been *awesome*."

Jay turned a very unnatural shade of red and tried to hide his face in his hands. He and Asta had recently reconciled thanks to Chase.

Chase gave a quick salute. "Happy to help."

Merrick scoffed. "Can we focus, please?"

"Yeah, yeah. Focusing. Totally focused. It's the star baby, right?" Chase looked around for confirmation. "We're saying the big, scary star baby is real? And it's Ell?"

Ollie took a break from drinking to reply, "Yup! It was Ell! Crazy, huh?"

Chase turned toward Ollie's voice. He laughed and headed over to give him a hug. "Hey! What are you doin' here?"

Ollie held up the cup. "I'm workin', Uncle Chase."

Loch wrapped his tentacles around Sloane and Pandora, saying, "We had a tiny mishap with a very small fire, but everything is all right. On a totally and completely unrelated note, we did not apparently fireproof the shower curtain."

"Oh, yes, totally unrelated." Sloane chuckled, appreciating the brief moment of levity. He knew there may not be many more to enjoy.

"What is happening now?" Merrick demanded. "Where are the others?"

"Robert and Lochlain are on the hunt for any less-than-legal items that might be able to help us. They're gonna let Milo and Lynnette know what's going on too. King Grell went with Fred and Ted to look for Ell at their place and a few other local spots, see if they can find him," Sloane replied. "There's a chance that Ell just needs a moment to calm down—"

"No, it is not that simple," Merrick cut in abruptly. "The Kindress is cursed to forever succumb to his corruption. I can only assume he has been able to resist this long because he was not aware of what he truly was."

"What are you saying, Uncle?" Loch frowned. "That now that he knows, he will be corrupted?"

"Yes."

"I would like to nominate placing the blame on King Grell."

"That does not matter," Merrick chided. "Whether it was King Grell or another or some other completely random act, this is destiny. The Kindress will always fail."

"Hey, but it ends too, right?" Chase squeezed Merrick's shoulder. "We just gotta wait for Big Azaethoth to come down and work up some tears, right?"

"That may also be a problem. Great Azaethoth remains in the dreaming and the fountain—"

Ollie swayed a little, and he sat in the closet chair with a loud belch. "Sorry, excuse me."

"How much have you had to drink?" Chase wrinkled his nose. "I can fuckin' smell you from here."

"My starsight thingie works better if I've had a few." Ollie stared long and hard at his cup. "This has been more than a few, so I'm thinking it's gonna work awesome."

"Can you see where Ell is?" Sloane asked gently. "Anything at all?"

"Sure! Totally. I've got this. I…." Ollie's head smacked into the table.

"I guess he don't drink like he used to." Chase made a face.

"It's all right." Sloane smiled patiently. "We'll wait. He's definitely our best hope for figuring out where Ell is now."

"So, let me get this straight because, you know, I'm slow at this Sage stuff." Chase pulled at his beard. "The star baby was Ell this whole fuckin' time, and we didn't know? Why didn't he ever go all murdery like he's supposed to?"

"If he did not know he was the Kindress, it may have created a mental barrier against the corruption," Merrick replied. "Now that it has been removed, it is only a matter of time."

"And the corruption is from Daddy Azaethoth bein' all sad over murdering him a whole bunch?"

"Yes." Merrick sighed. "However, it may be more complicated than that."

"Oh. Fuck. Great." Chase hesitated before asking, "And why exactly?"

"Do not forget what the song said—"

"Ah, I got it!" Ollie whipped his head up. He hiccupped and glanced around the room in a drunken daze.

"Got what, kiddo?" Chase asked gently.

"The answer to your question."

"What question?"

Ollie's eyes fell on Sloane, and he pointed at him. "Your question."

Sloane blinked. "Me? You mean about Ell?"

"No, the other one." Ollie shook his head. "You wanted to know what changed. I can see it. I can see all the things, and they fit together like a neat lil' puzzle. No, like one of those machine thingies where a ball will go down a tube and hits a sock, and then that fills up a tub with jam or something."

"I believe our starsight witch has had a little too much," Loch whispered loudly, "or he hit his head hard enough to sustain a brain injury."

Sloane eyed Asta, who shrugged and batted his eyes innocently. "What exactly was in that cup?"

"The Kindress," Ollie insisted, his words slurring faster now. "It's the Kindress. No, not that he's in my cup. That would be weird. Alcohol was in my cup. *Is* in my cup. But you! You wanted to know what changed the cycle."

"Yes." Sloane tried not to be alarmed that Ollie knew about a question he'd only thought about.

"Yup, that's the one." Ollie beamed.

Sloane cleared his throat. "Well, what was it?"
"Huh? What?"
"What broke the cycle, Ollie?"
"Oh! You did, Sloane."

CHAPTER 2.

"ME?" SLOANE'S pulse thudded.

"Okay. Follow me here for a second 'cause we're going on a ride." Ollie took a deep breath, rocking in his chair. "This all started, like, twenty years ago when your parents were killed in that ritual thing. You woke up Tollmathan—"

"I know." Sloane flushed with shame. "What does that have to do with the Kindress?"

"Everything." Ollie smiled sadly.

"Explain, intoxicated mop," Loch demanded, hugging Sloane a bit closer.

"Sloane's prayer broke the wall thing between worlds," Ollie said. "It made that big Xenon tree thingie appear and went all the way to Zebulon. Yes, it woke up Tollmathan, but it didn't stop there. It hit Great Azaethoth just as he rezzed the Kindress and boom! Smacko! He dropped the baby!"

"What?" Sloane gasped.

"Yes! Great Azaethoth should have had a slang. Slung? Like, one of those baby carrier things—"

"A sling," Chase supplied.

"Yeah! Them things! Anyway." Ollie rubbed his face. "Lil' baby Kindress fell to Aeon. I think he, like, followed the path of your starlight back through the hole? Then he, like, floated around for a little bit and then landed right smack on the doorstep of Ted's family. That's how he got here. I can't... I can't see the rest yet, but that's what changed. It was you."

Sloane's pulse decided to move up into his ears, and he clung to Pandora and Loch to steady himself. He'd carried the guilt of waking Tollmathan for some time, his prayer arguably causing the current wave of crises as Tollmathan was the god who first began plotting to awaken Salgumel. Tollmathan's efforts to rally the old gods inspired his brother, Gronoch, and his cousin, Cleus, to also rise up and cause heaps of trouble for the world at large....

And wasn't that all Sloane's fault too?

Loch had often assured Sloane that wasn't the case as such trouble was inevitable. After all, many of the gods lost to the dreaming longed for the world to return to the old ways when they were adored. It didn't always make Sloane feel any better, especially right now since the prayer he'd attempted to save his parents had inadvertently interrupted an eons-old cycle of rebirth and death of the second most powerful being in the universe.

He felt like shit.

"The cause is irrelevant," Merrick declared, his voice rising as he spoke. "I believe we need to focus on the issue at hand. *Where* is the Kindress? Where has he gone? How far into the *corruption* has he fallen?"

"Hey, hey, calm down," Chase soothed as he rubbed Merrick's shoulders. "Big breaths. We'll find him."

Merrick initially bristled at the open affection, but he gave in with a sigh. "I… I do not like this."

"I know. Just keep on breathin'."

"Can you take her?" Sloane asked, gently pushing Pandora into Loch's tentacles.

"Of course, my beautiful husband." Loch frowned. "What is wrong?"

"It's me." Ollie was slurring now. "It's 'cause of what I said." He put his head down again. "I'm sorry. It's just… it's what I see. Please don't be mad at me. I hate when people are mad at me."

"It's okay. I'm not mad. I just need a moment," Sloane insisted. "Really."

Loch did not appear convinced, and he quirked his brows in concern even as he held Pandora against his chest.

Pandora gurgled, amusing herself by pulling on Loch's tentacles. She had no idea that Sloane was upset, beautifully oblivious, and by all the gods, how he envied her in that moment.

She had no clue that her father had maybe sort of doomed the entire universe a tiny bit, and—

No.

Sloane took a deep breath.

Ell was their friend, an absolute sweetheart of a guy, and Sloane wanted to believe with all of his soul that even as the Kindress that he would never….

Sloane remembered Jeff's face.

Shit.

If Sloane broke the cycle when Ell was a baby, maybe there was a chance he wouldn't be affected by the corruption of Great Azaethoth's grief? That had to be a thing, right? Did the Kindress keep his memories throughout his many lives? Or was there a chance Ell didn't have them and could be free from it?

The thought only had a few seconds to linger in Sloane's brain before there was a loud crash and the entire building shook with the force of something big coming through.

"Firahhh!" Pandora roared, throwing up her hands. Her fingers morphed into thick tentacles and sparked with flames. "Maff destructionnn!"

"No, no, no—!" Loch scolded.

A large portal popped open near the doorway and the furniture in its path was blown away by a swath of translucent shimmering tentacles. Out of the swirling hole came a very unhappy young man with white hair, red eyes, and a black trench coat. The beast with him was fully revealed when he roared, his invisible skin turning an opaque red-violet as his tentacles whipped around in a frenzy.

Sloane actually smiled.

Of the many possible terrible things that could bust in here, it was just Alexander and Rota.

Alexander was a Silenced mortal whose body had been bound with the soul of an old god, Rota, through an involuntary and most heinous experiment. They were also Ollie's boyfriends.

Ollie lifted his head with a loud hiccup. "Oh! Hey, babes!"

Ollie! You're all right! Rota's voice filled Sloane's head like a deep rumble that echoed like thunder. His tentacles reached out to wrap Ollie up and squeeze him. *Oh, sweet boy. I'm so glad you're safe.*

"I'm super!" Ollie grinned. "Sooo super."

"You're drunk," Alexander complained, even though he was obviously relieved to see him.

"Yeah." Ollie kept grinning. "And you're sexy. Comin' to rescue me all sexy-like."

"That's...." Alexander blushed. "Whatever. Let's fuckin' go."

That's very sweet, Ollie, Rota said, ignoring Alexander as he petted Ollie's hair. He spoke out loud now, noting, "Oh! And Starkiller is here. And Chase. Hello. And.... Oh, lots of other people."

Chase waved. "What's up?"

"All the more reason to leave," Alexander mumbled. "We'll be taking Ollie now. Bye-bye."

"I'm so sorry we had to borrow him, but listen—" Sloane tried.

"*Borrow?*" Alexander snarled. "You sent that fucking Asra douche over to break our wards and fuckin' kidnapped him. Fuck you."

"Douche, huh?" Asta hummed. "If I was a douche, I think I'd be Delicate Blossom scented. You'd be Hot Topic Dumpster."

"Fuck you too, right in the—"

Wait, what's wrong? Rota sounded afraid. *Hold on, my love. Please. Something terrible has happened.*

Alexander paused long enough to perhaps take stock of the room—the specific people present, the rotten floor, the old magic that still clung to the very air around them. "The fuck?"

"It's the star baby," Chase said. "You just missed 'em."

"The what now?"

"The Kindress was here," Merrick said solemnly. "Elliam Sturm."

"*What?*" Alexander hesitated and then added, "Wait, who?"

"Ted's younger brother," Sloane replied. "Uh, you know, Fred's boyfriend?"

Ollie's ex-boyfriend's little brother! Rota added helpfully.

Alexander sighed and reached into his coat for a cigarette. He lit up using one of Rota's tentacles to create the flame. "Fuck this shit."

I thought you quit! Rota scolded. *We've talked about—*

"I think this place is nonsmoking," Asta chimed in, speaking over Rota since he couldn't hear him when he used his inside voice.

Only those who had been blessed by Great Azaethoth, like Sloane with his sword of starlight or Ollie with his starsight, could hear Rota and Alexander's psychic conversations. It was also what allowed them to be physical vessels for Rota even though Rota's soul was already bound to Alexander's.

"I think you can choke on a hairball and die," Alexander said with syrupy sweetness, pausing to take a long drag from his cigarette. He exhaled slowly. "So, what's the plan, then? Let me guess. You're trying to reason with the Kindress and make him all better with cuddly good feelings?"

"Did Alexander recently develop a psychic ability?" Loch whispered loudly.

"No, I just know Starkiller and how much he loves bein' the good guy." Alexander smirked. "I'm right, aren't I?"

"Ted and Fred went with King Grell to look for Ell," Sloane said firmly. "He was pretty upset when he left here. He apparently didn't know he was the Kindress, but when Grell sniffed him out, it sort of... woke something up."

Oh dear, Rota murmured. *We need to tell them.*

"No," Alexander said.

"Tell them what?" Ollie asked with another hiccup. "Am I part of the them?" He frowned. "Wait, did he just say Ted?"

It was never a concern before, but now that we've confirmed the Kindress is actually here? Rota huffed. *That changes things, Alexander.*

"What is it?" Sloane demanded. "You know I can still hear you guys when you do that!"

"It's very rude!" Loch agreed. "Because I cannot hear you!"

"Rude!" Pandora shouted. "Ruuuude!"

Rota spoke out loud again so everyone could hear him, snapping at Alexander, "If you don't tell them, I will."

"Tell us what?" Merrick asked. "If you have any information that may be pertinent to this situation, I must insist that you share it."

Alexander, Rota pressed. *Please.*

"*Now* if you would be so kind," Merrick said, his eyes narrowing.

"Fine, don't get your panties in a twist, Gordoth." Alexander rolled his eyes. "We've been tracking Daisy and the other cultists, all right? Workin' for Stoker." He paused to take another drag. "We've found some of them, and all they're babbling about is getting this fruit to the Kindress to get their wish."

"The fruit?" Sloane gasped. "Oh no."

"Oh fuck," Merrick said, his eyes wide.

"Did you just fuckin' say *fuck*?" Chase blinked. "What fruit? Wait... oh *fuck*."

"I wanna curse too!" Ollie announced. "What's going on?"

"Yes, please, do share with the rest of the class," Grell called out as he strolled back into the room with a toothy leer. "Cursing is ever so much fun." He eyed Ollie, Alexander, and Rota. "Oh, look, darling. More guests."

Ted was right behind Grell, and he was pale. "Just give me a second, okay? I'm not really feelin' that fuckin' great."

"What's happened now?" Merrick asked urgently.

"Look, we went upstairs to cancel the fuckin' party, and my parents are fuckin' here," Ted said with a miserable scowl. "I had no fuckin' idea what to tell 'em. Oops, sorry, we're kinda not having the reception anymore and my brother isn't here at the moment. He ran off because my new husband scared him the fuck off?"

Asta looked like he was ready to say something sarcastic, but Jay shook his head and shushed him with a pleading smile. Asta rolled his eyes, but he kept whatever the comment was to himself.

"May I suggest erasing their memories?" Loch said.

"No!" Ted scoffed. "I just told them the place flooded out! Who the fuck erases somebody's fuckin' memories?"

"I do."

"For fuck's sake." Ted sighed, and then he noticed Ollie. He gasped. "Ollie? Is that… Is that you?"

"It is! I think." Ollie stared back at Ted. "Ted…?"

"That's Ted?" Alexander narrowed his eyes into venomous slits. *Ted, as in, your dumb ex-boyfriend that broke your fucking heart? That Ted?*

"Yeah, that's him!" Ollie grinned and waved at Ted. "Hey! Congrats on getting married and stu-fahfah!"

"Uh. Thanks?" Ted blinked. "What the hell are you doing here?"

He's much bigger than I thought he'd be. Rota coughed. *Does he… work out?*

"Ollie's with us," Alexander said coldly. *Who cares? I don't mind digging a bigger hole.*

"A hole for what?" Ollie asked with big eyes. "I'm so *confused.*"

"I think he means a hole for me," Ted said with a smirk. "I think your little boyfriend over there is jealous."

Alexander's eyes widened ever so slightly. *The fuck?*

Oh! He has starsight as well? Rota sounded intrigued.

"That he does, whoever is talking right now." Ted glanced around warily. "Wait, so is that a ghost or what? Is anyone else hearing this?"

"Boyfriend number two," Rota explained out loud, allowing himself to be visible for a brief moment.

"Whoa. Good for you, Ollie."

"Yeah! I got two sexy boyfriends, I got starsight, and I see stu-fahfah, and ohhh…." Ollie ducked his head. "That's a secret. Shush. *Big* secret."

"It's, uh, good to see you," Ted said with a strained smile. "We'll have to catch up later or somethin'. Let your new boyfriends talk some more trash about me."

It might have been Sloane's imagination, but he swore Alexander tried to stand up taller.

"Always in such terrible taste when your old flames show up uninvited," Grell teased. He didn't appear the least bit bothered, though he did curl his arm around Ted's waist and smirk over at the trio confidently.

"Wow." Asta cackled. "This is fuckin' awesome."

Alexander turned his death stare on Asta.

"Hey! Attention over here please! You guys didn't find Ell, then?" Chase asked, quickly redirecting the conversation. "And hey, where's ghoul guy? Fred?"

"He stayed back at his place," Ted replied. "Wanted to be there in case Ell came back."

"I left a little magical surprise with him that will alert me should the Kindress return," Grell said. "If it goes back to that apartment, we'll know immediately."

"Alexander was in the process of sharing some vital information with us." Merrick nodded toward where Alexander was standing now beside Ollie, and Rota's mirage-like image hovered around them. "The cultists were apparently successful creating fruit from a Great Tide in Babbeth's Orchard."

"And that's what again?" Chase muttered out of the side of his mouth.

"A fruit that was used as an offering to the Kindress," Merrick said. "In exchange, it was said the Kindress would offer any boon."

"Chainsaw for a hammer," Sloane said quietly, recalling the absurdity of the cultists going to insane lengths seeking out the Kindress for the comparatively simple task of wanting to awaken Salgumel. "But hey, we checked the Orchard. And Umbriech's Glen. The stream never flowed there."

"It was moist at best," Loch added.

"No stream flowing over into the orchard means no fruit, right?"

"Well, those *moist* bits were apparently enough," Alexander drawled. "Every cultist we talked to wouldn't shut the fuck up about it.

Said they were waiting for some special day to give it to the Kindress so ol' Sally boy could rise up." He flicked his ashes onto the floor.

"And you are very sure they were not lying to you about this?" Merrick narrowed his eyes. "Do you even know how to conduct a proper interrogation?"

"Trust me. Stoker and I interrogated them very properly." *A few of them even survived.* Alexander smiled, and he made sure to look at Ted, knowing now he could hear him.

Ted grimaced, but he didn't say anything.

Sloane pretended not to hear that thought. He knew better than Ted how far Alexander was willing to go to get what he wanted, Stoker too. He noticed Pandora reaching out for him, and he nodded at Loch so he could take her. He cuddled her against his chest, saying, "So. We don't know where Ell is, but the cultists are still out there with the very item that they need to get him to do what they want and wake up Salgumel?"

"Sounds about right." Chase scrubbed his hands over his face. "Maybe the fruit will suck and he'll tell 'em no?"

"That is actually a possibility," Merrick said. "The Kindress is not obligated to grant their request, so there is a chance that he will refuse."

"And there's a really big chance that we can talk to Ell and fix this before it even starts," Sloane said firmly. "Yes, he is the Kindress, but he's our friend—"

"A chance I am not willing to take," Grell declared. "You. Little Robert Smith."

Alexander blinked. "Me?"

"Yes, you."

Ollie laughed suddenly. "Oh, 'cause your hair—"

"Whatever." Alexander cut his eyes at Grell. "What do you want, *Voltaire?*"

"Thank you. I respect a man who's not afraid to wear eyeliner." Grell flashed a fanged smile. "Now! I want you to take me to where you found these cultists."

"Why?"

"So I can track them myself."

"The last one was fuckin' days ago." Alexander scoffed. "Even an Asra isn't that good—"

"Exsqueeze me, ahem, *King* of the Asra, and yes, I am." Grell glanced back at Jay and Asta. "You two, go to Xenon immediately. The safest place to be right now is anywhere not on Aeon."

Jay frowned. "But wait, shouldn't we stay—"

"We're outtie!" Asta grabbed Jay and flipped backward into a portal that opened up in the floor behind them.

It closed with a pop and they were gone.

"You should go home as well," Merrick said solemnly to Chase.

"What?" Chase scowled. "I know you didn't just—"

"Elwood," Merrick soothed. "In light of the current circumstances, I believe it is more than appropriate to take what is known as a personal day in order to shelter from the impending destruction of the universe."

"He is welcome to shelter in Xenon," Grell offered. "Not you, of course. Whole no gods allowed thing, I'm sure you understand."

"Hey! What the fuck happened to reasoning with Ell?" Ted barked. "We're right back to he's gonna destroy the fuckin' universe already?"

"Yes, that is exactly where we are."

"Are you fuckin' high?"

"No, perhaps later, but you're going back to Xenon too, darling," Grell said firmly. "I love you. Sorry our wedding sucked. I'll make it up to you later with my mouth."

"The fuck you will—!" Ted disappeared through a seamless portal.

"Oh, fuck to the no." Chase straightened his hat, and he glared furiously at Merrick. "You just try that sneaky portal shit with me and see what the fuck happens. I'm not goin' fuckin' nowhere. End of the world or whatever, I'm staying right fuckin' here. We're partners, remember? Together until the fuckin' end, Merry."

While Chase was ranting, Grell very quietly opened up a new portal in the floor right behind him. He nodded at Merrick, very conspicuously clearing his throat and glancing at the portal.

Merrick hesitated, but then he shook his head.

"Wait!" Chase huffed. "What the fuck are you assholes doing?" He saw the portal and then leaped forward, shouting, "You fucker! You were gonna let him push me into another world?"

"No!" Merrick cringed. "Although I did perhaps consider it...."

"Fuck you," Chase spat.

"If we're going, let's go, Your Highness," Alexander drawled. "We gotta make a pitstop first."

"Where are we going?" Ollie asked.

You're going somewhere safe, Rota said sweetly.

I'll bring a TV so you can put on your cartoons, Alexander added. *Whatever you want.*

"But what if I need to see stu-fahfah?" Ollie pouted. "I wanna help too!"

"You're going," Alexander said out loud. "Right now."

Ollie stood from the chair and rose to his full height, glaring down at Alexander. "Make me."

"You know I can—"

Ollie took off, running at full speed toward the door. He nearly fell as he clearly could not run in a straight line, but off he went, pushing by Grell and zooming out of the room.

"Motherfucker," Alexander grumbled as he stalked after him. "Be right back."

"I guess we need to figure out what to do with you." Sloane kissed Pandora's forehead. "As much as I would rather have you with us, maybe we should take precautions too...."

"We could get a sling," Loch suggested. "We will be more responsible than Great Azaethoth."

"Loch."

"Okay, two slings."

Sloane snorted.

"My sister and mother are on their way," Loch said. "We can see if Galgareth will accompany us—"

"Wait, you're all going?" Chase demanded. "That would be what? Four fuckin' gods, a cat monster, Sloane, and that little emo guy?"

"The ginger daddy has a point," Grell mused. "We may be better off if we divide and conquer."

"What do you mean?" Sloane asked.

"If I may, I would suggest that I accompany said emo guy with his godly counterpart to track the cultists. Gordoth is welcome to come with us as well—"

"What about me?" Chase snapped.

"Sorry, no mortals allowed. Very exclusive club. Starkiller, that'll give you time to sort out care for your spawn and wait for the others. It will also allow you to prepare yourself for what is to come."

"Which is what?"

Grell's smile dimmed. "Killing the Kindress."

"No." Sloane grimaced. "We're going to find Ell and *talk* to him. He's my friend and your brother-in-law by the way!"

"A brother-in-law who could destroy the entire universe. I'm a pretty big fan of that place seeing as how I live here."

"We don't know that Ell is going to do that—"

"I've seen the great bridge of Xenon fall dark when his mere soul passes through. His power is endless. Ell or not, he is still the Kindress, and you might be the only one who can stop him. Unless someone knows where the Fountain is—"

"We do." Sloane sighed. "Well, Alexander and Rota do. But they said it's empty."

"I will personally crawl to the very bottom of it to look myself. If only a drop, better to have it and not need it, blah blah blah."

"We won't need it," Sloane insisted stubbornly.

"I am not trusting my family and kingdom to the power of friendship, Starkiller." Grell's jovial demeanor slipped further, and he raised a hand to rub his temple. "May Great Azaethoth have mercy on us all."

"I'll drink to that." Chase headed over to the table where Ollie had been sitting and found the neverending cup of alcohol. He took a big gulp and hissed. "You guys have fun on your little adventure to save the world without me. Hope you get turned into fuckin' soup. See if I care."

"I know that you care very much and you are angry with me," Merrick said. "But I love you. Always."

Chase flipped him off and kept drinking.

Merrick stood up straight, marched right over, and planted a passionate kiss to Chase's lips.

Alexander popped back in, and he immediately grimaced at the sight. "Whoa, ew." He looked to Grell. "Can we fuckin' go?"

Chase cleared his throat as Merrick pulled away, and he asked, "Hey! Where's Ollie?"

"Safe."

"He's in a world between worlds," Rota added. "We gave him television and snacks, but he is still not very happy with us."

"Hey! I'm not happy either! Fuck it, send me there with him!" Chase barked. "Just let me take this damn cup with me."

"Have fun." Alexander snapped his fingers and opened a portal.

Cup in hand, Chase paused only to blow Merrick a kiss and then jumped through. The portal closed with a loud pop, leaving only Sloane, Loch, Pandora, Merrick, Grell, Alexander, and Rota.

"I guess we're gonna head home to wait for Gal and Urilith," Sloane said. "Let us know what you find?"

"Of course." Merrick nodded. "If we do see Ell... we...." He took a deep breath. "We will try to speak with him first."

"Thank you. Good luck, guys."

"Let's fuckin' go," Alexander said impatiently.

"Lead the way, Mr. Smith." Grell bowed.

"Try to keep up." Alexander vanished away into a portal.

Grell and Merrick disappeared behind them, and the once crowded room was now almost empty.

"Now that we're alone...." Loch licked his lips.

"Loch!" Sloane made a face. "Pandora is right here!"

"No, not *that*. That's for later." Loch caressed Sloane's cheek. "I know your shoulders are heavy right now with many burdens. I want to know how I can alleviate them."

"I wish... I wish I had an answer for you." Sloane had to pause, surprised by a sudden well of emotion rising up in his chest that made it hard to breathe. "Some of our friends just fled Aeon because everyone is afraid of what Ell is going to do. Hell, King Grell just told me to be ready because I'll have to kill him. And oh, oops, my favorite part, it's my fault."

"My beautiful husband, no—"

Another portal tore open, prompting Sloane to shout, "For the love of all the gods! What the *fuck* is it now?"

"Fuck, fuck, fuck!" Pandora cheered.

From out of the portal came Sullivan Stoker, dressed in a dark gray three-piece suit, his prismatic black tentacles writhing all around him as he seethed, "Azaethoth the Lesser—" He took a breath. "—you are *dead*!"

Stoker's skin was covered in a thick layer of fine neon green glitter.

"Loch!" Sloane groaned. "What did you do?"

"You said it didn't matter how I delivered the message!" Loch said immediately. "I chose glitter bomb."

"Loch! Fix it!"

"But he matches Madame Sprinkles—"

"Fix! Now!"

"Fuck, fuck, fuck, fuck," Pandora continued to chant.

"Pandora!" Sloane warned. "That's a bad word, quit it."

Pandora dropped her voice to a little whisper. "Fuck?"

"*No.*"

Though Stoker was free of glitter now, he still brushed himself as if there was more hiding in the folds of his suit. "Thank you. Much appreciated. Now. What the hell was so damn important?"

Sloane sighed, bouncing Pandora lightly. "Ell is the Kindress."

"*What?*"

Sloane did his best to give Stoker a detailed and full explanation of what had happened, including where everyone was and what they were planning next. "We were just getting ready to head home to wait for Galgareth and Urilith. Robert and Lochlain are hopefully trying to find some kind of magical anything that could help us, and Milo... oh gods, Milo and Lynnette." He sighed. "They don't know!"

Milo was Sloane's best friend, and Lynnette was Lochlain's sister. They were expecting their first child any day now, and the last Sloane had heard from them was that Milo was trying to get Lynnette to take it easy while Lynnette was trying everything she could to induce labor.

"Yes, they do," Loch gently reminded him. "You already instructed Lochlain and Robert to inform them, remember?"

"Yes. Shit." Sloane took a deep breath. "You're right."

"Yes, I am."

"We should try to check on Fred, see if he's heard anything from Ell yet."

Stoker had been very quiet, and his expression was grim as he drawled, "I don't suppose it ever occurred to either of you to simply try a location spell?"

Sloane scoffed. "Well, it... they don't...."

"Always work? I know." Stoker scowled. "But I'd say it's damn well worth a try, wouldn't you?" He gestured to the rotten floor. "Ell certainly left us quite a sample to work with. Shall we?"

"Fine." Sloane passed Pandora over to Loch so he could approach the rotted-out wood. He reached out toward it with his magic, summoning his starlight to pull at the fetid essence. It sparked in protest as if it was resisting, and he focused more power.

There!

He was able to gather some of it up in a small orb of starlight, but he could feel it was unstable. "We need to hurry."

"Go." Stoker immediately sent out his tentacles to rest on Sloane's shoulders, sharing his power with him.

Loch's tentacles joined them, and he grumbled, "Remind me to hit you later for touching my husband."

"Will do."

Pandora watched them with wide eyes, and she quickly reached out to Sloane, copying Loch. Her hands turned into long tentacles, and she squeezed Sloane's shoulders, laughing.

Sloane smiled a little, but he remained focused on the task at hand. He let the magic from Stoker and Loch flow through him, the experience like two waves crashing over him—one cool and deep, the other hot and fast, and there was a small sprinkle like a sun shower he assumed was Pandora.

Location spells were notoriously inaccurate as they often resulted in places where the person in question hadn't been for days, or it could be a place they were going to be in the future. Anything at this point would be better than nothing, so Sloane closed his eyes and concentrated on the spell. When he'd attempted these spells before, he'd see splashes of color and blurry shapes until something—if anything—ever came into focus.

But right now there was nothing.

Darkness.

A deep void that was freezing cold, endless, and....

Ell was there!

Sloane could see Ell standing in the middle of the darkness, his eyes drawn to the glowing stars of the crown that hovered over Ell's magnificent horns. His head was bowed, and he was crying quietly, each sob causing the strange void to shudder around him. His tears had formed a small puddle around his feet, reflecting the bright stars of the crown above.

Sloane summoned more magic, pulling from both Loch and Stoker, struggling to see more—

Ell turned and he *looked right at Sloane*. Somehow he was looking right at him through the spell. Ell raised his hand out toward him, his tears evaporating off his face in a cloud of steam. His eyes were turning a brilliant purple, and he bared his teeth in an unexpectedly angry snarl.

Don't.

Sloane heard it, a single word, and then everything exploded.

"Sloane!" Stoker cried.

"My love!" Loch shouted.

Sloane hit the far wall with a groan. "Ow?"

"Birdy!" Pandora clapped her tentacles excitedly.

"Oh, my sweet love," Loch cooed as he hurried over to help Sloane up, wrapping his tentacles around his waist. "Are you all right? Are you hurt?"

Sloane's entire body throbbed. "Feel like I just got hit by a fuckin' car."

"What the fuck happened?" Stoker demanded.

"I think…." Sloane took a deep breath. "I think that was a warning."

CHAPTER 3.

"I COULDN'T SEE where Ell was," Sloane said quickly. "It was pitch-black, like he was in a room with the lights turned off, and then he looked right at me. He *saw* me looking for him, and then *bam*." He leaned into Loch's tentacles, cringing in pain. "He pushed me *through* the vision."

"Here, love," Loch said as he offered him a tentacle to drink from. "Let me help you."

"Later." Sloane blushed.

What was a casual gift to share with ancient worshippers for Loch was an awkward sexual act by modern standards for Sloane. While Loch's seed did indeed have many powerful healing properties, Sloane wasn't desperate enough to partake of it with an audience.

Stoker appeared ready to comment with something coy, but instead said, "You couldn't see anything else? Nothing at all?"

"No." Sloane shook his head. "It was just darkness. I could see Ell. He was crying, and he still had his horns and…." He fought to remember anything that might help, but the vision was fading. "I'm sorry. It happened too fast."

Stoker sighed. "We will have to try something else. We must find the Kindress before the cultists do."

"Ell isn't just going to give in the second he sees the stupid fruit," Sloane said stubbornly.

"But the Kindress might."

Sloane didn't have a good argument for that, asking instead, "Alexander and Rota told us you guys have been tracking the cultists, right? Trying to find Daisy?"

Stoker's lip twitched in annoyance. "Yes. We have, unfortunately, been unable to locate her or the fruit they plan to offer. My suspicion is that she is hiding it and herself off world. There is a specific day they wish to summon him."

"Let me guess." Sloane grimaced. "November fifth?"

"How did you know that?" Stoker demanded. "I hadn't even told Alexander or Rota yet."

"Because my husband is both beautiful and utterly brilliant." Loch beamed. He cleared his throat. "And how did you know that, my gorgeous mate?"

"It's the anniversary of my parents' death," Sloane replied glumly. "Just had a feeling."

"If they had been aiming for a more powerful summoning, they missed the perihelic opposition by a full year." Stoker scoffed. "It must be something else."

"Maybe the day is important to Ell? It's the day he fell to Aeon. Maybe it's his birthday?" Sloane took a deep breath and then regretted it when his ribs burned. "I think it's time to go home."

"Let's," Loch agreed. "Mother will be here very soon, and then I can feed you my seed—"

"*Later!*"

"That will be later," Loch said indignantly.

"That's it?" Stoker scoffed. "The Kindress is here, and you're going home to have sex?"

"I am going home to *rest* and make sure my daughter is safe before I do anything else," Sloane said firmly. "We just saw Ell. He's a mess. He doesn't look like he's about to go on a crazy murdering rampage right this second, okay?"

Stoker approached, his eyes growing dark as he said, "That could change very quickly."

"I'm well aware, but we're all doing our best, okay?" Sloane ignored his ribs and stood tall, staring Stoker down. "Everyone is looking for Ell, a way to stop him, or something we can use against him if the worst should happen. Unless you have any information about the cultists to share with us or anything else that might be helpful, we're going."

"I have the totem Jeff used to protect himself from the Kindress's rot."

"See? Now that's helpful!"

"I have been attempting to replicate the unique enchantment without success. So, as it stands, it is one of a kind."

"You should give it to Sloane," Loch said, eyeing Stoker in a way Sloane didn't understand and didn't like one bit. "He will need it."

"I will." Stoker eyeballed Loch back in the same unsettling way. "When it's time."

"Why not give it to Ollie?" Sloane asked. "See if he can figure it out? We should really use everyone's gifts to the fullest right now."

"Alexander said he quit drinking," Stoker drawled. "My understanding is that Ollie's starsight works best when he's on the sauce."

"He's pretty sloshed right now."

"Very well." Stoker looked thoughtful. "I'll see about having Ollie identify the enchantment and make as many totems as I can."

"And the cultists?" Sloane pressed.

"Their plan is simple. Use the fruit to ask the Kindress to awaken Salgumel."

"They have to know how stupid that is."

"What?"

"If what we know about the Kindress is true, then the cultists have to know that he might destroy the very world they want Salgumel to take over." Sloane sighed. "Chainsaw and hammer, all that. I think we're missing something."

"Does it really matter?" Stoker raised his brow. "We know this is what they want."

"It was different before we knew the Kindress was actually here with us." Sloane sagged, wishing he could pick out exactly what was bothering him. "Look, we will call you later if we hear anything, okay? Let me know about the totems?"

"Will do, Mr. Beaumont." Stoker bowed to him and then managed a civil nod at Loch. "Azaethoth."

"Jake," Loch sneered.

"Jake!" Pandora echoed.

Stoker actually smiled at Pandora, saying politely, "Farewell, Miss Pandora. Please take care of your father for me." He smirked as it was obvious he was talking about Sloane, and not Loch. "Goodbye, Mr. Beaumont."

"Bye, Stoker." Sloane waved.

"Bye-bye, Jake!" Pandora waved excitedly.

Loch smiled, which immediately made Sloane think he'd done something to Stoker.

Stoker vanished, but Sloane wouldn't have been surprised if he angrily portaled right back painted green or something.

"Are you ready to go home, sweet husband?" Loch asked. "I wish to take care of you. I know you are in pain."

"I'm ready," Sloane replied. "Let's go before anyone else shows up."

"Of course, my love." Loch gathered Sloane close with his tentacles and then transported them home to the living room of their apartment. He put Pandora down in her playpen with her favorite toy, Loch's old rattle.

Pandora eagerly shook the toy, chanting, "Jake, Jake, Jake!"

"Very good, my spawn." Loch nodded in approval. "You shake Jake like that the next time you see him."

Sloane collapsed on the couch, sore all over and mentally drained. He checked his phone to see if there were any new messages from anyone, and there was only one from Lochlain saying they hadn't found anything yet.

To ease communication, Sloane created a group text with the members of the Super Secret Sages' Club plus Stoker. He typed a brief explanation of the failed location spell and Stoker's promise to seek Ollie out to make more totems so everyone was on the same page.

An unknown number added itself to the group message, replying: *busy now doing hot girl shit. will let you know if we find tears. xxx*

Sloane assumed it was King Grell.

"My love?" Loch prompted.

"What is it?" Sloane set his phone down.

"I have been instructing our spawn to mangle Stoker on sight, and you haven't scolded me once."

"Sorry." Sloane smiled weakly. "Just letting everybody know what's going on and that so far we've got a whole lot of nothing."

"We have plenty." Loch sat beside Sloane, reaching for his hand to kiss it. "We have a shiny new watch, my potent seed, and a *plan*."

"Wait, whose watch?"

"Here, my sweet mate." Loch offered one of his slitted tentacles for Sloane to drink from.

Sloane narrowed his eyes, but he let Loch slide the thick tentacle into his mouth. A rush of sweet fluid splashed over his tongue and he gulped it down. The magic of Loch's seed was indeed quite potent, instantly soothing Sloane's aching body.

Loch smiled as he withdrew, dragging his thumb over Sloane's lips before planting a kiss there. "Feeling better now, my beloved mate?"

"Yes, thank you. Now what's this about a watch and a plan?"

"Ah yes. Our brilliant plan. Find Ell, convince him to not destroy the world, and if he refuses, we unleash my godly wrath and your beautiful sword."

Sloane smiled sadly. "I really wish it was gonna be that simple. I really do."

"I will make it so," Loch insisted. "I hate to see you so troubled, and I know you are blaming yourself—"

"Because it's literally my fault—"

"No, my love," Loch cut in, squeezing Sloane's hand. "It is not your fault."

"Right." Sloane laughed miserably. "Then whose is it?"

Loch was thoughtful for a moment, and then he replied, "Great Azaethoth's."

"What?"

"I love my great-great-great-grandfather very much. He has been a father to me in many ways where my own father failed." Loch sighed. "However, this cycle with the Kindress, this eternal circle of pain, is one Great Azaethoth has perpetuated because he cannot let go of his firstborn." He smiled sadly over at Pandora. "It is a pain I hope that I never fully understand, but it is one I can empathize with now that I am a parent myself.

"However, mourning is still no excuse for allowing so many others to suffer, especially you, my sweet mate. You feel responsible because of your prayer's repercussions, an outpouring of your own grief over losing your parents that had incredible unforeseen consequences, but it was Great Azaethoth's grief that first created the potential for such catastrophe. Not you."

Sloane's heart thumped heavily, and he hugged Loch tight. "I love you."

"I love you, my beautiful Starkiller." Loch embraced Sloane, dragging him into his lap. "I will love you until the stars fall from the sky and the lights of the universe all grow dim. There in the darkness, my love for you will still burn bright and we will bask forever in its glow."

"Azaethoth," Sloane murmured, surprised and deeply touched by the depth of Loch's words. He had to blink back tears, and he was mesmerized by the stars swirling around in Loch's eyes now.

"My mate." Loch kissed Sloane softly, and his tentacles wrapped around him to hold him close.

Sloane kissed him back, his passion surging wildly as his pulse skyrocketed. He wanted Loch to take him right there on the couch, to rip off his clothes and—

"Jake, Jake, Jake!" Pandora suddenly declared as something crashed.

Loch and Sloane broke apart to stare at their daughter, who had managed to silently escape her playpen and pull over the neat stacks of DVDs that were previously nestled under the television.

"Bad spawn, bad!" Loch tutted. He reached out with a tentacle to pick her up and then gently return her to the playpen.

Sloane laughed at Pandora's adorable pout. "She's mad at you now."

"Well, I'm mad at her." Loch snorted. "I alphabetized those myself, thank you."

Sloane kissed Loch's cheek. "Thank you."

"You're welcome. My organizational skills are quite flawless."

"No, for what you said. About this not being my fault."

"Ah yes. Because it is not."

"But I'm definitely going to help fix it. We will help Ell," Sloane said firmly. He glanced at Loch's wrist. "You didn't tell me where you got the new watch from."

"Focus on the plan, my sweet mate."

"You stole it from Stoker, didn't you?"

"That's not important right now. What matters is finding Ell."

"And fast."

"We shall, my love." Loch hummed. "He is likely still on Aeon."

"You really think so?"

"He was unaware that he was the Kindress, yes? He may not understand how to use his powers and navigate the worlds between worlds. I would imagine he will eventually return to see Fred. He will want what is familiar to him."

"But they had that big fight at the wedding. Ell is mad at him too."

"Then he will return to seek out make-up sex."

Sloane laughed. "Strong maybe."

"I know these things. Even if I was mad at you, I would come back for mating."

"I know."

Urilith suddenly appeared in the middle of the living room in the vessel of a heavyset elderly black man in a dark gray suit. "Oh! Hello, darlings!"

"Mother!" Loch got up to greet her, their tentacles unfurling as they embraced. "Thank you for coming."

"Of course! Galgareth is on her way. Something about Toby's parents, a concert, and an F-I-R-E."

"Why is your jacket cut up the back?"

"I borrowed this man from a casket."

"At a funeral?" Sloane grimaced.

"I'm only borrowing him for a little bit. I will put him back, I promise." Urilith smiled reassuringly.

Sloane stood to give her a hug. "It's good to see you."

"Nana! Nana!" Pandora used her tentacles to crawl over the side of the playpen.

"Oh! Hello, my little sweetie." Urilith swept Pandora up into her arms and then gave her a big kiss. "Look at how much you've grown! You are beautiful."

"We would like you to take her somewhere very safe," Loch said. "Perhaps... off world."

Urilith frowned, but she nodded. "Of course. I can take her to my temple."

"Loch already caught you up on what's going on with Ell?" Sloane asked.

"Yes. And—"

Galgareth popped in then, and she was in her usual vessel of Toby, a teenager with several piercings and rainbow hair. Today it was neon green and purple. "Hey! Sorry I'm so late."

"I heard there was a little something about an F-I-R-E?" Sloane chuckled as he greeted her with a hug.

"Just a small one!" Galgareth smirked. "Toby and his parents are still coming to an understanding about being more active in his life. The you-know-what with the F-I-R-E helps."

"She's gonna figure out what that means, you know." Sloane smirked. "We're gonna have to come up with a code word or something."

Pandora blinked over at them as if she knew they were talking about her, but she couldn't quite decipher the exact nature of the conversation. She looked up at Urilith, asking, "Jake?"

"Jake?" Urilith raised her brows.

"Jake, Jake, Jake!"

"Ah yes. Your cousin. I think. Hmm. I'm trying to figure out the exact relationship—"

"Strangled," Loch said sourly.

"Estranged?"

"Both. Strangled and estranged."

Sloane's phone beeped with a new text. He frowned as he read it out loud, "Incoming, have snacks ready?"

"Who's coming?" Galgareth asked.

"I guess... everyone?"

A portal opened, forcing Sloane and Loch to take a step back. King Grell came through first, and he was followed by Alexander and Rota. Merrick was a few seconds behind them, and Stoker appeared last, leaning against the kitchen counter in a fresh black suit.

Urilith and Galgareth clamored to greet Merrick, Alexander went to the fridge, and Stoker remained as he was. Urilith surprised Stoker with a big tentacled hug that he awkwardly returned amid Loch rolling his eyes as hard as he could.

Grell summoned a drink to his hand, seating himself in the recliner by the television as if it were a throne. He politely cleared his throat. "This godly family reunion is very touching, but perhaps we could get to the business at hand?"

"Let's." Stoker loosened his tie. "Ollie has successfully unlocked the technique to make the totems that will resist the Kindress's rot. When he sobers up, he and Chase will begin production. Oh, and I have a message for you, Detective Merrick." He smirked and flipped him off. "Chase told me to pass that along. I think he's still a touch mad at you."

Merrick glared.

"Now that we're done sharing love letters, let's talk good news, bad news, and worse news." Grell peeked over his sunglasses. "Good news is I've learned how to order a venti mocha cookie crumble with soy milk with whip and an extra shot of espresso. Bad news is that the fountain is indeed bone-dry. Not a drop."

"Were you able to find the cultists?" Merrick demanded.

"Yes, that's the worse news." Grell paused to sip his drink.

"And?"

Grell held up his finger, waiting until he emptied the glass to reply, "They were quite chatty after I ate one of them whole—"

"You *what*?" Merrick's eyes bulged.

"They attacked us, I was feeling peckish, and it's a convincing tactic." Grell scoffed. "You should be glad I didn't eat all of them and left a few alive to talk!"

"What did they say?" Sloane pressed. "Did they say where Daisy is?"

"Yes." Grell refilled his glass with a snap. "They gave it right up. Small wrinkle, however."

"What?"

"She wasn't fuckin' there," Alexander replied since Grell was actively chugging again. "The world was fuckin' empty. No Daisy, no fruit, no nothing."

Grell came up for air long enough to say, "And there are at least three old gods helping her. I tracked their scents, but we lost them once we returned to Aeon. Allow me to refuel and I will head back out again."

"So, there are *three* more old gods here now?" Sloane asked, his heart sinking.

"Yes. Isn't that just ducky? No doubt they're here in anticipation of the big day."

"Is there anything else to report?" Merrick asked briskly. "No news from Mr. Wilder?"

"Fred?" Sloane shook his head. "Nothing. Grell? Anything from the spells you cast at his house?"

Grell smiled sweetly. "Don't you think I would have led with that, and not my coffee order if I had?"

"I honestly don't know."

"Fair, but no, not even a ripple."

"Then I suggest we all join King Grell in his search of the old gods hiding here with Daisy," Merrick said. "I believe our chances of finding them are greater than they would be of locating the Kindress."

Stoker pushed off the counter and then took a few slow steps forward into the living room. "And that would be foolish."

"Excuse me?" Merrick bristled.

"The cultists and old gods are not the immediate danger," Stoker replied coolly. "It is the Kindress. Finding him should be our priority."

"To talk to him," Sloane cut in.

"As soon as one of you knows how to successfully track a being of pure starlight, please let me know and we can have all the little chats you'd like," Grell cooed. "I can sniff out a god and a mortal. I only need more time."

"Time we may not have," Merrick said glumly. "Stoker is... *right*." He grimaced as if the admission was painful to say. "We should divide our forces more strategically."

"What would you suggest, Uncle?" Galgareth asked.

Merrick pinched the bridge of his nose. "I will accompany King Grell, Alexander, and Rota in their search for Daisy and the fruit. Should any old gods make an appearance, we are a formidable team."

"Team Best Dressed." Grell raised his drink.

Stoker scoffed.

"You lost points for taking off your tie, and my shirt-and-vest combo is on fleek."

Merrick ignored him, speaking now to Sloane as he said, "You and Azzath should take Galgareth and continue to search for the Kindress. Stoker as well because of his ability to wield a sword of starlight."

Urilith cradled Pandora close. "I will be taking the little one to my temple. If anyone else wishes to seek shelter there, I will watch over them as well."

"I will bring over Chase and Oleander," Merrick said. "I will feel better having you there with them. Thank you."

"Of course."

"Let's go," Alexander said shortly. "Next time we decide to have one of these stupid bullshit meetings, let's make sure we actually have something worth talking about."

You're getting very cranky, Rota warned. *You need to eat something.*

Whatever. Alexander rolled his eyes, but he snatched a banana off the counter.

"I'm inclined to agree. Let's hope our next little get-together is more productive." Grell's glass vanished as he stood. "And please, remember to provide snacks."

"All over it, Your Highness," Sloane said dryly.

Urilith passed Pandora over to Sloane. "Say bye-bye, sweet one. You and Nana are going on a little adventure!"

Grell and Alexander portaled without another word, and Merrick was right behind them. He at least paused long to mumble a farewell, and then he was gone.

Sloane hugged Pandora tight and smothered kisses in her hair. "You be good for Nana. I love you so much, baby girl."

Loch embraced them with his tentacles, and he smooched the top of her head. "Behave yourself, my spawn. Don't do anything I wouldn't do." He paused. "But also don't do anything I would do."

"Jake, Jake, Jake!" Pandora chanted, wiggling in Sloane's arms.

Stoker quirked his brows in questioning.

"Don't ask," Sloane muttered.

Galgareth ruffled Pandora's hair. "Have fun with Nana Uri!"

Sloane rubbed Pandora's back, and he found himself hesitant to let her go. He knew she would be safe with a powerful goddess like Urilith, not to mention Chase was a capable mortal, and Ollie had his unique starsight ability that was often useful in a pinch. Still, Sloane didn't want to leave her.

The only way he would know without a doubt that she would be all right was if she stayed, but that would be putting her in danger because they had no idea what Ell or the cultists might do. He wanted to believe with all of his heart that Ell was still his friend, and not the monster everyone was saying he was, but Sloane couldn't stop a shred of doubt eating away at the back of his mind.

Off-world was the best place for Pandora until he knew for certain what they were truly up against, he knew that, but Sloane's eyes were getting damp as he held her tight.

"It will only be for a short while, my love," Loch soothed. "She will just be a quick portal away, all right?"

"Yeah. Totally." Sloane kissed her forehead. "You be good. See you soon, baby girl."

Pandora nuzzled Sloane's cheek, and her hands turned into tentacles to hug his neck. "Da-Da."

Sloane couldn't help the tear that managed to slip out then, and he handed her off to Loch so he could say his goodbyes. He took a step away to clear his head and found himself standing beside Stoker.

"She'll be fine," Stoker said quietly. "Don't worry."

"Do you have any kids?" Sloane asked.

"No."

Sloane smiled. "Well, if you ever do, you'll understand that not worrying is never an option."

Loch gave Pandora a final smooch before giving her to Urilith. "Love you, my little spawn." He kissed Urilith's cheek. "And you too, Mother."

"I love you all," Urilith said. "Take care."

"Love you, Mother," Galgareth said, giving her and Pandora a hug. "Take care. Be safe."

"You as well. Come. Before I go, I have a gift for you. My blessing of protection." Urilith stretched out one of her tentacles, bopping Galgareth, Loch, and Sloane on the head. She smirked at Stoker and then bopped him as well. "You too, Jake."

"Thank you," Stoker said. "We will need all the help we can get."

"Goodbye, darlings! Bye-bye!" Urilith waved, and Pandora waved as well, gurgling happily.

Sloane resisted the urge to steal Pandora back for one more hug, and he sighed when Urilith blinked away with her. He reached for Loch's hand, asking glumly, "Well, now what?"

"We look for Ell," Loch replied carefully. "I do believe that was the plan?"

"But how? The damn location spell didn't work, I have no idea how to track a being of starlight, and literally no clue to where he might be."

"Toby has a suggestion," Galgareth said.

"If it's about waiting for Ell to return home to Fred for mating, I already thought of that," Loch declared.

"No." Galgareth wrinkled her nose. "He says we should try looking for Ell in chill places. Right now, he's probably scared and upset, so he's definitely hiding. And if he can't go between worlds, he might be at a park or a library! Somewhere that won't have a lot of people."

"Where did Ell live before he moved in with Fred?" Stoker asked.

"Oh! It was some little cottage out in the woods or something."

"Sounds pretty chill, don't you think?"

"Right, except we already looked there, and—" Sloane's phone rang. "Hold that thought. It's Milo." He paused to answer. "Hey, Milo! What's—"

"It's Lynnette," Lynnette said anxiously. "Sorry, I'm using Milo's phone. You've got to get to the damn hospital right now!"

"Gods, what's wrong? Is it the baby?"

"No, no! The baby is fine!" Lynnette grunted. "Milo had an accident driving home from work after Lochlain and Robert told him about the you-know-what, and they brought him to the hospital. He's okay, but—"

"Gods, I'm so sorry!"

"No, no, it's fine! He's fine! Really! But listen to me. You need to get down here now. Portal right the fuck into the lobby. I don't care. Tell Azaethoth to bring out his big badass dragon and go. As fast as you can!"

"Lynnette, what's going on?"

"It was Jeff Martin!"

CHAPTER 4.

"JEFF MARTIN, whose face I saw decompose into soup? *That* Jeff Martin?"

"Yes!" Lynnette hissed. "Milo is positive it was him! He's alive, and he's the one who caused the wreck! He plowed his car right into Milo's and drove him off the damn road!"

"That's…. That's not possible." Sloane sat heavily on the couch.

"What's going on?" Stoker demanded.

Sloane switched the call to speaker as he said, "Milo and Lynnette are at the hospital. He was in an accident, and he says it was Jeff Martin who caused it."

Stoker's eyes widened and then narrowed into venomous slits. He had a personal vendetta against Jeff for killing one of his friends, and Jeff's suicide had denied him the chance for the justice he sought.

"I haven't seen him or any other cultist trash," Lynnette went on, "but I trust Milo. If he says he saw Jeff, then he fucking saw him, and he might come back to finish the job."

"We'll be right there," Sloane promised. "Don't worry."

"I won't." Lynnette sounded like she was trying to smile. "I trust in the gods. See you soon. Love you, Sloane."

"Love you too. Bye." Sloane hung up. "*Fuck.*"

"Let's go." Stoker's shirt and tie were magically fixed. "That bastard is not getting away from me this time."

"We don't know that it was actually him."

"You don't trust your friend?"

"I do, but we saw Jeff die! All of us!" Sloane frowned. "I don't understand how he could still be alive."

"He could be a ghoul," Galgareth suggested, "or the cultists unlocked the secrets of necromancy. That's doubtful, but… possible."

"We shall be ready to unleash our wrath either way," Loch said firmly. "I like the fuzzy bearded one, and Jeff will pay for harming him."

"Jeff is mine," Stoker warned. "I'm going to tell Alexander and Rota what's going on since they also have unfinished business with him."

"But they're supposed to be helping Merrick and King Grell!" Sloane said. "We shouldn't pull them back yet."

"This is personal."

"We don't even know if Jeff is really there." Sloane stood back up, glaring at Stoker. "And if he is, this might be a trap to draw me out."

"A trap?"

"I am the only Starkiller running around. Would make perfect sense that they'd want to get rid of me since I'm the only one who could wreck their end of the world party with Salgumel. What better way to get me to come out than to attack my best friend?"

"If you truly believe it to be some kind of ruse, then perhaps we shouldn't go," Galgareth said with a little frown. "We don't know what we'd be walking into."

"Nonsense!" Loch scoffed. "My beautiful mate is a very capable witch, and he'll be escorted by two very powerful and exceedingly attractive gods."

"And me." Stoker crossed his arms. "My personal interest aside, this is our best lead yet. Getting to Jeff would certainly lead us to the fruit and the other cultists."

"We have no idea where Ell is or where to even look. I don't think this is a good idea," Sloane mumbled, "but you're right. Let's go."

"I'm also right," Loch chimed in. "About everything."

"Yes, you are." Sloane couldn't help but smile.

Stoker rolled his eyes.

Loch was especially smug as he transported them to the hospital. They popped out in a discreet corner of the pristine lobby with Galgareth right behind them. It wasn't too crowded, and no one else seemed to notice the four people appear out of thin air.

Wait—only *three* people because there was no sign of Stoker.

"Shit." Sloane scowled as he looked around. "Where the hell is Stoker?"

"He's probably going to look for Jeff." Galgareth patted Sloane's shoulder. "It's all right. We know he's not far away at least."

"Let us go see the bearded one." Loch took Sloane's hand. "We'll worry about the big dumb loser who had his watch stolen later."

They got checked in at the visitors' desk and then headed upstairs to find Milo's room. He was out of the ER and already admitted into a room, which worried Sloane that he might be more hurt than Lynnette let on.

Sloane squeezed Loch's hand as they walked down the hall the receptionist directed them to, and he found himself glancing ahead and trying to feel for any magic that might be out of place. Knowing how risky this was put him on edge, and he wouldn't have been surprised if Jeff simply popped around a corner and yelled *boo*.

Seeing Milo bundled up in a big hospital bed, sleepy but smiling, was a huge relief.

Milo's bearded face was flushed, and he waved drowsily. His left arm was in a blue splint, and he had a small bandage on his forehead. "Hey guys! Wow, hey, full house. I think that was the name of a show. There was a guy who had really cool hair."

"That's the drugs talking." Lynnette smirked, lounging in a recliner next to Milo's bed. She was a redhead like Loch and Lochlain, radiantly pregnant, and munching on a bag of sliced turkey and what appeared to be jelly beans.

"Hey!" Sloane surged forward to hug Milo, trying to be careful of the splint. "Are you okay?"

"I'm so good." Milo grinned. "They gave me something that looked like blue milk and I feel yummy."

"He has a concussion, bruised ribs, and a distal radial head fracture that they're going to have to cast," Lynnette said. "They said with a good healing sigil, it should be off in a few days."

"That's great!" Sloane turned his attention to Lynnette, walking over to give her a gentle hug. "Hey! How are you doing? How's little Mara?"

"We're fine. Just exhausted and ready to escape." Lynnette smirked. "Sorry I didn't get up to greet you all, especially you, your god and goddessness." She bowed her head respectfully to Loch and Galgareth.

"You're forgiven, dear mortal." Loch bowed his head. "You're with child and as such, you are to be as revered as we are."

"Tell that to my swollen feet." Lynnette chuckled. "They could use some worship right about now."

Loch winked, and a foot massage tub appeared in front of Lynnette's chair and her shoes vanished.

"Bless all the stars, the gods are good." Lynnette eagerly dipped her feet into the tub and groaned when the water started to bubble. "*So* good."

"Thanks, Loch." Milo shot a finger gun in Loch's direction. "You're awesome."

"Yes, I am." Loch beamed.

"Here." Galgareth walked around to the side of Milo's bed. She slipped out a tentacle from her sleeve to touch his broken arm, saying, "I think we can take care of this a little faster than a healing sigil can."

"Wow! Thank you!" Milo stared at her with big eyes. "Your face is so shiny. And I think your hair is melting like a rainbow. It's so cool."

"How much have they given him?" Sloane asked Lynnette.

"So much." Lynnette replied. "So very much."

"Hey, Milo?" Sloane sat on the edge of the bed. "I know your brain is probably painting with all the colors of the wind right now, but I need to talk to you about what happened, okay? Can you tell me about the wreck?"

"Totally!" Milo nodded, and he blinked a few times as if trying to focus. "I'm driving, trying to get home, and then wham! This truck plows right into me and I swerve into oncoming traffic! Wham, I get hit again. When everything finally stops moving, I turn my head to see who the fuck hit me, and there he was. Jeff, in some big shitty pickup truck, cruising right by me with this awful smile."

"And you're sure it was him?"

"As sure as I am that this feels fantastic." Milo groaned as Galgareth withdrew her tentacle. "Thank you so much, goddess person who I forget what you're the goddess of."

Galgareth petted Milo's hair. "We'll get you some flash cards."

"So, Milo, you're positive it was Jeff?" Sloane asked again.

"Yeah." Milo nodded firmly. "Oh! But his face. He didn't have the thing, the rot stuff. No bandage, no handprint, nothing." He closed his eyes. "I'm sorry I can't remember anything else, but seriously. Trust me. It was Jeff Martin."

"Do you recall anything about the truck he was driving? Maybe we can talk to Merrick about getting an APB out."

"Dark. Maybe blue or black. Big. Shitty. Like it was dirty."

"Okay, that's a start." Sloane paused to get his phone out so he could text in the group chat the new information. He expected Alexander and Rota were probably already aware of Jeff's possible return thanks to Stoker, but he urged them to stay with Grell and Merrick.

He didn't get a text back, but he had a feeling it would have said "whatever" with a middle finger emoji if Alexander had replied.

"Okay." Sloane paused to read the incoming messages. "Merrick is going to contact the AVPD about Jeff. He's also letting them know he got an anonymous tip about another big cultist attack, so they should be on high alert."

"Yeah, and what are they going to do?" Lynnette scoffed. "Try to put cuffs on an old god if one shows up?"

"Well, they can get the mayor involved. Set up a curfew and get people off the streets. Maybe even try to evacuate while there's still time. As much as I want to hope we can stop this thing before it starts, there is a very real chance that it might get pretty bad."

"You mean like the last time a bunch of gods ran around and caused a wee bit of mass panic?"

"Yeah, like that."

"That wasn't fun," Milo chirped. "Like, at all."

"And there's still no sign of Ell yet?" Lynnette asked, her brow creased.

"No." Sloane sighed. "I don't think he wants to be found. I'm sure it's a lot to learn that you're actually the firstborn child of Great Azaethoth and... well." He cringed. "Everyone wanting to kill him on sight definitely isn't helping."

"Team Kill Ell is quite vocal," Loch grumbled. "It is highly unfair. Ell has such great taste in personal lubricant. I believe he will listen to reason."

"He's our friend," Lynnette said firmly. "I'm more worried about Jeff Martin being very much alive and doing gods know what."

"I promise you all that when we find Ell, we are going to talk to him," Sloane swore. "He's scared, he's hurting, and we need to show him that we're not afraid of him. We're going to help him and stop the cultists."

"What about the corruption?" Galgareth asked quietly. "Do you think... he can resist it?"

"I know Merrick said the Kindress is doomed to fail, but Ell isn't *just* the Kindress," Sloane replied. "He's part of our family, and we have to act like it."

"He is also Fred's mate, and they found a way to do things with his penis," Loch chimed in.

"Yes, that too." Sloane shook his head. "If Ell turns into a monster, it's only because we treated him like one."

"We should get him some tampons," Milo said with a stern nod. "That will fix it."

Sloane barked out a laugh. "Wow. Really?"

"It's a very thoughtful gift."

"And why would Ell be in need of such hygiene products?" Galgareth asked.

"Right. Uh." Sloane laughed again. "Feels like a lifetime ago now, but Milo and I first met at a concert back in college."

"I punched him in the face!" Milo smiled brightly.

Galgareth blinked. "Is that how... you normally made friends?"

"It was an accident," Sloane explained. "He got really excited, we'd both had a little bit to drink...."

"And I punched him in the face!" Milo cheerfully repeated.

"Right. My nose was bleeding everywhere, he's apologizing, says he feels awful, and just takes off. When he comes back, he has a pack of tampons."

"Totally went into the wrong bathroom." Milo groaned, laughing lightly. "I was so damn freaked out, all of the stalls were out of toilet paper and they only had those air dry things so no paper towels either. Then I saw the dispenser thing! The one on the wall that you stick quarters in and bammo!"

"Tampons?" Galgareth smiled.

"Yup! We stuck one of those bad boys up his nose, got to talking, and figured out we were going to the same college. Been friends ever since."

"It became a big running joke between us, and we'd give each other tampons to celebrate special occasions," Sloane added. "If I remember right, that had a little something to do with how he and Lynnette started dating?"

"Sure did." Lynnette laughed. "Started my period a few days early while we were hanging out, and he just so happened to have a box of tampons."

"I promised to buy her all the pads and tampons in the world if she'd go out with me." Milo grinned over at her. "We stayed up all night, eating chocolate and talking about our favorite scenes in that holiday special. It just took a few *whip, whip, stirs*, and I was in love. Wait, or is it stir, whip, stir, whip, whip, stir?"

"Whip, whip, *whip*, stir," Lynnette corrected with a wink.

"You're so sexy."

"You're high."

"And you're still really sexy. Hell, I'm sexy. We're all sexy."

"Well, listen up, sexy man," Sloane teased, "I think we need to get you guys out of here. Until we find Ell and get a handle on what Jeff is doing, you should go to Urilith's temple. She's watching Pandora for us, and Chase and Ollie are there too."

"Is it okay to portal to worlds far, far away?" Milo glanced at Lynnette worriedly. "With her very pregnant condition?"

"We would literally be there with the goddess of motherhood." Lynnette smiled. "I can't imagine a safer place for us."

"So, you'll go?" Sloane asked.

"Of course."

Sloane hesitated, choosing his words carefully as he said, "I expected more of a fight…."

"I'm *very* pregnant. As long as I can bring this tub with me, I'll go anywhere you want."

"Deal." Sloane chuckled.

"Hey, do you think Robert and Lochlain can come too?" Lynnette perked up. "As long as we're trying to keep everyone safe from old gods and cultists, I'd rather not have my brother die again."

"Of course. We can do that as soon as…." Sloane paused.

Something was wrong.

The hum of activity in the hallway had fallen silent, the air was charged with something sinister, and dread gnawed once more at Sloane's stomach.

Loch and Galgareth sensed it too, judging by how quickly their heads turned toward the door. Loch stepped forward protectively in front of Sloane, and Galgareth quickly booped them both with her tentacle, no doubt a blessing of her serendipity.

"What's going on?" Lynnette demanded.

"It's a trap," Milo croaked in his very best impersonation of a certain aquatic admiral.

"We thought there was a chance this might be a trap, yes," Sloane said quickly. "Galgareth, can you please take Milo and Lynnette? We need to get them out of here now."

"On it." Galgareth hurried to take Lynnette's hands, stretching out her tentacles to grab a hold of Milo. "I'll be right back!"

"Whoa, that feels—" Milo didn't have a chance to finish before he and Lynnette vanished with Galgareth.

"Remember." Sloane took a deep breath. "No matter what happens, we can't have your godly wrath unleashed here."

"And we can't do that because?" Loch asked.

"Hospital. Full of innocent sick people."

"Ah yes. Of course. I'll behave. Mostly." Loch opened the door and stepped into the hall, his tentacles moving beneath his shirt like a writhing nest of snakes as he struggled to keep his true form hidden.

Sloane followed him, starlight dancing across his palms as he prepared himself for the worst. He could *taste* the magic churning around them, and he flinched when he saw the source.

Jeff Martin was standing at the far end of the hall, smiling as he strolled toward Sloane and Loch. Sloane dared to train a perception spell on him to verify that he was indeed alive, and not a ghoul, which meant he had to have been resurrected. There was an odd glow to Jeff's aura that hadn't been there before, something *godly*, and Sloane shuddered.

Jeff was very much alive and more powerful than ever.

His face was healed as Milo had said, and his restored smile was somehow even worse as he leered at him and Loch.

The hallway was empty, the doors were shut, and there was no evidence that any other patients or staff were there. Sloane didn't know if it was an illusion or if Jeff had done something to them, but he couldn't even hear the beeps of heart monitors now.

Everything about this was *wrong*.

Sloane hoped Galgareth would return soon if only to keep the odds in their favor.

"Ah, there you are!" Jeff laughed as he continued his leisurely approach. "The mighty Starkiller and his godly bitch, Azaethoth the Lesser."

"Why, yes, I am beautiful and in total control of myself, thank you," Loch quipped.

"You're supposed to be dead," Sloane said.

"We can fix that—" Loch whispered loudly.

"What the hell do you want, Jeff?" Sloane demanded firmly.

"The same thing every boy wants," Jeff teased. "For my patron god to awaken and remake the world anew, to destroy the Lucian heathens who nearly wiped out our people, and then maybe have a refreshing drink. Maybe a pop."

"We already know about the fruit, the boon you want to offer the Kindress. We're not going to let that happen."

"And how exactly do you plan to stop me when you don't know where I'm keeping it, and the last time I checked, you actually *lost* the Kindress?" Jeff smirked. "I think I'm doing all right for a recently dead man."

"You don't know where he is either," Sloane accused. "Do you?"

"Maybe I do, maybe I don't. You know I'm not much for villainous monologuing. Spoils all the fun, you know." Jeff chuckled. "The important thing is that you're both here now and—" A prismatic black tentacle whipped around his throat. He gasped, clawing at it as he wheezed, "Son of a bitch!"

"Son of a Starkiller actually," Stoker purred as he stepped into view, appearing out of thin air. His tentacle tightened around Jeff's neck. "Quiet down now."

"Stoker!" Sloane scowled. "Where have you been?"

"Waiting for this little worm to show himself." Stoker kept strangling Jeff, forcing him to drop to his knees. "Don't worry. I won't kill him. Yet." He glanced to Sloane. "I don't suppose he's said anything useful?"

"No."

"I was just about to do that, you know," Loch said stubbornly. "Stoker simply beat me to it."

Stoker rolled his eyes and then glanced at his watch. "Alexander and Rota should be here soon. We'll be taking Jeff—"

"The hell you are!" Sloane barked. "We're going with you."

"You're not going to want to see what we do to him."

"Wait, when did you get your watch back?" Loch snapped, staring at Stoker's wrist.

"Does it really matter?"

"The god of thieves has been *robbed*!"

"You robbed me first, you ridiculous twerp."

"Can we please fucking focus?" Sloane hissed. "Jeff is turning purple!"

Stoker made a face, but he loosened his hold on Jeff's throat.

"I am not letting him out of my sight!" Sloane glared at Stoker. "I understand that you want this because of what Jeff did to your friend. I know it's important to Alexander and Rota, too, because they think there's a chance he knows something about Rota's body. But *none* of that is going to matter if we don't find Ell and destroy the fruit."

"Obviously that is my first priority," Stoker said coolly. "After that—"

Jeff clapped his hands.

The room doors that had been shut now opened in unison. People emerged—some of them were nurses, others appeared to be civilians, and one was even in a doctor's coat. They took a single step to stand outside the rooms in perfect sync, and every last one of them was staring at Sloane.

Sloane shuddered, feeling surges of powerful magic thumping around him. He threw up a shield of starlight, and he heard Loch's tentacles unfurl, whipping across the floor.

This had most definitely been a trap.

"You really thought I'd come alone?" Jeff laughed weakly. "You... fools!"

"This changes nothing," Stoker warned, giving Jeff's throat a mean squeeze.

Loch held up his hand and time froze in an instant. The people were totally motionless, and only himself, Sloane, and Stoker were unaffected.

"Fuck you!" Jeff shouted. "This... is nothing!"

Ugh, and Jeff.

"So!" Loch said, "I think it's time to go."

"Agreed." Stoker squeezed Jeff's neck until his face darkened again. "I have a place we can—"

Glass shattered behind Sloane, and he turned just in time to see a bundle of giant purple tentacles thrusting through the now broken window at the end of the hall. He raised his shield, but he was too slow. It didn't matter anyway as he was not the tentacles' target.

Stoker was.

The tentacles grabbed Stoker and dragged him forward, forcing him to release Jeff as his body skidded across the floor.

"Stoker!" Sloane summoned his sword of starlight and swung as Stoker flew by them, striking the tentacles. The brilliant blade cut them clean in half.

"Much obliged!" Stoker grunted as he struggled to his feet.

"Aunt Zarnorach?" Loch scoffed, swatting at the remaining tentacles with some of his own. "Is that you?"

There was an angry responding roar outside.

"The goddess of *victory*?" Sloane groaned. "Great. Wonderful. Fabulous."

Loch frowned. "It's really not—"

"I *know*!" Sloane swung again when one of Zarnorach's tentacles got too close. He could see some of the people surrounding them starting to twitch as Loch's hold on time weakened. "Someone grab Jeff and get us the fuck out of here!"

Jeff was still gasping on the floor as he fought to catch his breath. He rubbed his raw throat as he reached out for Zarnorach's tentacles, likely trying to catch a ride out the window.

"What's the matter, Jeff?" Stoker sneered as he stalked back toward him. "Your pathetic little wards too much for you to portal through?" His thick prismatic tentacles seized Jeff and then lifted him into the air.

Jeff gurgled angrily, and a flurry of Zarnorach's tentacles surged toward him.

Stoker saw them coming this time, spreading his own tentacles out like a wall to keep Zarnorach's back. "Ah, ah! Not so fast."

"Come on!" Sloane shouted. "Let's get out of here!"

"Can we leave him?" Loch asked, his face furrowed now in concentration. "We should leave him." He gritted his teeth. "Something is… fighting me."

"Shit!" Sloane tilted his shield to deflect a small fireball cast by one of the nurses who was breaking out of Loch's hold. "We need to go! Now!"

"Prick's warded himself too! I can't take him!" Stoker growled.

"Whose… wards… are puny now?" Jeff heaved. "Ha… ha… urghhh…."

"Shut the fuck up!"

"Stoker!" Sloane pleaded, fending off another fireball.

"My mate," Loch grunted. "We have to go!"

"*Stoker*!" Sloane shouted.

"One moment please!" Stoker declared in an impatient singsong voice.

"We don't have—"

More of Zarnorach's long tentacles pushed into the hallway, nearly blocking out the sun. She was said to be a mass of tentacles like Urilith except a few of her appendages had giant claws at the end—

Exactly like the one that just grabbed Sloane.

He looked down, staring dumbly at the claw curling around his middle. He had enough time to think how shiny it looked before he was yanked forward fast enough to make his stomach flip.

"Sloane!" Loch screamed.

Sloane lost the sword of starlight in his struggle to get free of Zarnorach's claw, and he grunted as he was pulled right out the broken window.

He was falling fast, screaming as he fought to bring back the sword. He could see Zarnorach beneath him, and he had every intention of slicing right through her as soon as she drew him close enough.

But she didn't.

Zarnorach whipped Sloane high up into the air....

And then let go.

CHAPTER 5.

THE WIND ripped through Sloane's ears as he fell, and he had just enough time to turn so he could see where he was about to fall.

The hospital parking lot.

If he was lucky, he'd hit a nice soft car.

He got a quick glimpse of Zarnorach, a giant ball of undulating violet tentacles and claws. She was as big as a house, crawling up the side of the hospital like a spider.

Sloane's thoughts were of Loch's smile, Pandora's sweet laugh, and really wishing he could summon a sword to hurl at Zarnorach as hard as he could—

Leathery wings flapped around him, and Sloane gasped as giant hands plucked him out of the air.

"Galgareth!" Sloane shouted, staring up at the goddess in awe.

Galgareth was a massive beast with a beard of writhing tentacles and great wings like a bat. She was cradling Sloane close as she flew up high, babbling, "I'm sorry! I'm so sorry! After I dropped off Milo and Lynnette, she begged me to go get Lochlain and Robert! And Robert had to pack so much—"

"It's okay! It's okay!" Sloane clung to thick fingers, well aware that her grip was the only thing keeping him from falling to the ground. "You're here now! Just in time!"

"Goddess of serendipity!" Galgareth flashed a quick smile. "Where is Azaethoth?"

"Still inside the hospital with Stoker and Jeff—"

"Jeff? Je-fahfah, *that* Jeff?"

"Yes!"

The window Zarnorach had pulled Sloane out of suddenly exploded, raining debris down on the parking lot and setting off multiple car alarms as Loch emerged as his true godly self, a grand dragon with a long neck, a tentacled tail, and tentacles hanging from his chin. His wings were massive, and the webbing in between the thick bony ridges shimmered beautifully as they flapped.

"Sloane!" Loch bellowed as he took to the air, having spotted Galgareth. "My mate!"

"I'm here!" Sloane shouted.

"Thank you, dear sister," Loch said as he approached, hovering in front of Galgareth to nuzzle against her cheek, "for saving my beloved."

"Thank me later." Galgareth smirked. "We still have to deal with our aunt."

"Where's Stoker?" Sloane asked. "Is he still inside?"

"Yes, but—"

A roar drew their attention to the sky, and there was an undulating flying worm headed right for them. It was impossibly long, covered in thin spikes, and its mouth was a gaping maw lined with thousands of sharp teeth.

Maybe Sloane was dizzy from the fall and being flown around, but he swore he was seeing double.

"Hey, uh…." Sloane blinked. "Is that two fucking worms or one?"

"It's two!" Galgareth groaned. "It's Eb and Ebbeth! Two of the nightmare triplets!"

"I really just wanted you to say one."

"So did I," Loch griped. "One would be so much easier."

"Come on!" Galgareth sat Sloane down at the base of Loch's neck. "They're about to—"

Eb, distinguishable from Ebbeth only by the faint green circling his many eyes, rammed into Galgareth. She grunted but was able to stay in the air, swinging her fists to pound into the side of Eb's head.

Eb snarled and twisted his long body around Galgareth's, trying to get a hold of her wings in an attempt to take her to the ground.

"Let go of her!" Loch snapped his big head forward, sinking his teeth into Eb's side.

Eb howled, but he still refused to release her.

Sloane raised his hand to summon forth the sword of starlight. He swung right as Ebbeth, an identical worm except for his red coloring, crashed into Loch and tore them out of reach of Eb.

Loch snarled, gracefully spinning away from Ebbeth's grasp. "Rude! That was just rude!"

"Get me closer!" Sloane shouted. "I can't hit them from here!"

"Hold on, my love!" Loch flew up high, taking off like a rocket.

Sloane clung to Loch with his legs and his free hand, and he glanced at the hospital beneath them.

Sirens were approaching, no doubt in response to the purple tentacle monster and part of the building exploding. Dozens of people were fleeing on foot, a panicked and screaming swarm trampling over each other to get away. Traffic around them had come to a halt, confused drivers honking their horns as others abandoned their cars to retreat.

Sloane snapped his attention back to the air as Loch was preparing to dive. He couldn't see Ebbeth, but Loch's target was Eb, still entangled with Galgareth as their battle took them down into the parking lot. "Let's go!"

Loch dove, his wings tucked against his body as he zoomed at Eb.

Sloane held the sword high, and he waited for the perfect moment to swing his blade across Eb's side. He sliced along Eb's middle, and Eb howled miserably. Sloane swung again, stabbing deeper this time.

Eb released Galgareth, and she quickly stumbled out of his grasp. "Uncle, you're a real ass!"

"Fools!" Eb wailed. "Fools! All of you!" He slithered away in retreat. "Salgumel is going to rise and you're all on the wrong side! Such wastes of godly flesh, the both of you!"

Loch landed, unleashing a barrage of prismatic flames with a furious roar. "The name-calling is very unnecessary, Uncle!"

"Your mate must die, Azaethoth!" Eb bit back. "The Starkiller must fall!"

"Never!"

Sloane slid off Loch's back, raising the sword high over his head. "Eb, listen to me! We don't have to do this! You can stop this right now—"

Ebbeth descended upon them, swinging his long body like a whip and crashing into Sloane. He went skidding across the parking lot, catching himself on the side of a car with a pained grunt. The world spun, and his head rang miserably.

Loch lunged for Ebbeth now, and he snapped his teeth into the side of his face. "How dare you! I will end every last one of you! I will drag your worthless soul across the bridge in tiny bite-sized fragments!"

"You foul little vermin!" Ebbeth snarled. "I will rip your precious mate apart, piece by piece, right before your very eyes! I will utterly destroy him and make you—"

"Not if I make your insides into your outsides first!" Loch latched on to Ebbeth's cheek, his wings flapping as he struggled to keep him from flying off.

Ebbeth's long body whipped frantically, and he thrust his wings forward, striking at Loch's head. Loch refused to let go, but the claws on Ebbeth's wing tips were drawing blood.

"Brother! I'm coming!" Galgareth had recovered and she came for Ebbeth, shoving Ebbeth's head into the pavement to pin him in place. "Sloane! Now!"

Sloane pushed off the car and sprinted forward, drawing on his magic to create the sword. The pommel was burning his palm now, but he didn't stop.

That is, until Eb lashed his tail.

Even wounded, Eb's strength was enormous, and the blow sent Sloane flying back across the parking lot with a panicked shout.

"Fuck, fuck, fu—!" Sloane grunted as he hit something surprisingly soft. He almost laughed when he saw he'd landed in the back of someone's truck who had been carrying a mattress. It still didn't feel great, but it was much better than the ground would have been.

He bounced out of the truck and looked around, trying to catch his breath and track where everyone was.

Zarnorach had left the side of the hospital and now had Loch's neck wrapped up in her tentacles. He was breathing burst after burst of wild prismatic fire, but as soon as one tentacle was reduced to cinder, it was immediately replaced by another. Galgareth was facing off against Eb and Ebbeth, and she'd managed to get them tangled with each other by stepping out of the way of their latest attack just in time.

Eb was slower since he was wounded, but Ebbeth was still fighting at his full strength and forcing Galgareth to take to the air to try and escape them.

Hearing a crash behind him, Sloane turned to see Stoker pulling himself off the top of the van he'd landed on. "Stoker!"

"In the flesh." Stoker's face was bloodied, and he'd lost his jacket and vest. His shining black tentacles helped him get to the ground, and he wiped his mouth off with his sleeve. He made a face at the bloody stain left behind. "Ugh. Really?"

"Where have you been?"

"Once Loch fled to help you, I was left all by my little lonesome with Jeff and his little cultist friends. Don't worry. They're all dead. You're welcome."

"Jeff?"

"No." Stoker scowled. "He left his comrades to die like the coward he is."

Sloane jerked his head back to the battle, his ear drawn by Loch's furious roars. He grabbed Stoker's shoulder. "Hey! Can you fight?"

"Always." Stoker held out his hand.

Sloane brought forth a new starlight sword and then passed it over to him. "I'm gonna go help Loch! Can you—"

"Galgareth. Eb and Ebbeth. On it."

Sloane sprinted ahead with Stoker racing right beside him. Chest heaving and thighs burning, Sloane pumped his arms and flew across the asphalt as fast as he could. He and Stoker split off as they got closer to the fray, and Sloane hurried to Loch. He threw the sword as hard as he could, shouting, "Get the fuck off him!"

His aim was true, and the blade sliced through Zarnorach's coils holding Loch's throat. She screamed in pain, and Sloane already had another sword ready to swing when she tried to grab him.

Free now, Loch reared back with an enraged roar that rattled every car in the parking lot. He inhaled deeply and then blasted a massive barrage of fire at Zarnorach that drove her away from the hospital and....

Right into the street in the middle of traffic.

"Shit, shit, shit!"

Zarnorach crushed the cars in her path, and Sloane prayed that their occupants had already fled. At the end of the block, he could see police cars setting up a roadblock and building a tall magical shield.

"That will not hold her back." Loch shook his head. "She will destroy them all."

"Can you get in front of her?" Sloane asked quickly. "Drive her back to me and away from them?"

"Yes, my love." Loch bowed his head to touch Sloane's brow with the tip of his snout. "I love you."

"And I love you. Let's go kick your aunt's ass!"

Loch took off into the air, the wind from his wings ruffling Sloane's hair as he tried to catch up to Zarnorach.

He heard the words of a spell being called, and he put up his shield just in time to fend off a spear of ice. It was followed by a fireball and a chunk of rock, and he scanned the street to find the source.

He spied a nurse peeking out from around one of the wrecked cars and groaned.

So much for the cultists being gone.

Sloane turned around to jog backward so he could keep his shield up to defend himself. He grimaced when he saw another handful of people creeping out to throw spells at him. At first, it was easy enough to dodge and ping the magical attacks away, but the number of cultists was growing.

And fast.

Sloane watched in horror as dozens of men and women emerged from the buildings lining the block to join the cultists in hospital apparel, and he knew he had to think fast before he got completely overwhelmed by a small army.

He ducked behind a mangled truck, cringing as a fireball whizzed by close enough to singe his hair.

Zarnorach had almost reached the roadblock, and Loch was flying overhead, blasting her with fire to push her back. She seemed mildly annoyed at best and continued to writhe forward undeterred.

Shield raised, Sloane jumped out from behind the car to throw giant bolts of starlight at the cultists closest to him. The road erupted wherever stray arcs of the bolts struck, and the cultists hit went right down. He kept firing spell after spell, but the cultists kept coming.

He tried advancing to join Loch's fight against Zarnorach, but he could not move more than a few feet at a time. He was constantly forced to take cover and sneak from car to car, and he was getting desperate to keep the cultists at bay.

He didn't want to call for Loch because he was still trying to keep Zarnorach from reaching the barricade. He couldn't see Stoker or Galgareth, but he was certain they had their hands full with Eb and Ebbeth. He was about to try something really crazy, but—

A portal popped open right next to Sloane.

"What in the actual fuck?" Alexander snapped as he came through, Rota's shimmer rising over him. "Where's Jeff?"

"Alexander! Rota!" Sloane gasped. "I'm so glad you're here! Zarnorach is here—"

Alexander barely looked her way. "I noticed. Where's Jeff?"

"He ran!"

Alexander turned as if he was going to leave.

Sloane grabbed Alexander's arm. "Hey! I could really use your help here! I'm trying to help Loch stop Zarnorach before she reaches that barricade—"

Alexander glared at Sloane's hand. "Do you like having two of those?"

Look, Alexander, Rota urged. *There are many cultists here. Perhaps one of them knows where Jeff has fled?*

Alexander eyed the small army closing in and smirked. "Let's go ask them."

Rota's mass grew solid for a brief moment, his red and purple flesh revealed as Alexander marched right down the middle of the street. He stretched out his arms, directing Rota's thick tentacles to pick up the crushed cars and fling them toward the cultists.

Sloane only watched long enough to be sure Alexander and Rota were going to be all right, and once he saw the cultists screaming in retreat, he bolted to the roadblock.

Loch had landed behind Zarnorach, grabbing at her tentacles and trying to drag her back as she shattered the shield.

"Loch!" Sloane shouted as he summoned the sword of starlight again. "I'm here!"

"Mah loff!" Loch's voice was muffled since he had a mouthful of tentacle. He had several new wounds along his neck and chest, no doubt from Zarnorach's flailing claws. "Hurreh!"

On the other side of the now broken shield, Merrick had appeared. He was still in his human vessel, screaming for the officers to fall back while he built a new shield to keep Zarnorach from reaching them.

"Duck!" Sloane jumped on Loch's hip, pulling himself up and then sprinting along his spine. He skidded down Loch's neck like he was running down a slide. He jumped when he reached Loch's head, diving into the air and pooling all of his magic to make the blade of his sword bigger.

He drove the sword through the tentacles Loch had latched on to with a strained growl. He kept going, dragging the blade with him as he fell, cutting through Zarnorach's countless coils.

Zarnorach wailed horribly, thrusting her clawed tentacles at Sloane. She couldn't move forward because Merrick's new shield wouldn't break, and she was now cornered by Sloane and Loch.

Loch continued to blast her with fire, using his wings to help shield Sloane as he hacked at her. Zarnorach's tentacles never seemed to end, and Sloane's arms were burning from exertion. The sword was getting heavier by the second, and he had no idea how to stop Zarnorach except to keep trying to take her apart.

Loch's head snapped to the side, listening to something Sloane couldn't hear, and his eyes widened in worry. "Sister! She needs us!"

Sloane's stomach clenched. He'd thought Galgareth and Stoker would be able to handle Eb and Ebbeth, especially since Stoker was armed with a sword of starlight.

Merrick must have also heard Galgareth's cry for help because he promptly vanished.

"Uncle is going to help them!" Loch confirmed.

"Hope he hurries back!" Sloane gritted his teeth as he struggled to raise his sword. He could see the shield cracking now that Merrick wasn't there to power it, and his arms were going numb.

"Help is coming to us!" Loch promised.

Sloane was too tired to think clearly. "Who?"

"Meow, motherfuckers!" King Grell's rumbling voice sang out. He appeared between Loch and Sloane in a blink in his glorious Asra body, a giant cat monster with a long tentacled tail and a mane of tentacles decorated with colorful beads framing his head. He was massive, as big as Loch's dragon, and he charged forward to attack Zarnorach.

Sloane stopped swinging then, grateful for the reprieve as his arms throbbed. "Grell!"

"Sorry we were a tad delayed!" Grell declared as he continued to shred Zarnorach's tentacles. Sloane swore he was getting bigger. "We'll catch up soon over tea and crumpets!"

"What?"

"Go help your family, Starkiller!" Grell scoffed. "I'll handle this one."

"Are you sure? We can stay and…." Sloane stared as Grell continued to grow until he was nearly large enough to bat Zarnorach around like a ball of yarn. "Holy *shit*."

"It's good to be the king." Grell winked. "Now go!"

"My love!" Loch bowed his head so Sloane could jump on his back.

Sloane let the sword fizzle out and then climbed up, saying, "We'll be back as soon as we can! I promise, we'll—" He turned his head when he heard the pop of a portal, and Grell and Zarnorach were both gone. "The fuck?"

"I am confident the kitty king can handle himself," Loch said as he leaped into the air. "They did win their little quarrel with us."

"It was a rebellion!"

"Details!" Loch flew at top speed back to the hospital.

Sloane clung to Loch tight, and he squinted, trying to make out what was going on.

Galgareth was crumpled against the front entrance of the hospital, tangled up in the broken awning. It looked as if she'd fallen and one of her wings was torn. She was still fighting, sending blasts of prismatic magic at Eb and Ebbeth whenever they got close enough.

Merrick had twisted himself around Ebbeth to keep him grounded, and they were exchanging brutal bites and tearing out chunks of flesh.

Stoker had lost his starlight sword, but his slick tentacles had fully erupted out of his body from his back. He was battling Eb and trying to keep him from attacking Galgareth.

Loch went for Eb first, landing right on top of him. He grabbed Eb's top and bottom jaw, forcing him to whip his head back and open wide so Loch could then breathe a blast of prismatic fire right down his throat.

Eb convulsed in agony, trying to shake Loch off. Loch held on tight, but it was enough to knock Sloane off his back.

"Sloane!" Stoker dove forward, and his tentacles snatched Sloane up before he could hit the ground.

"Thanks!" Sloane grunted.

"Are you all right?" Stoker held Sloane close, looking over him worriedly.

"I'm fine!" Sloane quickly pulled away. "Grell is here! He portaled off somewhere with Zarnorach! And Alexander—"

"Is turning cultists inside out, I know. He and Rota are fine." Stoker held out his hand. "Sword, if you please?"

"On it!" Nodding, Sloane fought through the pain to bring out another sword. He handed it to Stoker, saying, "Try not to lose this one!"

"I'll do my best." Stoker winked and then ran over to aid in Merrick's twisting scuffle with Ebbeth.

Eb let out a fearsome shriek, and he was finally able to buck Loch off him. The moment he was free, he slithered away like a blobby bolt of lightning. He was headed around the other side of the hospital to the road that ran behind it.

"Shit!" Sloane took off behind him, but he skidded to a stop as he passed by Galgareth. "Gal! Are you okay?"

"Go get that son of a bitch and I will be!" Galgareth groaned as she struggled to her feet.

"Sister!" Loch had flown over, and he offered out his long neck to help Galgareth stand. "You are wounded."

"I'm fine!" Galgareth tucked her hurt wing back, fixing her sights on Merrick and Ebbeth. "You and Sloane go! We've got this. Go stop Eb before he hurts anyone!"

"Okay!" Sloane jumped back up on Loch's neck. He was exhausted, his palm was stinging, but he knew they had to keep going. "Let's go!"

"Yes! It is time to unleash my godly wrath!" Loch took off like a shot, zooming through the air to catch up with Eb.

Eb had already made his way onto the road and was smashing through the sea of abandoned cars. He didn't seem to know where he was going, and he left a sticky trail of blood in his wake.

Sloane didn't see any people at first, thankful that the AVPD had been able to get innocent citizens out of harms' way. All too soon, however, Eb cut through an alley and was headed right for a crowded street. Traffic was backed up for blocks, doubtlessly because of the roads being closed around the hospital, and those vehicles were still occupied.

"Loch!" Sloane cried. "Fly faster! We have to head him off!"

"Hang on tight, my love!" Loch twirled high in the air to build momentum for a dive. He tucked his wings back and down he went, crashing into Eb just as he emerged from the alley.

Sloane winced as he fought not to get thrown off by the force of the collision. He heard terrified screams erupting behind him and the building roar of a panicked crowd.

Loch forced Eb back into the alley, but he was too big to actually fit through himself. Eb squirmed backward until he was just out of reach, and Loch hit him with a blast of godly fire. "Hey! Get back here so that I may unleash my wrath upon you!"

"Surrender your mate, Azaethoth!" Eb croaked. "The Kindress is going to wake Salgumel! We will be triumphant! You cannot stop us!"

"I'm sorry, I can't hear you. Could you come a little closer?" Loch stretched out his neck, snapping his teeth at Eb. "Come here, damn you!"

Sloane hopped off Loch's neck, landing in a crouch just in front of him. He slowly stood and brought his hands together, focusing his magic to bring out the sword. "Last chance, Eb," he warned. "I do not want to kill you, but I will if I have to."

"It is you who will perish, Starkiller!" Eb snarled. "You will fall!"

The sword of starlight scalded Sloane's fingers, but he kept going until the weapon was fully formed. He raised it high, narrowing his eyes. "You first!"

Eb scuttled backward when Sloane swung, wailing as he retreated out of the alley.

Sloane gave chase, but he only managed to nick his tail before Eb was out of range. He chased after Eb, and he was so focused on his pursuit that he didn't even notice that Loch wasn't behind him.

Eb had found another alley to cut through, and this one opened up into the city park. Eb didn't hesitate to surge forward, slithering through the trees and over picnic tables.

Sloane cringed when he heard children screaming in terror. He could see a whole group of them fleeing the playground right in Eb's path. There was no way they would be able to get out of the way in time.

"Loch!" Sloane shouted. "We have to—"

He didn't get a chance to ask Loch for help.

He didn't need to.

Eb came to a sudden halt as if he'd hit a brick wall. He twitched and howled as the spikes that covered his body fell out in big patches. His skin darkened and then slid off, revealing the muscle beneath that quickly turned black. It fell away until only bones were left, and then those, too, melted into a thick liquid.

It was over in seconds.

Eb the First was dead.

Sloane froze, his heart pounding as he searched for what had killed an old god in mere seconds.

He already knew who he would find.

Cautiously, he walked into the park and let the sword drop from his blistered hand. He could see the children fleeing to safety with their families and just a few yards ahead of him, he saw what he was looking for.

Sitting there on a bench surrounded by a bright glittering bubble of light was the one responsible.

It was Ell.

CHAPTER 6.

"ELL?" SLOANE called out hesitantly. "Can you hear me?"

Ell was staring at the puddle that used to be Eb with wide eyes, and all the color had drained from his face. His horns had shrunk, and his crown was gone, but the strange bubble of light around him remained.

Sloane didn't know what the bubble was, but he was certain touching it was a terrible idea.

Ell showed no sign that he could hear Sloane, and he appeared to be in shock at what had happened. He also looked like he was about to be sick.

"I'm so sorry, my love!" Loch ran up behind him. "I'm too thick for my own good, and I'm afraid I got a tiny bit stuck in the alley. Then I remembered that I can, of course, simply shrink myself...." He trailed off as he approached, bowing his head to nudge Sloane. "What has happened? Where is Eb?"

"See that big puddle?" Sloane grimaced.

"By all the gods.... It's Ell!" Loch dropped his voice to a dramatic whisper to hiss, "He's right there."

"I know." Sloane took a deep breath. "Whatever you do, don't touch that bubble around him."

"Is that what made Eb into the puddle?"

"Yes."

"Got it."

"Okay." Sloane tried to take a step forward, but Loch's tail snatched him around his waist. "Loch! Let go!"

"We just agreed that the puddle bubble is very bad, and yet you are walking right to it."

"Because I'm going to go talk to Ell!" Sloane pushed his way out of Loch's tail. "Can you let Fred know we found him? With your godly messaging?"

"Of course. He can't reply, naturally, but I will let him know."

"Thank you. Tell the others to get here as soon as they can."

"As you wish, my beautiful mate."

"And... stay here for a second."

"But why?"

"Please trust me." Sloane reached out to pet Loch's snout.

"I always trust you." Loch's eyes glittered. "Please be careful, my beautiful husband."

"I will, I promise." Sloane slowly approached Ell, his pulse firing away at top speed. He wasn't sure if Ell was even aware he was here, and he called out to him again, "Ell! Hey! It's Sloane—"

The bubble around Ell expanded, stopping only a few inches away from Sloane's face.

Sloane stayed where he was and raised his hands. "It's okay, Ell. It's just me. Sloane Beaumont. Do you know who I am?"

"Starkiller," Ell said quietly. His brow furrowed. "I knew another like you. Abigail."

"Right. Stoker's mom." Sloane tried to smile. "Do you remember Stoker?"

"I... I don't know." Ell looked up at Sloane, and his eyes were filling with tears. "I don't even remember who I am."

"You're Elliam Sturm," Sloane said firmly. "You have an older brother, Tedward, a boyfriend named Fred Wilder, and a lot more friends and family who care a lot about you."

"I don't think that's true. That can't be right."

"It is," Sloane insisted. "I'm your friend. You and Fred came to my wedding. Do you remember that?"

"A wedding?"

"Yes! When I got married to Loch, you were there. You gave me a copy of *Starlight Bright*. I read it to my daughter, Pandora, all the time."

"Don't forget the strawberry-flavored lubricant!" Loch shouted over.

"That too." Sloane offered a reassuring smile. "It's okay. Really. I just want to help you. Just tell me what I can do."

"Nothing." Ell blinked, his tears falling down his face. "There's nothing anyone can do for me."

"No, hey, there has to be something—"

"No!" Ell snapped. "You don't understand!"

"Then tell me! Tell me what's going on!"

"I don't know who Ell is! Don't you get it? Please go away," Ell whispered, hanging his head and digging his fingers into his hair. He pulled at his horns as he cried. "Please just go!"

As Ell's sobs grew, the bubble grew.

"My love?" Loch called out worriedly.

"It's okay! It's okay!" Sloane took a few steps back. "Everything is fine."

The bubble stopped growing, though Ell was still crying.

Sloane was afraid to say anything else for fear of upsetting Ell more, and he figured he had no choice but to retreat for now. "I'll be right over here, Ell. Okay? Just…. You just hang out over there." He headed back to Loch with a grimace. "Well, I guess that went okay."

"He doesn't remember who he is?" Loch frowned. "That's probably not good."

"No, it's not. Maybe seeing Fred will help him remember?"

"I hope so." Loch leaned down to bump the tip of his nose against Sloane's chest. "The others are on their way. Ebbeth managed to escape them."

"Shit." Sloane glanced at the puddle. "Well, at least we have one less god to worry about now."

"I imagine Ebbeth is going to be a tad upset about his brother."

"Well, him trying to help end the world is a tad upsetting to me."

"Fair."

The pop of a portal signaled King Grell's arrival, though he had now returned to his human form. He smoothed back his hair as he approached, drawling, "Zarnorach is trapped in a maze I concocted off world. Don't expect her to stay there long. If you want to go give a little, you know—" He made a stabbing motion. "—then I suggest you go now. We should…." He trailed off, noticing Ell. "Well, look at that. You have someone right here."

"I'm not going anywhere or stabbing anyone right now," Sloane declared. "Fred is on his way here—"

"On his way? To do what exactly? Be a fetching distraction?"

"No!" Sloane narrowed his eyes. "Ell doesn't remember who he is. He's confused. We need to help him remember."

"And the puddle?"

"Uncle Eb," Loch said cheerfully. "Don't touch Ell's bubble."

"Lovely." Grell grimaced. "So, this is the plan, is it? Try to make the Kindress all better with the warm fuzzies and maybe he won't end the universe?"

"Yes," Sloane confirmed. "We can talk to him. We can reason with him. There's no reason to think he's going to hurt us."

"Tell that to the puddle."

"That was an accident."

"Right." Grell was definitely not convinced. "We are all very probably going to die because this plan is insane. I'm so happy that I'm a part of it. Now where is the rest of our dear little club? Wouldn't want them to miss this."

"On their way to us," Loch replied. "Ebbeth has fled."

"Such a shame he got away. If only we knew where another old god was in need of an intimate appointment with a Starkiller." Grell snapped his fingers. "Oh! Right!"

Sloane rolled his eyes. "Look, I'm not leaving Ell. Especially with you being more than a little eager to freakin' unalive him! We wait until Fred gets here and we can try to talk to him again."

"So, we're just leaving the old god I trapped especially for you to kill?"

"I'm not some kind of a murderer for hire!"

"I never said you were." Grell wrinkled his nose. "As if I'd pay for it."

Sloane groaned.

"Here's a thought. Instead of waiting here for Fred to drive his very mortal self over here, why didn't you have your godly hubby run over and grab him?"

"I didn't want to leave Sloane alone with Ell." Loch huffed. "There is still a puddle bubble."

"Fine!" Grell threw his hands up. "I'll go do it." He mumbled something under his breath.

It didn't sound kind.

Grell's seamless portal vanished him away in an instant, and Sloane glanced worriedly toward Ell.

Ell had drawn his legs up, hugging them to his chest. He didn't seem to be crying now, and the bubble around him had shrunk back to the size it was when Sloane first saw it.

That was a good sign.

Or so Sloane hoped.

He didn't have much time to think it over before Galgareth crashed into the sidewalk right behind them. She'd been carrying Toby, and he landed over in a bush.

"Oh! Toby!" She struggled to right herself. "Are you all right?"

"Great!" Toby croaked. "The bush is so soft!"

Loch and Sloane rushed over to help. Loch lifted Galgareth to her feet while Sloane helped untangle Toby from the bush.

"Thanks!" Toby said, brushing himself off.

"Of course!" Sloane said. "Are you really okay?"

"Yeah, I'm—oof!" Toby grunted as Galgareth scooped him up into a crushing hug. "Gal! I'm okay!"

"I'm so sorry! I didn't mean to drop you!" Galgareth fussed. "You're the best vessel ever!"

Toby looked like a tiny kitten trying to wiggle out his mama cat's grasp. "Yes, thank you! But please! I'm all right, I promise! Can you put me down now?"

"Oh! Yes. Sorry." Galgareth gently set Toby on the ground and then patted his head.

"Come on." Toby grinned up at her. "Hop aboard. You need to rest up."

"Thank you." Galgareth smiled and nodded. She did look weary from battle, and her wing was more wounded than before. She disappeared, and then Toby flinched.

"Seriously the best vessel in the history of vessels," Galgareth said now in Toby's voice. She gave herself a hug, but she froze when she finally saw Ell over on the bench. She also noticed the puddle. "So, uh, is that Ell?"

"Yes. Right. So, about Ell…." Sloane heard someone running toward them, turning toward the sound to see Merrick racing up to them.

"AVPD has secured the hospital grounds in the absence of old gods and cultists, and they are currently coordinating evacuation efforts! This area and a full block radius shall remain clear!" Merrick skidded to a stop. "I have given strict orders for no one to engage with any godly or otherwise otherworldly entities. We are attempting…. Wait, is that Ell?"

"That's what I just asked!" Galgareth exclaimed.

"I told you to tell them what was going on!" Sloane said with a sigh.

"You told me to tell them to come here as soon as possible," Loch corrected.

Sloane put his face in his hands.

"We should inform them about the puddle bubble," Loch urged.

"I thought you were…! Okay, look." Sloane took a deep breath. "Loch and I chased Eb over here—"

"The puddle is Eb?" Merrick gasped.

"Yes, but! *But* Eb was about to crush a bunch of kids, so Ell totally saved them. Maybe unintentionally. Still." Sloane cleared his throat. "Ell doesn't seem to know who he is. Grell just left to go get Fred and bring him here so we can try to talk to him."

"Stoker, are you getting all this?" Galgareth glanced over her shoulder, frowning when she saw he wasn't there. "I swear he was right behind me."

"He fought very bravely," Merrick said as if he didn't want to admit it. "Perhaps he needed a moment?"

"Was he hurt?" Sloane asked.

"No."

Loch snorted.

Merrick managed a small smirk. "Try not to look so disappointed, Azzath."

"Maybe he's meeting back up with Alexander and Rota?" Galgareth suggested. "Haven't seen them since they went on their cultist cleanse, right?"

"I hate to think what they're up to." Sloane grimaced.

"Probably better not to."

Grell and a very perturbed Fred popped up then, and Fred immediately jerked away from Grell.

"You're welcome." Grell scoffed.

Fred glared. "If you think I'm helping any of you fuckers hurt Ell, you can fuck—"

"No!" Sloane cut in. "No, not at all. That's not why I asked Grell to bring you here. Please, Fred. Ell needs us. He needs you."

Fred noticed the bubble, and his eyes widened when he saw how visibly upset Ell was. Then he saw the puddle. "What the fuck is that?"

"Long story. Short version is that we chased Eb over here and, well, the puddle is what happened."

"Eb, as in…."

"Yeah. That Eb."

Fred's brow wrinkled. "You try talkin' to him yet?"

"Yes, I did." Sloane sighed. "Didn't go so great. He doesn't seem to remember who he is, who *Ell* is. He got upset, so I backed off and have just been waiting for you."

Fred hesitated, but he grunted, "Thanks."

"Wonderful. Superb. Love that the gang is back together again." Grell scowled. "We're going to now let the ghoulish one try to go sweet talk his very capable of destroying the universe boyfriend?"

"Yes," Sloane replied. "It's just us here, no Jeff, no fruit. We can try to talk to him, nice and calm, and no one has to get hurt."

"Have I mentioned how fabulous I think this plan is?"

"You're being sarcastic," Loch accused.

"No shit, Azaethoth. And where is your vessel?"

"Oh! It's back at the hospital. I don't suppose you'd be willing—"

"No."

"We will go get it *later!*" Sloane took a deep breath, turning to Fred. "Okay, Fred, now I thought we could—" He stopped when he saw Fred was already halfway to Ell. "Shit! Uh, everybody else stay here."

Fred had stopped a few feet shy of the bubble, calling out, "Ell! Hey!"

Ell jerked his head up, and he looked confused. "I... I'm sorry. Who are you?"

"It's me, Fred."

Sloane caught up to Fred, but he stood off to the side to give Fred and Ell some semblance of privacy. He kept his eye on the bubble, hoping for the best but preparing himself to drag Fred out of harm's way if he had to.

"I don't know anyone by that name...." Ell frowned. "But I know your voice."

"Yeah, you heard it a lot." Fred smiled sadly. "We live together, me and you."

"What?" Ell scoffed. "I find that very hard to believe."

"But it's true," Fred insisted. "You're my boyfriend. You're the love of my fucking life, Ell. We were gonna get married. You kept one of them scales for our wedding. I found it right before—"

"No, wait. Please just... please just stop!" Ell held the sides of his head. "I don't know you! I, I don't remember any of that! I don't want to!"

"But why?" Fred demanded.

"Because it *hurts!*" Ell shouted, fresh tears streaming down his face. "I have so many memories. Lifetime after lifetime of pain, of *dying*, of never being enough—"

"You're enough for me," Fred said passionately. "You're more than enough. You're fucking everything to me, Ell. I love you."

Ell whimpered as his horns shot up a few inches, and he let out a choked sob. "No. No one loves me. That's a lie. I am so fucking empty inside, and all I see is death and suffering, and it's always my fault. It's eating me up! It hurts so much! What's the point of anything if death is all there is?"

"No! You don't believe that!" Fred argued. "There is so much more! I used to think that same fuckin' way! I was gonna let myself rot! But then I met you." His eyes were damp. "I met you, and you changed my whole fuckin' world. You, Elliam Sturm."

"I'm not Elliam... I'm not anyone." Ell cried miserably.

"Yes, you are. You're fuckin' Ell, I love you, and there's nothing you can do to change that." Fred looked over the bubble, and he took a step forward.

"Fred! Don't!" Sloane yelled.

"What are you doing?" Ell's eyes widened. "No! Stay back!"

"This is just like when Blix had to go through the Forest of Madness to save his friends," Fred said stubbornly. "He knew the fuckin' risk, but he did it anyway. Because he loved them." He stepped right up to the bubble. "They meant everything to him, just like you mean fuckin' everything to me."

"Stop!" Ell pleaded. "Don't come any closer!"

"Fred! Don't!" Sloane raced toward him, but he was too late.

Fred put his hand through first, and it rotted away instantly. It burst back to life with fresh skin only to rot again. It was happening over and over, an endless cycle of decomposition and restoration, and Fred was clearly in horrible pain, but he tried to step through the bubble anyway.

Sloane wasn't fast enough, but Ell was.

Ell stood from the bench, throwing up his arms as he shouted, "Stay away!"

Fred suddenly went flying, thrown from the bubble by an invisible wave of energy. He landed with a grunt, and Sloane hurried over to help him sit up.

"Are you okay?" Sloane asked.

"Fine." Fred held his hand against his chest. The rot appeared to have stopped for now, but Fred was still wincing in pain.

"No, no!" Ell cried. "I'm sorry! I didn't mean to! I just, I just wanted you to stay back!"

Sloane sighed, glancing back to Loch and the others. They looked worried, though Grell was grinning and giving him a thumbs-up. Sloane ignored him, turning his attention back to Ell as he said, "It's okay, Ell. Really. We love you. We forgive you."

"No." Ell's horns grew taller. "No, you don't. You don't know what I've done. All the terrible things I've done…."

"It doesn't matter!" Fred growled through gritted teeth. "I love you! And Sloane does too! Milo and Lynnette, Robert and Lochlain, all of us do!"

"You're afraid of me," Ell realized with a small sob. "Oh no. No, please. You're all afraid of me, aren't you?"

"No," Fred replied without hesitation. "No, we're fuckin' not!"

"Yes, you are!" Ell's horns had become their former grand size, and the crown of stars reappeared in a violent swirl above them. His eyes glowed as he took a step forward, the bubble around him expanding. "I do remember you. I remember you turning your back on me when I needed you. Because you were *afraid*. You were afraid then, just like you are now."

"I'm afraid of losing you!" Fred broke away from Sloane, pleading, "Listen to me, Ell! Please!"

"No." Ell's tears had dried, and his face was contorted in an angry snarl. "I'm done talking. I want you to go away now."

The bubble was getting bigger.

Much bigger.

The grass inside the bubble turned brown and then faded into nothing until only raw earth was left behind. There was no sign of returning life this time, and the bubble only continued to grow.

"Uh, Fred." Sloane backpedaled. "I think, uh, maybe we should take a break. You know, a *big* break, and then we can come back later."

"No!" Fred grunted. "I ain't done talkin' to him yet."

"The giant puddle bubble says otherwise."

"Fuck it!" Fred held out his arms and remained where he was. "No point if I don't have him. Go on. Leave if you gotta. But I ain't goin' anywhere."

"Fred! Shit!" Sloane looked back at the others. "Someone grab Fred. It's time to go! Right now!"

"Going!" Grell snapped his fingers, and he and Fred disappeared through another smooth portal.

"To the temple!" Merrick shouted, reaching for Galgareth to transport her away.

Galgareth had looked as if she was about to say something, but Merrick took her away before she could.

Sloane ran right for Loch, well aware of the bubble closing right in behind him. He hated to be running away again, but he didn't know what else to do. One touch from Ell's bubble spelled the end for any of them, and it was too dangerous to risk it.

Loch bounded over to meet Sloane halfway. He scooped him into his arms as he took off into the air to avoid the bubble, soothing, "I've got you, my love."

Sloane held on tight. "I fucked up. I fucked it up again."

"No, no." Loch shook his head. "You did not fuck up. These are… unfortunate circumstances." He hugged Sloane. "Let us go, all right?"

"Okay." Sloane looked back down at Ell through the bubble, and he shouted, "We'll be back, Ell! We love you!"

Ell did not reply, but the bubble was definitely still getting bigger. It had almost overtaken the entire park, and Sloane prayed people would stay away and listen to the AVPD's evacuation orders. He tried not to think about what would happen if they didn't.

Loch brought them to Urilith's temple, a stone step-style pyramid that was built in her honor long ago on a lushly forested world between worlds.

Lynnette was lounging in a plush bed of pillows and blankets, snoring lightly. Milo was next to her, his arm as good as new as he adjusted the pillows under her feet.

Robert and Lochlain were seated nearby, and Merrick had all but tackled Chase where he'd been hanging out beside them.

Ollie was passed out in a hammock that Urilith was gently rocking with her tentacles while she held an equally zonked Pandora. Galgareth went to her to greet her with a big hug.

Grell had made himself a drink and then headed over to one of the open terraces, no doubt seeking some solitude.

And Fred….

Sloane didn't see him.

"What happened?" Urilith asked urgently. "Did something go wrong?"

"It definitely didn't go right," Sloane mumbled. He walked over to Urilith so he could press a soft kiss to Pandora's brow.

"We found Ell," Loch said, "but he is not quite himself. His memories appear to be a bit scrambled. We tried to speak with him…."

"But?" Urilith prompted.

"But it went about as well as a three-legged dog trying to bury shit on an icy pond!" Grell called out from the balcony.

"Colorful, and yes, perhaps even accurate," Loch mused.

"Ell doesn't fully remember who we are, and he got pretty angry when we tried to push him," Sloane said. "What little he does remember is apparently not that great, and he's created this death bubble—"

"Puddle bubble," Loch corrected.

"This bubble that turns anything that touches it into a puddle." Sloane sighed miserably. "Eb is dead. He crashed right into it and poof. Fred tried touching it, and it sort of freaked out on him. I guess it didn't know how to react to a ghoul."

"I must report back," Merrick said. "I have to make sure the AVPD is able to evacuate that area and keep it secure. At the rate that bubble was growing, it could easily overtake the city in mere hours."

"Now that we left, it should stop, right?" Sloane frowned. "Ell should calm down and it'll shrink."

"How certain are you of that?"

"Not very, I guess. I don't know."

"I'm going back with you," Chase said firmly. "I can help you. You know I can. We gotta get this shit sorted out and fast. If we really gotta evacuate the whole damn city, you know it's gonna be a fuckin' nightmare."

"I am aware," Merrick said, "but I would still be much more comfortable if you remained here."

"Fuck you, and fuck you being comfortable! How about my comfort, huh? Knowing you're out there fighting gods and star babies while I'm stuck out here is worse than havin' fuckin' hemorrhoids!"

"Elwood!"

"Well, it is!"

"Where's Fred?" Sloane asked, hoping to change the subject and ease some of the tension.

"He said he wanted to go for a walk," Milo said quietly, glancing at Lynnette to make sure his voice didn't rouse her. "Not sure how long he's planning to be gone, but, uh, he didn't look very happy."

"How are you guys all holding up?"

"We're good. Promise. Lynnette's been snoozing, Robert and Lochlain are watching her snooze, and uh, well, I'm just here."

"Sobered up now?" Sloane smirked.

"Yeah! And my arm's as good as new thanks to Galgareth." Milo wiggled both of his hands, his arm now free of its cast, and he smiled wearily. "Ollie over there finally passed out, but the totems are finished. Made, like, a hundred of them before he went night-night. Urilith's been the best hostess goddess ever taking care of everybody."

"Aw, such a sweet mortal," Urilith cooed. "Thank you, Milo. You're very kind."

"My pleasure, your goddessness."

"And Panda? She's okay?" Sloane petted Pandora's hair. He didn't want to wake her, but he very much wanted to cuddle her.

"She's been a delight," Urilith replied. "She's very spunky. Just like her father."

"I am still quite spunky," Loch said proudly.

"Where is your vessel, my darling child?"

"Ah. It is at the hospital." Loch nudged Sloane's shoulder. "I shall return. Just a moment."

Sloane waved, watching Loch vanish. He turned his attention back to Pandora, and he smiled when Urilith offered her out to him. "Am I that obvious?"

"Just a bit." Urilith winked.

Sloane scooped Pandora up, cradling her against his chest. He loved how warm she was, and he rubbed her back gently. "Hey, little girl. Missed you."

He didn't have long to enjoy their reunion cuddle because Loch reappeared in his human body with Stoker, Alexander, and Rota. They landed in a messy pile on the floor with Alexander trapped on the bottom, and he wheezed angrily, "Get the fuck off me!"

Loch snorted. "Aren't you glad I took the time to find my vessel now? Imagine how uncomfortable that would have been if I had been in my full godly glory!"

"Fuck you," Alexander panted.

Stoker rolled off with a grunt, but he didn't bother trying to sit or stand. "There. Happy?"

"Fuckin' great," Alexander snapped. "My ribs are still broken, but no, really, that's so much better!"

Easy, sweet boy, Rota soothed. *We're safe now.*

"What happened? Where have you guys been?" Sloane asked with a frown. "You kinda look like you got the crap kicked out of you."

"We have a small problem," Stoker said.

"What is it now?"

"An army of cultists and old gods is marching right to the city park as we speak. Jeff and Daisy are with them, and yes, they have the fruit. No, we could not stop them, and no, I don't see how we can."

"Well... *fuck*."

CHAPTER 7.

"HOW MANY?" Merrick demanded.

"At least a thousand cultists, maybe more," Stoker replied. "It seems Je-fahfah and Daisy really amped up their recruiting efforts. They probably got people from all over the world to come here."

"And the gods?"

"About a dozen, I believe. Ebbeth and Zarnorach are with them." Grell snorted loudly.

Sloane ignored him. "And they're headed to the park? Are you sure?"

"That's where Ell is, isn't it?" Alexander rolled his eyes. "You thought they couldn't figure out that something was going down in that part of the city? The giant roadblocks are a pretty big clue."

"I guess I'd hoped not." Sloane hugged Pandora closer. "I'm sure it's all over the news by now too. Even if they're not reporting exactly what's happening."

"So, can we kill him now?"

"What? No!" Sloane scoffed. "We need to worry about the army that's marching toward him right now with the damn fruit!"

"You all must rest," Urilith said firmly. "You are exhausted from battle. Please, take a few moments to recover so that I can heal you. It would be foolish to rush back while you are weak."

"We don't have time," Stoker said. "They will reach the park in a matter of *minutes*."

"What happened to them waiting for that special date?" Chase asked. "Ell's birthday or whatever the hell it was?"

"I guess they decided to move things up."

"We should wake Oleander." Merrick crossed his arms. "His starsight might be able to help us deduce what our next move should be."

"Fine." Alexander walked over to the hammock. He leaned down to shake Ollie's shoulder, saying quietly, "Ollie? Hey. Hey, baby. Wake up."

Sweet boy, it's time to wakey wakey, Rota said in a singsong voice.

Ollie grunted, but he didn't open his eyes.

With a sigh, Stoker walked right over and flipped the hammock.

Ollie hit the floor face-first. "Ow."

"Stoker! You fucker!" Alexander snarled, shoving him hard.

Stoker barely flinched.

Rota pushed him with one of his tentacles and put Stoker flat on his ass. "That was very rude!"

"We do not have time for this!" Stoker grumbled as he picked himself up. "Come on!"

"What's going on?" Ollie asked, rubbing at his eyes.

"We need your help," Alexander explained as he helped Ollie to his feet. "Short version is that a fucking army of cultists and olds gods are headed right for Ell with the fruit. Got any bright ideas on what the fuck we should do?"

Ollie's eyes widened. "I really, really need a drink."

Grell appeared beside him with a glass of something purple. "Drink up."

Ollie tipped the glass back without hesitation, belched, and then nodded. "Okay. So, we need to see what to do. We have to...." He swayed. "Whoa. We have to do nothing."

"What do you mean, do nothing?" Alexander scowled. "We can't do nothing."

"But that's what we have to do." Ollie shook his head. "It's not time yet."

"Time for what?"

"To do stu-fahfah."

"That's not very helpful," Sloane said carefully.

"Come on, Ollie." Chase came over to give Ollie a small shake. "Can't you starsight somethin' else?"

"I'm not a magical cue ball! You can't wiggle the answers out of me!" Ollie swatted at Chase. "It's what I see!" He took a deep breath. "If we want to win, this is what we do. We have to wait. It's not time yet. If we try to go fight now...." He frowned. "We will lose."

Silence fell over the temple.

Lynnette stirred, grumbling, "What's going on? What have I missed?"

"A lot." Milo patted her shoulder. "I'll catch you up, okay?"

Sloane glanced around, noting the many injuries among them and overall exhaustion. "Ollie is right, you know. It's just like Urilith said too. We're hurt, we're tired, and we need to rest."

"You're willing to trust the fate of the universe to the whims of an alcoholic ginger?" Grell asked sourly.

"Yes," Sloane replied without hesitation. "Ollie is our friend, and his starsight has never been wrong. I trust him. We all do. If he says we have to wait to win, then waiting is what we do."

"Thank you, Sloane." Ollie smiled warmly. He cut his eyes at Grell. "And I'm a *former* alcoholic, thank you!"

Grell put his face in his hands and sighed.

"Hey, uh, Ollie. Don't suppose you can see how long we're supposed to wait?" Sloane asked.

Ollie hiccupped. "Uh. Two hours, thirteen minutes, ten seconds. Nine. Eight. Six. Five...."

"You skipped seven." Alexander affectionately ruffled Ollie's hair.

"No. That's important. We'll need it later."

"Okay." Sloane cuddled Pandora, trying to ignore the clenching in his stomach. "So. We rest up, we heal, and hopefully try to come up with some kind of plan."

"And that means you are coming with me," Loch declared, gently plucking Pandora from Sloane's arms. He turned to Urilith. "Mother?"

Urilith smiled as her tentacles wrapped around Pandora, gathering her close. "Of course."

"Loch, wait—" Sloane protested.

"Can't wait. We only have two hours." Loch hugged Sloane against his chest. "You are entirely too tense, you need to rest, and that can only mean one thing."

"Loch!" Sloane blushed furiously. "This is not the time for *that*!"

"Oh, but it most certainly is."

The temple vanished, and Sloane found himself at the edge of a giant city floating in outer space. He recognized the shiny black stone immediately, staring in awe at the endless maze of floors and hallways connected by high arches and long halls. The dark stone reflected the starry skies around them and gave the illusion that they were floating out amongst the heavens.

"Zebulon." Sloane breathed in sharply. "You brought me to Zebulon?"

"Yes, my love." Loch took Sloane's hand. "Where I first bedded you and took you as my mate."

A waterfall of liquid gold appeared out of nothing, gushing into the center of the platform they were standing on. The gold flowed over the edge into the void, and a bed took form where it had struck the floor. The linens were gray and white, the plush pillows were stitched with bright silver thread, and Sloane was certain it was the same bed from before.

"This is amazing," Sloane said. "Just as amazing as it was the first time, but we should head back."

"No, we should head this way. In the direction of the very large bed."

"Loch," Sloane said firmly, "I love you, but we really do not have the time. We need to come up with a plan."

"This is part of the plan."

"We can't waste time *mating*."

"Mating is never a waste of time!" Loch gasped.

"Might be a tiny bit when the fate of the world is at stake." Sloane snorted as he let Loch lead him over to the bed. "Your seed does have incredible healing powers, but can't we just, you know, have a quickie or something?"

"My love," Loch soothed. "Here in this place, while we are together, I will stop time. For me and you."

"Wait, are you serious?"

"Yes, my beautiful love." Loch smiled warmly, and his eyes filled with stars. "For as long as we share this bed, time will not exist. It is my gift to you."

"Loch...." Sloane's heart fluttered. "We...."

"If we are truly about to fight for the fate of the world in two hours and eight minutes, then I wish to worship your body in preparation for the battle." Loch winked. "You always feel much better after you've had my seed, you know."

"I can't believe you're trying to convince me to get laid to save the universe."

"I can't believe you're not in this bed yet."

Sloane laughed.

Loch wagged his brows as he hopped into bed, his clothes magically disappearing as he spread himself out. "Well? Time is fleeting, my beautiful mate."

Sloane licked his lips as he gazed over Loch. "Okay. Fine. For the sake of the universe."

Loch grinned, and his tentacles unfurled from his arms and shoulders, reaching out to grab Sloane. He dragged him on top of him and then kissed him sweetly, cupping the sides of Sloane's face with his hands. "Mmm, my gorgeous mate."

"Yours. Forever." Sloane closed his eyes as he kissed Loch back and straddled his hips. The tension he'd been carrying melted away, and he focused on the slide of Loch's hot tongue in his mouth. It was easy to block out the insane reality that awaited them back on Aeon when he had Loch's tentacles peeling away his clothes, and he gave himself over to the raw pleasure of divine flesh meeting his.

They were going to save the universe, and they were going to save Ell—from himself, from those that would harm him and abuse his power.

They just had to.

A new urgency fueled Sloane's kisses, and he impatiently reached for one of Loch's tentacles. He stroked around the tip to find that it was slitted, and he then immediately pushed it between his legs to his aching cock.

"Sloane." Loch chuckled breathlessly. "Impatient, are we?"

"Please." Sloane whimpered, bucking forward.

"Anything for you, my love." Loch's tentacle swallowed down Sloane's cock into sweet, impossibly tight heat. It created magnificent suction, and its steady pulsing was incredible. Loch mouthed his way down Sloane's throat, and his other slitted tentacle slid around Sloane's hip.

Sloane shuddered as his body became open and wet, magically preparing itself to take Loch inside of him. He rocked into the tentacle sucking on his cock and leaned his head back to give Loch more room to suck and kiss his neck. "Gods, yes.... Loch."

"Yes, my beautiful mate." Loch sat up, wrapping Sloane's legs around him. He slid his hands up Sloane's back and traced his fingers along his spine as he pressed a searing kiss to his lips.

Sloane was already panting, grinding down in Loch's lap. He could feel one of Loch's other tentacles teasing at his hole, and he groaned as it circled back and forth in torturous loops. The pressure wasn't enough to penetrate yet, and the friction was intense. He grabbed Loch's shoulders and then reached for the base of the tentacles where they erupted from Loch's upper back.

He knew this was a tender spot for Loch, and he traced the base of the thick tentacles with soft caresses in hopes he was getting Loch just as turned on as he was. Judging by the sound of Loch's happy groans, it was working perfectly.

The tip of the tentacle playing with Sloane's hole finally breached him, a taunting dip that was far too shallow to offer any relief. Sloane tried arching back for more, but the tentacle shied away before he could.

"Loch," Sloane pleaded. "Come on."

"We have time." Loch nosed Sloane's cheek. "There is no need to rush."

Sloane stroked the base of Loch's tentacles more frantically, but it didn't spur Loch to action as he'd hoped. His cock was throbbing, and thrusting into the tentacle that was sucking on it didn't give him the friction he wanted. He wanted Loch inside of him, he wanted that sweet pressure, and he wanted it now.

"*Loch*." Sloane surged forward so he could press his teeth into Loch's neck. He sucked as he bit down, grinding his hips more forcefully.

"Sloane!" Loch made a funny sound that was a cross between a moan and a giggle, and he squeezed Sloane's hips. "That, that is unexpectedly pleasant."

"Come on, baby." Sloane licked at the bite mark he'd left. With a little more effort, it could be a respectable hickey. He latched back on, reaching down to find Loch's tentacle and guide it back to his ass as he sucked at Loch's throat.

"My love!" Loch flinched, and he thrust the tentacle into Sloane's slick hole. His fingers dug into Sloane's hips and he fucked up inside of him with short, feverish bursts.

Sloane snapped his head back to moan, the force of Loch's slams lifting him up off his lap. More of Loch's tentacles spiraled around his waist and thighs, and he pressed breathless kisses to Loch's lips, praising, "Gods, yes. Just like that, that's it! Mmm, just like that!"

"There are not words for what you do to me," Loch purred. "The desire you stir, the lust you set aflame deep within me… It's indescribable." He pushed Sloane onto his back, moving on top of him and spreading his legs wide.

Sloane grunted from the change in position and the new depth it offered. He couldn't tell how far the tentacle was inside of him now, but the sensation was white-hot and the ache left in its wake blissful. It was thrusting impossibly fast now, a pace that only a god could sustain, and Sloane went limp against the bed, moaning happily.

Loch's tentacles squeezed Sloane's thighs and lifted his ass off the mattress as he continued to fuck him hard.

The tentacle that had been sucking Sloane's cock suddenly increased its efforts, and Sloane cried out, "F-fuck! Loch!" It was so intense that his eyes watered, and Loch's tentacle was driving into his prostate relentlessly. Combined with the wonderful suction and the awesome pressure of being fucked like this was sending him right to the edge. "Loch! I'm—!"

Loch's voice was rumbling with a low growl as he commanded, "Come for me, my mate... now!"

Sloane's entire body trembled as he surrendered himself over to Loch's demands, and he came with an excited sob. The tentacle on his cock swallowed down his load, and it added an extra layer of pleasure that made his hips jerk. His chest felt light, his face and neck flashed hot, and he pushed down on the tentacle inside of him to drag the pleasure on for as long as he could.

His entire body was tingling with it now as wave after wave of sweet sensation crashed over him until he had to grit his teeth and hiss to breathe through it. He stretched his thighs and his hips popped, finally able to speak as he croaked, "Wow."

"A fair review," Loch said huskily, "but I think I can do better than that."

Sloane yelped in surprise as Loch flipped him onto his face. The bed rose beneath him, morphing under his body to support his chest and stomach. He managed a small chuckle. "There you go again, showing off. You could have just bent me over the edge of the bed."

"How crass." Loch tutted as he got settled behind Sloane, his tentacles withdrawing.

Sloane's lashes fluttered as the tentacle that had been sucking him now slid inside his hole. The tentacle previously fucking him teased over his cock, and he hugged the edge of the raised mattress as he lifted his hips. "Mmm, this is nice too."

"Yes. It is." Loch ran his hands over Sloane's cheeks and up his back. "The view is extraordinary."

"Glad you're enjoying yourself back there." Sloane chuckled.

"You shall be enjoying yourself in front of me shortly," Loch declared as he thrust his tentacle forward.

"Mmm! Yeah." Sloane groaned into the sheets, grinning wide. He spread his legs as Loch got going, loving the way his thick tentacle rubbed against his most intimate places and set every delicate nerve ablaze with ecstasy. The tentacle felt so much bigger in this position, and Sloane's asshole throbbed as it dared to push deeper than the other had.

There was never pain, not with Loch, but there was a brilliant pressure building that flooded his senses until all he could do was moan and beg for more with breathless cries. He was so full that he was certain Loch's tentacle was pushing against his heart, and bolts of electricity were tingling up his spine from every staggering slam.

He couldn't even hold on to the mattress now, his arms hanging limp as Loch continued to drill into him. He was lost to the fiery escalation, and his vision was blurred with tears as he looked out to the stars around him. He could hear Loch's low growls, the wet smack of the tentacle fucking his ass, and his own labored breathing.

It was incredible.

Nothing would ever compare to making love with a god.

Loch's tentacles grabbed Sloane's wrists, pulling them back and forcing his spine to arch. The new angle was devastating, and Sloane was worried his moans might actually wake the gods from their dreaming as Loch fucked him ruthlessly. The tentacle on his cock barely had to twitch and Sloane was coming again, his head hanging back with a groan.

His climax was slower this time, pulsing in steady jerks that sent the most delicious heat surging through his core. He melted forward into the mattress, and he smiled dreamily as Loch's many tentacles massaged his back and hips. The tender caresses were the perfect complement to the orgasmic shivers, and it was only then Sloane noticed....

"You haven't come yet," Sloane murmured.

"Not yet."

"Why?"

"Because." Loch gently picked Sloane up to stretch him across the bed on his back. He settled between his legs, smirking down at him. His eyes had a sly twinkle in them as he said, "I'm waiting."

"You? Waiting?" Sloane cupped Loch's cheek.

"Yes. It happens."

"Mm." Sloane kissed him, wiggling as the slitted tentacle pulled out of his body. He let his legs come up on Loch's hips, and he slid his fingers through Loch's unruly curls. "Not very often."

"Ah, but this is for a good reason," Loch promised. "I wish to bring you the most pleasure imaginable."

"Yeah? So? You're what, edging yourself?" Sloane chuckled.

Loch's reply was a kiss, and he slid his arms beneath Sloane to embrace him as his tentacock pressed against Sloane's hole.

The mere tease of it made Sloane clench with anticipation, and he took a deep breath to prepare himself. The other tentacles always felt amazing, but the tentacock was in its own league. The very fact it could even fit inside of him probably defied the laws of physics, and Sloane relished being able to take it on.

It was here in this bed that Sloane had tasted it for the very first time, a gift from Loch that he'd never shared with anyone else before. He knew Loch bringing him here was meant to be special, and he couldn't help the fluttery feeling stirring in his chest that dried his mouth and wet his eyes.

"I love you," Sloane whispered.

"And I love you," Loch replied. "Always."

The head pressed in, summoning a rapturous wealth of heat and feeling that made Sloane shiver. His cock twitched, already stirring back to hardness once more as Loch continued to push in. Sloane clung to Loch's shoulders to brace himself, and he gasped, his voice cracking as he said, "Gods... it's so good... it's always so good...."

Loch's tentacles swarmed around Sloane's body as he thrust into him, patiently working the massive tentacock deeper and deeper. He buried his face in the crook of Sloane's shoulder as he murmured, "You are so beautiful... you are everything to me... absolutely *everything.*"

Sloane was so wrapped up in Loch's tentacles that he could barely move, and he loved the warmth of the powerful muscles holding him so tight. He surrendered himself to Loch's embrace, soft moans tumbling over his lips as Loch buried the tentacock down to the knot.

It was right on the precipice of being simply too much, and Sloane's chest heaved as he breathed through the overflow of sensations. Loch's tentacock was filling him up so perfectly, and the tentacles around him were cradling him with such reverence. The pace was syrupy slow and sweet, and Sloane was losing all sense of self as he and Loch blurred together.

Intertwined while stars swirled in the surrounding skies, it truly felt as if they were one being. Their flush chests were rising and falling in sync, and there wasn't an increment of space left between them. Sloane's entire body was thrumming with the beat of his heart, and he could feel Loch's echoing alongside it in an intimate symphony. He groaned as Loch slipped the knot of the tentacock inside of him.

And gods, there was *more.*

Loch's other two tentacles were pushing inside of Sloane, leaving him so stuffed that he forgot how to breathe. His pulse pounded in his ears as he swore his very soul left his body, and he was left gasping from the desperate ache of having all three tentacles inside of him. They moved as one massive girth, and the first thrust immediately brought on a mind-shattering orgasm that stole Sloane's breath away.

He saw stars whether his eyes were open or closed, and he sobbed joyously as his hole was flooded with pulse after pulse of Loch's thick come. He trembled in the wake of such raw ecstasy, and he lost track of how long his climax had been carrying on for. He was afraid to breathe because it might end, but it simply didn't.

It went on and on until he thought he was going to pass out, going limp in Loch's arms and whispering weakly, "I love you."

"I love you," Loch whispered in reply, placing an adoring kiss to Sloane's lips.

A final burst of pleasure signaled the end of the impossibly intense orgasm, and Sloane quivered helplessly. He could hardly catch his breath, he was confident that he was glowing, and he could not stop smiling. "G-Gods... I love you so much."

"And I love you, my most beautiful mate." Loch kissed him again, letting some of his tentacles retreat.

Sloane gasped as the tentacles withdrew from inside of him, and he tried to close his legs to stem the gush of come threatening to leak out. He was pleased to find that it didn't happen, no doubt thanks to magical intervention from Loch. He still felt wet and full, and he hugged Loch's neck. "Mmm, that was incredible."

"I know." Loch beamed as he rolled onto his back, laying down beside Sloane with a happy sigh. "You were magnificent, my love."

Sloane managed to flop onto his side so he could cuddle on Loch's chest, and he smiled as Loch's tentacles drew the sheets over him. "Mm. Thank you."

"Of course, my love."

Sloane stretched his legs and let out a very satisfied groan.

"So." Loch smiled smugly. "How do you feel, my beautiful mate?"

"Like I'm ready to go to save the universe. Thank you. You were right. I did need this."

"I am always right." Loch winked. "Shall we return to begin the plan making?"

"Just a few more minutes?" Sloane rubbed Loch's stomach. "Please?"

"Yes, my sweet husband. We can spare a few more for this."

Sloane closed his eyes, listening to the steady thump of Loch's heartbeat beneath his ear. He rubbed his chest and smiled when Loch's fingers tangled with his own. It was peaceful, quiet, and he found himself whispering when he said, "Are my parents here?"

"They are close," Loch replied quietly. "Would you like to see them?"

"No. Not now." Sloane smiled. "We can come see after. So we can tell them that I fixed everything."

Loch kissed Sloane's brow. "Of course, my love."

"Okay." Sloane took a deep breath, and then he nodded. "I'm ready."

"Let's go."

Wind rushed around Sloane's body, and he was very thankful that he was wearing fresh clothes when he opened his eyes again. They were back in Urilith's temple and judging from how everyone was standing almost exactly as they'd left them, not very much time had passed.

The exception was Alexander, who was sitting on the floor now with a loudly snoring Ollie sleeping in his lap and Rota curled around them both like a giant cat.

"Welcome back!" Urilith waved a tentacle.

Galgareth was now holding a still snoozing Pandora, and she smiled. "Hey, guys!"

"Well." Stoker could barely contain his amusement. "That was quick."

"One day you'll learn how to manipulate the very fabric of the universe to make love to your mate for hours and have only but a few fragments of time pass by. Oh wait." Loch grinned. "No, you won't. Because you're only *half* a god."

"Still more of a man than you, little *Azzath*."

"How original, *Jake*. But I'm not even a man."

"That much has long been obvious since the moment we met."

"I am going to eat you—"

Sloane playfully smacked Loch's shoulder. "Come on. Time to plan, right?"

"Plan! Yes!" Ollie jerked up. "Plan! I see the plan."

"Easy," Alexander soothed, rubbing Ollie's back.

"I'm not gonna throw up." Ollie made a face. "Mostly sure that I'm not gonna throw up. But no, I see the thing. I see…." He squinted. "I see how we're connected."

"What is it?" Sloane asked urgently. "Is that important?"

"We are all, like, mad connected. So connected. Your prayer did a lot more than you think it did. When I was a little kid, I got hit by something. I was trying to turn o-fahfah a light and get ready for bed, but I got majorly zapped."

"Your stutter," Alexander said suddenly. "Your fahfah." He exchanged a quick glance with Rota. "That's when it happened, isn't it?"

"It… it is." Ollie seemed surprised. "Huh. I guess that's not how you say double F's after all. Okay. Focus. Gotta focus." He shook his head. "My parents thought at first it was bad wiring, but then they realized it was a bolt of magic. Big, crazy powerful magic."

"I remember that," Chase chimed in. "I helped them file the report. We thought it was some rogue witch gone nuts. It's why I got into magic enforcement in the first place, to try and track down the asshole who did it. We never found 'em." He frowned. "It was Sloane? This whole time?"

Sloane cringed.

"Hey, you wouldn't have met Merrick if you hadn't gone into magic law whatever!" Ollie said firmly. "Just like I wouldn't have met Ted. He always told me he liked the way I talked. He thought it was cute." He smiled sadly. "But, uh, also? Alexander's parents heard about what was being labeled as a rogue witch attack and they decided to study ways to give magic to Silenced people."

"Their research," Alexander said quietly. "That was the whole reason for their research." *The fucking research that got Gronoch's attention. The research that got them fucking killed.*

"I'm sorry. I'm really, really sorry." Ollie grimaced. "Everything that's happened is one of those butter effects from Sloane's prayer. Like, I would have never got my starsight if Ted hadn't drowned and we had to break up so Ted would be living with Jay at the right time to get all tangled up with the cat people."

"You." Grell's eyes widened. "You're the one who brought Ted back."

"Yup. That's me. I did that."

"Well." Grell laughed in disbelief. "Then the king of the cat people knows why he's here. Other than gracing you all with my charming personality and witty commentary, of course."

"Why?" Sloane asked.

"We need an army, don't we? Just so happens I know where to get one."

CHAPTER 8.

"You." Grell pointed at Sloane. "You're coming with me to Xenon."

"Me?" Sloane scoffed. "Why me?"

"Gods aren't allowed, and that includes halflings and those who have a godly soul bound to them," Grell drawled.

"Hey! What about me and Ollie?" Chase demanded. "We're human."

"Ah, allow me to rephrase." Grell bowed his head. "No gods, no halflings, no godly souls, and no gingers."

"Fuckin' rude!" Chase huffed.

"Hey! Are we invisible?" Milo spoke up. "Hello! Very important section of the Super Secret Sages' Club right over here who are non-ginger! Why can't we go?"

"Yeah!" Robert crossed his arms. "We're very capable witches—"

"Capable enough to kill a god? No? Didn't think so." Grell took a sip from his drink.

"But there are no gods in Xenon," Lochlain said slowly.

"What we're going to wake up is just as dangerous," Grell said. "If not more so."

"And what is that exactly?" Loch demanded.

"Sorry, the Q and A portion of our segment is now over. Any further concerns can be submitted in writing with a self-addressed stamped envelope." Grell turned to Sloane and offered out his hand. "Are we ready, Starkiller?"

Loch wrapped his tentacles around Sloane protectively. "No, we are not. We definitely have more questions, and I have no stamps. Or envelopes."

"We really do not have time for this," Grell said firmly. "Trust that I will watch over your mate as I would watch over my own, all right?"

"It's okay." Sloane passed Pandora over to Loch, being careful not to wake her. "I'll be back as soon as I can."

"And what exactly should the rest of us do?" Stoker asked warily. "Wait here for your triumphant return?"

"Yes," Grell replied. "Exactly that. Oh, and I would suggest putting together a buffet. With a focus on meat dishes, if you please."

Stoker scoffed.

"While I'm gone, you guys can work on distributing the totems to everyone," Sloane said. "Hopefully we won't need them, but we should be ready. Maybe do some recon and see what's going on with Ell? Alexander and Rota?"

"Yeah. Whatever." Alexander flinched when Rota nudged him. "We're on it. We'll go see what's going on."

Sloane looked around the temple. "And we should probably find Fred. He's still not back?"

"No." Lochlain frowned.

"I can go look for him," Galgareth offered. "I'll be quick."

"I'll come too," Lochlain said. "Official best friend business, you know?"

"Of course."

"Starkiller," Grell pressed. "Ticktock."

"Right." Sloane sighed, and he turned to kiss Loch. "I love you."

"Love you, my sweet husband." Loch's eyes darkened, filling with galaxies as he pressed his brow to Sloane's. He held him for a long moment before finally letting go, saying, "Please be safe."

"I will." Sloane kissed Pandora's forehead, whispering, "Love you too, baby girl."

Pandora cooed softly, wiggled, but remained asleep.

"If anything happens to him, I will make a macramé tapestry out of your entrails," Loch promised Grell.

"You would certainly be welcome to try, Azaethoth, but I promise we will return." Grell tipped his head. "After all, we need him to save the universe, don't we?"

Sloane grimaced at the unspoken implication, and he turned to address the others. "I'll be back as soon as I can. Love you guys."

"Love you, man!" Milo came lumbering over for a big hug. "You be good. Or be good at it. Whatever it is you're going to do."

Lynnette waved farewell, but she paused, reaching for her stomach. Her eyes widened. "Oh! Oh! I think… I think it's happening?"

Milo whirled back around. "Wait, what? You mean it? *It* it? It as in—"

"Yes! Yes! Baby! Now!"

"By all the gods, right now? That's—" Sloane gasped as the temple vanished, and he was now standing out on the balcony of a massive stone castle.

The castle was made of a strange lavender stone, and there were flowering vines crawling all over it that gave off a spicy scent. The sky was dark and full of stars, and there was an absolutely giant bridge off in the distance. It was so large that it filled the horizon from one side to the other, and it glowed with a beautiful white light that pulsed like a steady heartbeat.

"It's... we...." Sloane tried to find the words for the incredible sight.

"Yes, beautiful, isn't it?" Grell had a new drink in his hand and slurped it noisily. "I'll make sure to give you some postcards to take home."

"Xenon," Sloane finally said. "We're in Xenon."

"Yes."

"That's the bridge."

"Yes."

"The bridge that souls use to pass through to Zebulon."

"*Yes.*"

"Wow." Sloane grinned.

There was a bustling city below them, and beyond its walls was a forest of glowing white trees and jagged mountains. There was so much to take in, and Sloane was in awe of being able to see this world. He didn't think he'd ever be able to see this magical place—well, not while he was alive anyway.

Sloane quickly recovered from his stupor, and he remembered what Grell had pulled him away from. "Hey! Lynnette was getting ready to go into labor! I didn't even have a chance to say anything to her."

"And what words of wisdom were you going to pass along?" Grell drawled. "Good luck? Don't drop it? If the child says they're going to throw up, never call their bluff?"

Sloane scoffed.

"I apologize for the rush, but the drunk ginger gave us a tight schedule."

"So, why are we in Xenon? You said you knew where to find an army."

"Yes, but first we have to find my beloved son. We're going to need his help too."

The balcony flickered, and they were now standing in a lavish bedroom. It was definitely still within the castle judging by the lavender stone walls, and it was bigger than Sloane's entire apartment. He tried not to be too impressed by the fancy furniture, the giant television, or the in-ground hot tub.

Jay was perched on the foot of the bed talking to Ted, who was sitting against the headboard with a sour grimace. Asta was in his fluffy cat form, playing on the floor with a big rag doll in the shape of a cat.

The doll had lopsided ears, mismatched button eyes, and it moved in a funny sort of floppy way as it chased Asta around in a clumsy circle.

Everyone froze to look up at Sloane and Grell as they appeared, except the rag doll cat. It kept running and promptly smacked into Asta.

"Oof! Why'd you stop?" the cat doll asked in a small voice.

Hardly the weirdest thing that had ever happened, but still, Sloane was surprised.

"Hello, my gorgeous husband. My beautiful son. My future son-in-law if my beautiful son doesn't fuck it up." Grell smiled down at the doll. "Ah, and my favorite possessed toy."

The doll waved.

Ted narrowed his eyes to venomous slits. "You here to tell me my brother's dead?"

"No," Sloane replied quickly, hoping to cut the palpable tension. "We found Ell. He's alive, he's still pretty upset, but things have gotten kinda complicated."

"Complicated how exactly?" Jay asked with a frown.

"What's going on?" Ted demanded.

"There's been a bit of trouble—" Grell started.

"No, not you," Ted snapped. "I don't wanna hear shit from you." He looked to Sloane. "You. Go."

"Uh, right." Sloane cleared his throat. "Short version is we found Ell in the park. He's created some sort of shield around himself that kills anything that touches it. We tried talking to him, me and Fred both. He doesn't seem to remember who he is. He's confused, and, eh...." He winced. "Jeff and Daisy are on their way to him now with the fruit."

"Shit." Ted bolted out of bed. "Okay, let's go."

"What?"

"I said, let's fuckin' go. I need to talk some fuckin' sense into him." Ted gave Sloane a pleading look. "Come on. You guys already tried and couldn't get through, yeah? Let me do it. I've known Ell since he was a fuckin' baby. He's my brother, for fuck's sake."

"We don't have time," Grell said gently. "Your lovely intoxicated ex-lover has used his starsight and given us about two hours in which to summon an army to fight the army currently en route to your brother."

"You're here for the dead," Asta realized with wide eyes.

"Yes. I'd say this is a time of need, wouldn't you?"

"Hey, hey!" Ted barked, coming over and getting right in Grell's face. "Two hours is plenty of fucking time! Why won't you let me at least try?"

"My love, my beautiful bounty of beefcake," Grell said, his patience clearly thin. "Your brother is too dangerous right now for you to go anywhere near him. I will not let you—"

"Let me?" Ted fumed. "You won't *let* me?"

"—risk your life because you think you can help!" Grell's voice rose as he passionately exclaimed, "I have already lost one queen who was just as stubborn and hopelessly foolish as you are, thinking they had to put themselves in danger to save everyone when there was no damn reason to, and I will not lose another!"

Ted fell silent, visibly stunned.

"I'm never going to apologize for doing whatever I can to keep you safe." Grell's eyes brimmed with tears, and he reached up to cup Ted's cheek.

Ted was equally emotional, laying his hand over Grell's as he visibly struggled not to cry. "I'm not Vael. I can do this."

Grell closed his eyes, and he didn't reply except to pull Ted into a soft kiss.

Sloane tried to make himself as small as possible to give them some sense of privacy. He was empathetic to Ted's situation as Loch had trapped him in Zebulon once upon a time in the name of safety, but he also understood Grell's desire to keep a loved one from harm.

Ell was their friend and family, but he wasn't the only one they had to worry about.

There was Jeff and his cultists, plus Ebbeth and Zarnorach, and who knows how many other gods and monsters who might wish to use Ell's powers for evil.

"Gross. Ulgh. Puke. Vomit." Asta made several dramatic retching sounds. "Dying from the severe grossness. Stop using so much tongue. There are minors present!"

Sloane noticed the rag doll cat was standing by his feet and staring at him, its head cocked in a curious sort of way. He waved. "Uh. Hi."

The ragdoll cat waved back.

"Starkiller, Graham. Graham, Starkiller." Asta gestured with his paw.

"You're Ted's... friend." Sloane didn't know what else to call him, given their strange situation.

"Yeah!" Graham perked up immediately. "Can I see your sword? The starlight sword? Please, please?"

Sloane smiled, summoning the sword. He was careful to keep it out of reach of curious little paws.

"Whoa!" Graham gasped. "That's so fuckin' cool!"

Ted broke away from Grell to scold, "Graham! Potty mouth!"

"Sorry," Graham muttered, ducking his head. "But it is really effing cool."

"Wonder where he got that kind of language from?" Grell batted his eyes.

"Don't you start with me," Ted warned. He shied away when Grell tried to kiss him again. "Look, I get you're all worried about something happening to me 'cause you lost Vael, but you're not gonna lose me. You—"

"You're absolutely right. Because you are staying here."

"Grell, don't you dare fuckin' leave—"

"Time to go, Starkiller!" Grell declared.

Sloane quickly banished the sword and then waved to Graham and Jay. "Later guys."

"BBL, babycakes." Asta blew a kiss to Jay.

Jay caught it and waved, cringing as Ted continued to yell.

"You are so dead, you motherfuckin' puss in *bitch*!" Ted raged.

Given that Ted was an absolute giant, Sloane took a step back, and he wasn't even the one Ted's anger was directed at. He saw Grell sigh sadly before the world moved again, and the new location appeared to be an underground cave.

Asta and Grell had both transformed into their Asran forms, and Grell was mumbling under his breath, "Puss in *bitch*? What does that even mean?"

"Maybe he meant it like a twist on Puss in Boots?" Asta nudged Grell's shoulder. "Hey, he's real stressed out."

"Apparently. Even his cussing is suffering."

Sloane shivered, all the hairs on the back of his neck standing up. He didn't know where he was, but he could practically taste the magic of this place. It was in the very stone beneath his feet and in the air all around him.

There were large open slots in the walls, rows upon rows of them, and Sloane had no idea what they were for. He could see hallways leading off into what he assumed were more caves, and there was a definite odor of something rotten.

Sloane cleared his throat. "Where are we exactly?"

"The pits. They are interdimensional tunnels that run underneath the city," Grell explained. "We Asra bury our dead here."

Sloane grimaced. "All those holes are… their tombs?"

"Yes."

"Okay, and how exactly is this gonna help? We need an army. A *living* one."

"And here it is." Asta waved a paw. "You see, Asra have many different levels of dead. There's, like, no-pulse dead, which is like *dead* dead. And then we have only kinda dead, which is like dead-*ish* or diet dead. Oh, and there's the ones who have been dead forever, and they are mega-dead."

"Huh?" Sloane blinked.

"We can live for thousands of years, and some will choose to pass on in a more symbolic sense," Grell clarified. "Symbolic as in we have a funeral, we bury them, but they're not dead by human standards. They have sort of a long nap before they actually die for realsies. Many of our warriors choose to pass on this way since there's not exactly a plethora of glorious battles happening. Or at least, there weren't until very recently."

"I have so many questions right now, but so, you're telling me not all of these Asra here are actually dead?" Sloane stared at the countless slots. "How many are alive?"

"Enough for an army," Grell replied with a wink. "I wasn't kidding about the buffet. They're going to be very hungry."

"Okay." Sloane took a deep breath. "So, what do we do?"

"I wake the dead, and you and Asta stop anyone trying to stop me."

"What?"

"Some of the Asra are going to be very grumpy when they first wake up. Not morning people at all, I'm afraid. They will try to stop me from waking the others, so you stop them."

"Seriously?" Sloane blinked.

"No, I just thought it would be fun to drag you along with me into one of the most sacred Asran spaces for a laugh."

"By all the gods." Sloane groaned as he summoned a sword of starlight and a shield. "You're saying they're going to try and kill you?"

"Yes. That. And I would appreciate it if you kill them back for me."

Sloane took a deep breath. "Okay, fine. Let's do this."

"Let's." Grell threw his head back and howled, a piercing cry that shook the rock beneath their feet. He howled again, louder this time, and the sound echoed throughout the cave until the entire space seemed to vibrate.

Asta bowed his head, as if the sound somehow commanded him to. His eyes were alert, however, scanning the cave and the connecting corridors.

Sloane cringed from how loud it was, watching the slots carefully. He wasn't sure what to expect, but he tried to be ready for anything.

Grell continued to howl, and Sloane caught a glimmer of movement from one of the slots.

A thin Asra emerged, slinking down from one of the highest levels of the crypts. It gracefully landed in front of Grell, bowing its head with a fierce growl.

Or maybe that was its stomach.

Sloane wasn't sure.

More Asra came, some from inside the cave they were standing in, but several others were coming from the connecting halls. Sloane lost count of how many there were after thirty or so, and he was in awe of being surrounded by so many magnificent creatures. They pushed as close to Grell as they could, no doubt drawn by his haunting cries and practically stacking on top of each other to reach him.

Asta was on the move, stalking around and cautiously sniffing the other Asra as if to make sure they were all right.

Sloane had to move carefully to avoid stepping on anyone's paws while he kept watch. He also had to fight the urge to pet the nearby Asra, many of whom looked particularly soft and fluffy.

He almost wasn't ready for the lone Asra racing right for Grell with a frenzied snarl.

This Asra looked bloated, sickly, and its eyes were flashing bright white as it roared brokenly. The other Asra appeared too dazed to intervene even as it ran right on top of them, but Sloane swung his shield with all of his might at the would-be attacker.

He caught the Asra right in the face, sending it sprawling into the surrounding crowd with a pained whine. The other Asra parted so that the sickly Asra was on his own, flailing as it struggled to stand again.

Sloane stood his ground as he warned, "I don't want to hurt you, but I will if I have to."

"You're gonna have to!" Asta called out.

The Asra growled and charged again.

"I'm really sorry about this!" Sloane raised his sword, jumping up high so he could slam the pommel into the top of the Asra's head.

The Asra whimpered and then collapsed.

"Booyah!" Asta hollered. "One point to Starkiller!"

Sloane hesitated, wanting to make sure it was truly incapacitated before he took his eyes off it.

Another sickly Asra was stalking toward Grell, but Asta was right there to intercept. He leaped into the air, achieving enough height to do a somersault before he pounced on top of it. His jaws seized its neck with a brutal crack, and then he declared, "One for me!"

Sloane flinched as sharp teeth tore into his shoe, and the Asra he'd thought he had knocked unconscious was merely dazed. He tried to yank his foot away. "Shit! Come on!"

"Yeah, you gotta make sure they're *dead* dead," Asta said cheerfully. "If they don't heed the royal meow meow, they're toast."

"Really?" Sloane kicked the Asra away, raising his sword to stab into its throat. He winced, but he didn't move until the Asra went limp. He tried to ignore the blood. "What are they, zombies?"

"Easy on the zed word. Their souls are pissed off and can't move on. They're Asra who have been trapped here and need help being released." Asta paused. "The royal meow meow is, like, cleaning out your fridge."

A new Asra appeared, and it was another ripe, bloated specimen, and it was on its way to Grell.

"So many questions!" Sloane hurried over to cut it off since he was closer than Asta. "Pardon me! Excuse me!" He pushed through the other Asra, keeping his sword raised high so he didn't accidentally hit any of them.

The attacking Asra dove at Grell, and Sloane hurled his shield at it.

The shield hit the side of its head, it huffed in annoyance, and it then focused its attention on Sloane.

"Well, I knew that was going to happen." Sloane brought out a new shield just as it lunged at him, and he went to the ground with the giant beast on top of him.

The Asra was foaming at its mouth, gnashing its teeth against the shield and growling.

"Little help here!" Sloane shouted.

"Little busy!" Asta replied, as he was now tangling with two more of the angry resurrected Asra.

Some of the Asra's hot bubbly spit dripped onto Sloane's forehead, and he groaned in disgust as it ran down into his eye. "Okay, okay! That's just gross!" He summoned his magic and used it to push the shield forward, heaving the giant Asra off him.

He leaped to his feet as it went flying into the far wall of the cave, and he had to drop his sword to wipe at his eye. His vision was blurred, but he could see the sickly Asra getting ready to attack again.

"Can't you please just stay down?" Sloane pleaded. "Pretty please?"

The Asra either didn't understand or didn't care, and it went for Grell again. Asta had taken down one of his foes but was still battling the other.

Sloane threw a bolt of starlight to slow it down, and he sprinted through the sea of Asra to head it off again.

There was a loud howl, and Sloane saw *another* new Asra appearing to fight, racing right toward them.

"Shit!" Sloane threw his shield at the new opponent, nailing it right in its snout. "Fuckin' give me a break already!"

"Ow! What the fuck?" Asta shook his head and huffed. "Starkiller, you dick!"

"Asta?" Sloane grimaced. "Sorry! I didn't know it was you!"

"Yeah, yeah. Whatever! Racist!" Asta was faster than Sloane, and he reached the sick Asra first. He jumped on top of it, sinking his teeth into the back of its neck.

The sickly Asra went down with a wretched cry and then didn't move.

Asta glared at Sloane.

"I'm so sorry—"

"You're a *dick*."

"And very sorry."

Asta remained poised for battle, though no more attacks seemed to be coming. Sloane didn't see any more signs of other disturbed Asra, only the peaceful crowd that was growing around them. There were so many now that they couldn't all fit inside the cave, and Sloane's hopes soared.

They'd done it.

They had an army.

Grell's howling finally drew to a close, and he declared, "I am King Thiazi desu Grell Tirana Diago Tasha Mondet. I have called you here to come to the aid of the kingdom of Xenon. The world of Aeon is in danger, under attack by old gods and the Kindress himself. If Aeon falls, then Xenon will surely be next."

There was a collective murmur, and many of the Asra bared their sharp teeth.

Sloane hoped that was a good thing.

"So." Grell clicked his tongue. "You can either go back to your extremely boring eternal snooze time or come with me and fight to save the universe. Tough choice, I know, but I trust you will make the right one. Many of you are warriors who wished to pass on for there was no longer any battle to seek glory in. Well, let me assure you that this is an absolutely fabulous opportunity for glory, pride, and bragging rights that you got to kick old god ass one final time."

The Asra cheered, several howling and roaring ferociously. They seemed to be moving faster now, their eyes bright and tails lashing like whips against the floor.

"Uh, question!" An Asra near the back had their paw raised.

"Yes?" Grell sighed.

"Will there be snacks?"

"Yes. Of course there will be snacks." Grell eyed Sloane. "A buffet, in fact."

"Right." Sloane cleared his throat when he realized that the army of Asra were all staring right at him. "With lots of meat?"

That seemed to be the right thing to say as the crowd of Asra roared happily in reply.

Sloane stood beside Grell with Asta on the other, and he said, "Well, we have an army. You were right."

"I often carry that burden." Grell smirked, his sharp teeth shining bright. "Once we give them some hot food and an unnatural dose of caffeine, they'll be ready to go."

"And a bath," Asta noted with a wrinkle of his nose.

"I'll open a portal that will take them to Urilith's temple. One of the non-orgy floors. By my count, we still have fifty-six minutes."

"Uh, and where are you going?" Asta demanded.

"To use at least thirty of those precious minutes to make amends with my husband," Grell said, his smile saddening. He butted his head against Asta's. "If that's all right with you, my dear spawn."

"Ew, vomit, gross." Asta made a face and retched.

"Yes, disgusting, I know."

"You really think...." Asta lowered his voice. "You really think I can handle this?" He glanced at the other Asra. "They're gonna have questions. They're gonna wanna know stuff. Like, all the stuff."

"I believe in you," Grell said firmly. "If... if this is still the path you wish to follow."

Asta seemed surprised, but he nodded. "I—It is. Okay? It really is. This is what I want. And you know, I appreciate you asking. Very cool of you." He narrowed his eyes. "But I'm not taking over for you anytime soon, so you don't get any funny ideas, okay?"

"Understood, son." Grell nuzzled Asta's brow.

"I love you," Asta said quietly.

"I love you too." Grell turned his head and a giant portal opened up in the wall of the cave. "Go now. I'll be with you as soon as I can, but—"

"Just, ew, no. Stop. I already know you're doing gross sex things with Cat Kicker."

"As many as I can in thirty minutes." Grell winked. He nodded to Sloane. "Thank you, Starkiller. For all of your assistance."

"Thank you for the army," Sloane replied. "We'll see you soon."

Grell smiled, and then he vanished away.

Asta seemed unusually nervous now. He fidgeted, and his eyes were flicking over the room as if unsure of what to do. He gulped audibly.

The other Asra were all looking to him now, and there was a palpable tension brewing. They were murmuring among themselves, their eyes cutting to Asta with uncertainty and clear distrust.

Sloane didn't know if Asra could sweat, but Asta certainly seemed to be under such scrutiny.

"You okay?" Sloane asked him quietly. "Do you need a second?"

"Huh?"

"Do you need a sec?"

Asta took a deep breath and then teased with his usual jovial sneer, "What I need is for you to buy me dinner or get off my dicks."

Sloane grinned, clapping his hand on Asta's back. "That's more like it."

"Easy! Hands off the merchandise."

"Right. Sorry."

"All right, listen up, motherfuckers!" Asta called out as he stood up on his hind legs, addressing the crowd with a deep rumbling shout. "I am Prince Asta desu Crem Dianah Kane Bavar Nico Lucet! Let's all head into the nice shiny portal in a single-file line, keep your tails and tentacles to yourselves, and let's hope that dumbass Azaethoth the Lesser actually put out the buffet! If not, I vote we eat him!"

CHAPTER 9.

FORTUNATELY, LOCH had indeed taken the order to create a buffet to heart and set one up on a lower level of the temple. Stoker was actually there to help serve, though he'd taken off his tie and jacket. It was adorable to see the two of them somewhat getting along, and they were ready to feed the incoming army of ravenous Asra.

Who all very much enjoyed being served by gods.

Asta helped steer the Asra into an orderly line, and Loch passed out trays while Stoker served a pair of whole roasts and a full rack of ribs to each individual cat monster.

"My love!" Loch called out when he saw Sloane wading through the crowd.

"Hey!" Sloane hurried over to greet him with a kiss.

"I see you found an army."

"We did indeed. Where's Panda Bear?"

"She is with Galgareth."

Sloane frowned. "I thought she was with Lochlain looking for Fred?"

"Ah." Loch paused to pass out a tray, placing it neatly in the awaiting Asra's mouth. "Lochlain wanted to be here for the birth of his niece!"

"Lynnette!" Sloane gasped. "The baby!"

"Is a bouncing beautiful baby girl named Mara Organa Evans-Fields." Loch smiled warmly as he continued to hand out trays. "My dear mother did promise Lynnette a very pleasant labor and delivery, and it was very quick. They're upstairs now. Milo is also recovering well."

"Milo? What happened to Milo?"

"Oh! He fainted."

"*What*?"

"He's fine. No tampons required."

The final Asra came through the line, and once Loch had given them each a tray, he swept Sloane off his feet with his tentacles. He pressed a deep kiss to his lips, letting it linger for a long moment and recall their earlier passion. "Mm, I missed you."

"Wow." Sloane's face grew hot. "Missed you too."

"How was Xenon?"

"Beautiful. I'll tell you all about it later." Sloane smooched Loch's forehead. "I want to go see our baby, the new baby, and talk to our friends and family while we still have some time left to plan."

"Ah, time to strategize, yes?"

"Yup. Alexander and Rota back yet?"

"I haven't seen them."

Stoker had just finished serving the last Asra and was approaching, saying, "They're on their way now. I would keep your visits brief."

Sloane resisted the urge to roll his eyes. "I know we don't have that much time. But hey." He gestured toward the Asra. "We have an army!"

"I see that. Well done, Mr. Beaumont."

The Asra were eating and seemed to be enjoying their meals. Those who had finished appeared to be resting, no doubt stuffed from such huge portions. Asta was with them, walking around and chatting with them. He looked confident, taking the time to talk to each Asra and trade a few jokes, and Sloane imagined that Grell would be proud to see him like this.

For the first time, Asta looked like a prince.

"Come on!" Sloane grinned. "Asta looks like he's got a handle on things here, and I wanna go see the baby."

Loch smirked. "Ours or theirs?"

"Both."

Loch and Sloane headed upstairs to the next level of the temple with Stoker in tow, and then Loch led the way into part of the inner sanctum. There was a large dais in the center stacked with pillows and blankets, and Lynnette was nestled right in the middle with a dark-haired baby at her breast.

Milo was massaging her feet, beaming at her and the baby adoringly.

Urilith was humming as she cooked away on a very out-of-place modern kitchenette that had no doubt been magically summoned there. Chase was with her, helping prep vegetables and pile them into a big pot.

Robert and Lochlain were hovering around Lynnette, cooing over the baby.

Galgareth was sitting inside a large playpen with Pandora, and they were playing with a toy kitchen, mimicking what Urilith and Chase were doing with plastic pots and pans.

Someone had brought a hammock down for Ollie, who was snoozing away in it and snoring lightly.

Sloane's heart swelled to see his friends and family all gathered together, and it reminded him of exactly what they were fighting to save. Loch must have felt it too, because he put his arm around Sloane's shoulders, stopping with him at the doorway to simply watch for a few moments.

Except Stoker was right behind them and he asked, "Any special reason why you decided to stand in the hallway?"

"Right. Sorry." Sloane chuckled as he moved forward out of the way.

Having heard his voice, Pandora whirled around to face Sloane. Her eyes widened and she gasped. "Da! Da-da! Dad!"

"Hey, baby girl!" Sloane gushed as he hurried over to the side of the playpen.

"Hey!" Milo waved. "You're back!"

"Welcome back!" Lynnette said.

"Thank you! And congratulations to you both!" Sloane reached down for Pandora, laughing as she snapped her tentacles around his shoulders to climb her way out of the playpen and up into his arms. He kissed her cheeks and gave her a big hug. "Hi, baby! Were you good?"

Pandora promptly launched into an intense babble, waving her tentacles and gesturing everywhere. The only word Sloane understood was "fuck."

"She was here while Mother was helping Lynnette give birth," Galgareth said, trying to hide a laugh behind her hand. "There was, uh, some very colorful language."

"I was nervous!" Lynnette protested.

"You did great, baby," Milo soothed, bowing his head to kiss the top of her foot.

Loch hugged Sloane, greeting Pandora with a smooch and tangling their tentacles together. "You can't keep saying that word, my sweet spawn. Not until you're at least ten."

"Loch," Sloane scolded.

"Okay, thirteen."

Sloane passed Pandora over to Loch, fussing, "Don't you listen to him. Don't say any of those bad words."

"Only sometimes," Loch whispered loudly.

Galgareth climbed out of the playpen so she could give Sloane a hug. "So, do we have an army?"

"We sure do." Sloane smiled. "Grell brought a bunch of Asra back from the dead kind of? It's complicated. But yes, we do. They're out there now eating, and Asta is with them. Grell is, uh, handling some personal business back in Xenon, but he'll be here soon."

"Ted?"

"Yeah. Ted." Sloane tried to remain cheerful, heading over to hug Milo. He grunted as Milo pulled him down for a giant bear hug. "Hey! Agh, need to breathe!"

"Sorry." Milo clapped him on the back before letting go with a sheepish grin. "I'm just really excited. I mean, I know we have a huge crazy battle for the universe coming up? But look! I have a baby. A perfect, beautiful, wonderful little baby."

Sloane walked around the side of the bed and then leaned down, kissing Lynnette's cheek. "Congratulations."

"Thank you." Lynnette sighed. She'd finished nursing, now cuddling the baby against her bare chest with a soft blanket over her. "She's pretty perfect, huh?"

"Damn right, she is." Sloane smiled down at the sleeping baby. "Hi, Mara. It's nice to finally meet you."

Mara seemed much more interested in napping than chatting.

"Can't wait until she's old enough to hold a lockpick and a tension wrench," Lochlain teased.

"Shush!" Lynnette snorted.

Sloane glanced around the room, finally taking note of someone who was missing aside from Fred. "Hey, where's Merrick?"

"Back in Archersville." Chase glanced up from his chopping. "We hadn't heard anything from Alexander and Rota yet, and he wanted to check in with the force. Make sure they were getting people out of the city."

Sloane grimaced. "Gods, I hope so."

"We have thirty-nine minutes!" Urilith declared, waving her tentacles over the big pot. "This soup will carry my most powerful blessing of protection. I want everyone to have a bowl and make sure our Asran friends get some too. Mm, just a few more carrots, Chase, sweetie."

"You got it, ma'am." Chase dumped the carrots into the pot.

"So! The Asra are eating, we can pass out the soup, and oh, the totems!" Sloane snapped his fingers. "Do we have enough totems for everyone?"

"We do!" Robert replied. "Ollie and the others didn't stop until we had a few hundred. I found some chain enchanted with a blessing of punctuality from Gramlinoth, and we used that to make bracelets for everyone."

A pop of a portal signaled Grell's return. He was in a new suit, this one all black with purple stripes and a violet corsage pinned to his lapel. Although his attire was dashing as always, his expression was haggard and forlorn.

Sloane waved. "Hey! You're back kinda early—"

"Universe needs to be saved, don't it?" Grell said briskly.

"Right." Sloane decided not to ask. "Ah shit. we really do need to go find Fred. We're running out of time."

"On it." Lochlain offered his hand to Galgareth and bowed. "M'lady?"

Galgareth actually giggled and then cleared her throat bashfully. She took Lochlain's hand, saying seriously, "We're going right now."

"Okay. Good luck!" Sloane nodded, watching them vanish before continuing, "Right. So, we need to think about planning. It's almost time—"

"Time!" Ollie suddenly shouted. He was awake, flailing to get out of the hammock. "It's almost time!"

Robert hurried over to help him. "Hey, hey! Easy!"

Right at that moment, Alexander and Rota came tumbling into the room from a portal that opened in the ceiling. Alexander landed on the floor with a heavy thump, groaning in pain. "Ow?"

I'm so sorry, my sweet boy! Rota quickly wrapped his tentacles around Alexander, trying to help him sit up. *Are you all right?*

"Peachy."

"Hey!" Sloane was close enough to offer Alexander a hand and pull him to his feet. "You guys okay?"

"Shit is getting bad," Alexander said, flinching away from Sloane as soon as he was standing. "They're all gathered in the park around Ell, and—" He stopped when Urilith shoved a bowl of soup in his hands. "What the fuck is this?"

"That is fucking soup!" Urilith patted the top of his head and then went on to pass out more bowls to everyone.

"We're almost out of time!" Ollie stumbled toward Alexander. "Quick. Eat it. Eat your soup. And drink it. Both. Definitely both."

"Hey, hey." Alexander caught Ollie, wrapping his arm around his waist. "Calm down, big guy. We got you."

Rota's tentacles shimmered as he embraced them both, soothing, *We're right here*.

"Right now, you are. But soon you won't be. And we, we have to hurry."

"We should get ready," Grell said somberly.

"Okay." Sloane steadied himself with a deep breath. "Urilith is passing out her soup, so we need to get the totems out too. Robert? Milo? Would you mind?"

"You got it!" Milo paused only to kiss Lynnette's cheek and the top of Mara's head before he joined Robert in passing out the totem bracelets from a large chest.

Urilith was carrying the giant pot of soup, and Chase trailed behind her with a stack of bowls that never seemed to end. They crossed paths with Robert and Milo, and they stopped to exchange bracelets and soup before moving on to finish distributing to everyone in the room. Urilith and Chase left to go distribute more soup while Robert and Milo continued to pass out bracelets.

Sloane adjusted the new bracelet around his wrist and then lifted the bowl of soup to his lips to take a sip of the broth. "Okay, Alexander. Quick. What did you guys see out there?"

"Right." Alexander sniffed the soup but didn't try it. "They got Ell surrounded in the park, but no one can get to him because of his puddle bubble. There are hundreds of cultists, at least ten old gods, and more. I saw people from the Hidden World there too. Some Absola, a few Eldress, and a bunch of Devarach. From what I can see, Ell is ignoring them, but Jeff has the fruit. We saw it."

"But Ell isn't interested?" Sloane dared to hope.

"No. He said it looked like shit."

"Well, he didn't say that exactly," Rota corrected, "but in so many words, yes, he was not impressed with the offering. Daisy was considering putting some sort of syrup on it, but I don't think that would help."

Robert and Milo headed out of the sanctum to continue passing out soup and totems, and they nearly crashed into Asta, who was bounding down the hallway.

"Whoa! Giant cat! Big, *big* cat!" Milo yelped.

"Watch the fur, man!" Asta bit back as he slinked around them, skidding to a stop beside Grell. "Yo. Hey. You. Yes, you. We got a problem."

"What's that?" Grell said smoothly. "More of a problem than the fact we're about to head into battle to decide the fate of the universe?"

"The Asra!" Asta hissed. "Those fuckers are going to sleep."

"Sleep?" Grell's eyes widened. "What in the everloving *fuck*?"

"Why are they sleeping?" Sloane demanded. "They just woke up from sleeping! We need them to fight in, like, what? Ten minutes?"

"Nine minutes, thirty-six seconds!" Ollie called out helpfully.

"I don't fucking know!" Asta groaned. "Why the fuck do you think I came to get you?"

"Come on." Grell charged out of the room with Asta right on his heels.

Stoker followed them, as did Alexander, Rota, and a very frantic Ollie.

"We should go too," Sloane said firmly. "We can't fight without an army, and we're almost out of time." He kissed Pandora and hugged her tight, closing his eyes as her tentacles wrapped around his neck. "Okay, little girl. I swear, after this, I am never letting you go again for a very, very long time."

Pandora didn't want Sloane to let go of her, and she cried when he tried.

Loch managed to wiggle her out of Sloane's arms and carry her to the playpen, but she started kicking him when he went to set her down. "Oh! She is extra spicy right now."

"She's probably mad we keep leaving her," Sloane grumbled.

"Hey, go ahead and go!" Lynnette said. "I can keep an eye on her until Milo or Urilith gets back."

"Are you sure?" Sloane frowned. "She can be… well, you know, a handful. And you literally just gave birth."

"And there is the spiciness to consider!" Loch winced as Pandora had now turned herself upside down, hugging Loch's chest with her tentacles so she could try to kick him in the face. "So spicy!"

"Just bring her over here," Lynnette said firmly. "Trust me."

"As you wish, dear mortal." Loch carried Pandora over to her, dodging most of Pandora's kicks, but not all of them. He peeled away her tentacles and then plunked her down next to Lynnette.

Lynnette was quick to wrap her arm around Pandora's shoulders, bringing her against her chest as she cooed, "Look, Panda Bear. This is Mara. Mara is your cousin. Sort of." She smiled. "Do you wanna say hi?"

Pandora squirmed, but she stopped when she saw Mara. Her eyes widened, she gasped, and she reached out with the tip of one tentacle to gently touch Mara's hair. "Baybeh!"

"That's right. Baby. Very good, Panda!" Lynnette cut her eyes to Sloane and Loch, saying out from the side of her mouth, "Time to go, boys."

"Thank you, Lynnette! We love you!"

"Love you too!"

Loch grabbed Sloane, instantly transporting them to the floor where the Asra had been feasting.

The crowd of Asra were indeed sleeping, several snoring loudly, and Urilith was bopping one in the head with a ladle. Grell and Asta were also trying to rouse the others and arguing back and forth.

"Why the fuck aren't they waking up?" Asta snapped. "What did you do?"

"I didn't do anything!" Grell barked. "I'm sorry if I don't understand all of the exact ramifications of waking the dead! I've never bloody done it before!"

"None of the other fucking kings ever mentioned, oh, yeah, you can wake these fucks up, but then they're just going to fuck off right back to sleep again?"

"No! Because that would have been *helpful!*"

"What do we do?" Sloane asked. "How can we help? We're supposed to be leaving for battle in a matter of minutes!"

"The ladle on head approach is not working," Urilith said glumly. "Some of them didn't even finish their soup."

"Did they eat too much?" Stoker snorted. "Sort of like when you eat too much turkey and pass out after a Dhankes feast?"

Grell narrowed his eyes. "What is in that soup?"

"Oh!" Urilith looked at the pot. "It's a bone broth base with lots of carrots, potatoes, onions, and there's some rosemary, mint—"

"What *kind* of mint?"

"Why, the mint that grows right outside the temple here! It's...." Urilith's eyes widened. "Oh no."

Grell dragged his hands over his face. "*Oh no* is an understatement."

Sloane's stomach twisted. "What's wrong?"

Urilith cringed. "The mint that grows here is by far the most potent strain in probably the universe, a special hybrid of my own design—"

"And it used to be called Asrawort," Grell grumbled.

"Asra-what?" Sloane tried to clarify.

"Are you familiar with catnip? Well, this is bloody Asra-nip. All right?" Grell groaned in frustration. "The goddess of fertility just *doped* our entire army."

"I am so terribly sorry!" Urilith clutched the pot to her chest. "It's been thousands of years since I've cooked for Asra, and I wanted just an extra pinch of protection—"

"There has to be something we can do," Sloane said firmly. "We cannot fight like this."

"We cannot do fuck all until that bloody mint wears off!" Grell argued.

"Why aren't you and Asta falling asleep?"

"I'm on a diet. I didn't eat any. Watching my girlish figure and all that." Grell looked to Asta. "What about you? Did you eat it?"

"No!" Asta wrinkled his nose. "I don't like onions! Besides, do you really *eat* soup or do you drink it and just chew occasionally?"

Galgareth and Lochlain suddenly appeared, and Galgareth scoffed in surprise at the crowd of snoozing Asra. "Uh, so, what did we miss?"

"The Asra all went back to sleep because Urilith accidentally drugged them, and we're almost out of time before we have to be in battle to win and save the universe?" Sloane choked back a hysterical laugh. "Did you guys find Fred?"

"No!" Lochlain grimaced. "There's no sign of him. It's like he portaled out, but I didn't think Fred even knew how to do that."

Ollie was counting down out loud, and he dropped to his knees, babbling out the numbers so frantically it was impossible to understand him. Alexander and Rota were quick to try and comfort him, but it didn't seem to be helping.

"What the hell do we do now?" Milo asked nervously. "What happens if you guys don't go?"

"I don't know, but it's going to be fine," Sloane insisted. "Did you and Robert get all the totems passed out?"

"If by passed out, you mean we tied them to their paws, then yeah."

"Okay. So. Milo, Robert, Lochlain, Chase. You guys should go back to the sanctum with the others."

"No squishy mortals in the way?" Lochlain teased halfheartedly.

Milo sagged. "Ain't gotta tell me twice."

"Go ahead." Sloane gave Milo a fierce hug. "We're gonna figure this out."

"Fuck, I hope so. I've got a bad feeling about this." Milo left with the others, following them back down the stairs to retreat into the sanctum.

"You guys should probably get Ollie in there too," Sloane said to Alexander and Rota. "One way or another, we've got to leave any second if we're going to make it in time."

"What about the army?" Stoker demanded. "You really think we stand a chance without them? We may be a powerful force, but the numbers are not in our favor here. We will be overwhelmed in seconds."

"Seconds!" Ollie whimpered. "Sixty… fifty-nine… fifty-eight…."

"We have to trust that Ollie's prediction was correct," Sloane said, hoping he sounded more confident than he felt. "We have to hope for the best and go."

"But without the army, the third best-dressed person here is right," Grell said. "We will not win."

"What the fuck are you saying?"

"I'm saying that we need to fucking stop and think of something else instead of plunging headfirst into a suicide mission! It could take *hours* for these Asra to sleep off their little nighty night potion.

"Ollie said—"

"By Great Azaethoth's profoundly pendulous gonads, I do not fucking care what that little twat said—"

"Wait, profoundly *what*?"

"Profoundly pendulous gonads. Glorious grand marbles. Wonderous wrinkle berries. Fantastic—"

"Hey! Enough!" Asta frowned, turning his head and sniffing the air. "Isn't this the same place where we fought that globby guy or something? And dude got his face melted?"

"Yes?" Sloane paused. "Why?"

"Because I smell a portal—"

"… two, one!" Ollie cried.

A portal opened—but not one opened by Grell or Stoker or anyone else there. It was someone portaling into the temple from another world, and Sloane's blood froze when he saw Daisy coming through.

"Hi, Sloane," she said with a wicked leer. "So nice to see you again."

"*Shit.*" Sloane immediately summoned a shield and a sword of starlight.

The portal behind Daisy continued to grow, and Zarnorach and Ebbeth were trying to push their way through, snarling and whipping their tentacles. There were more old gods behind them, so many that Sloane could barely recount their names.

No.

No.

This couldn't be happening.

"Hey, Captain Bitch Face!" Asta bolted forward, slamming himself into Daisy with his entire weight.

She went flying back into the portal with a startled scream.

Amazingly, the portal started to shrink.

Asta was clearly behind it, grunting with effort as he hissed. "Okay, could use a little help here!"

"I'm here!" Grell transformed in a blink, standing beside Asta in his glorious Asra body. He bowed his head and used his magic to help Asta try to close the portal. "We need… to get out of here… very soon!"

"Rota and I can make a portal!" Alexander said hurriedly. "We can get everyone out!"

"And what about the army of sleeping Asra? What are you going to do? Drag them one by one?" Stoker spat. "No, we have to do something else." He reached his arms above his head, his prismatic tentacles slithering out to touch the ceiling.

Alexander's eyes widened. "What the fuck are you doing?"

"Go help Grell and Asta close that fucking portal!" Stoker snapped. "Now!"

Alexander flinched at Stoker's tone, but he obeyed. He hurried over, sending Rota's invisible tentacles to start pulling at the sides of the portal.

The gods on the other side were fighting just as hard to keep it open, and a new tear opened up from which more of Ebbeth's tentacles swung through.

Loch and Galgareth ran over to help close the tear, but then a second portal opened up next to the first.

"Fuck, fuck, fuck!" Sloane saw more tentacles forcing their way through, and he sliced through them with the sword of starlight as fast as he could. He kept dancing between the two portals, swinging with all his strength to keep the old gods back.

"Mother!" Loch screamed.

"I'm here!" she cried, rushing to him.

"Pandora! Mara! Go get them! Get them and the others to safety!"

"But son—"

"Mother, *now!*"

Urilith vanished and Loch leaped back into the battle, roaring as he slammed his tentacles into the others still trying to bust through.

Alexander split Rota's massive tentacles between the two portals, clawing at their edges and summoning more magic until his skin audibly sizzled.

My sweet boy! Rota cried. *No!*

"Shut up and help me close this fucking bullshit!" Alexander snarled. "Now!"

Stoker was grunting, louder and louder until it was a thundering roar, and the entire temple trembled.

"Stoker! What are you doing?" Sloane shouted, daring to look back long enough to see Stoker flash a quick smile.

"Do you trust me?" Stoker asked.

"No, fucking never."

Stoker grinned. "Smart man. Keep them from coming through… just a few more seconds!"

"Stoker, what are—"

Everything went black, and gravity turned so that Sloane was falling into the ceiling. He gasped as his back struck the hard stone, and a few of the sleeping Asra were suddenly on top of him. He tried to scream for help, but he couldn't breathe.

Gravity righted itself, and then Sloane was falling down again into the floor with the Asra. He was dazed, groaning as Loch's strong tentacles wrapped around him. "Loch…?"

"I'm here!" Loch hugged him tight. "My love, are you all right?"

"I'm okay… I think. What the fuck…?" Sloane struggled to focus his vision, seeing first that the invading portals were gone.

Grell and Asta were up, shaking themselves off and bumping their noses together. Ollie was still down, but Alexander and Rota were tending to him. Urilith was untangling the sleeping Asra from one another with Galgareth's help. Everyone seemed to be shaken up but otherwise unharmed.

It had felt like the temple had been through an earthquake, but no….

It had *moved*.

Sloane stared out into a barren wasteland dotted with random oases of vibrant flowering plants that now surrounded them. At its center was a cluster of tall modern buildings complete with roads and sidewalks. It couldn't have been more than a few city blocks, and the skyline was eerily familiar.

The temple had been moved to this new world a few hundred yards from the edge of the little city, and Sloane could not hide how stunned he was by such a raw display of power.

Not to mention that it had saved all of their lives because there was no sign of Daisy or any of the old gods.

"Stoker!" Sloane gasped. "How did you...."

Stoker was standing a few yards away, having just dragged himself out from underneath one of the sleeping Asra. He was swaying back and forth, and his gaze was cloudy.

"Stoker?" Sloane started toward him. "Hey, are you okay?"

Stoker's nose gushed blood down onto his shirt.

"Stoker?" Sloane reached for him.

Stoker smiled, inhaled deeply, and then he collapsed.

"Stoker!"

CHAPTER 10.

SLOANE DROPPED beside Stoker, easing his head into his lap. "Hey, hey! Wake up!"

Stoker stirred, but his eyes did not open.

"Loch!" Sloane pleaded. "Help him, please."

Loch extended his tentacles, laying a few across Stoker's neck and chest. They glowed alongside Sloane's hands as they tried to heal him, but even after a few seconds, Stoker did not wake.

"He portaled the entire fucking temple," Asta murmured. "Boss fuckin' move."

"But we're still in Aeon." Grell scowled. "How?"

"Boss magic?"

"Is he going to be all right?" Sloane asked worriedly. "He's not waking up."

"I am trying, my love," Loch said, offering a tentacle to nuzzle Sloane's cheek.

"Here!" Galgareth came over, and she slid her tentacles down to add to Loch's and Sloane's hands. The glow burned brighter, but still Stoker remained unconscious.

Rota helped Ollie into a sitting position, and Ollie mumbled miserably, "I threw up on one of the big kitties. And then I threw down. And maybe sideways too."

"Take some deep breaths." Alexander rubbed his back. "I think you've done enough drinking for one day."

For a lifetime, Rota agreed.

"No, no... I have to keep going." Ollie put his face in his hands. "I have to see... what went wrong."

"You said the countdown was for the battle, right?" Sloane said. "The battle to save Ell?"

"I don't know now." Ollie grimaced, belching loudly. "Ugh."

"Please, Ollie. We need to know—"

"Give him a fucking minute," Alexander warned.

"We don't have a fucking minute," Grell snarled as he stalked toward Alexander and Ollie. "He predicted that we would lose if we didn't go to battle by the time the clock ticked down. Well, ticktock, ticktock, that time has come and gone, and we were fucking *blindsided*."

"Back off," Alexander cautioned again, his eyes narrowing.

Rota made himself visible, his true size too large to fit inside the confines of the temple floor, but his massive arms and tentacles curled around Ollie and Alexander protectively.

Grell scoffed at the display, but he did not advance.

"But hey, we did fight," Sloane said, "and we won, didn't we? We survived, and—" His heart jolted. "Pandora. The others."

"Go," Loch said. "I'll take care of Stoker."

"I love you." Sloane took off his jacket and then folded it up so he could place it beneath Stoker's head. He petted Stoker's hair, saying, "And *you*, you better wake up, so I can yell at you for being such an idiot and saving all of us."

"Don't worry. I will do lots of yelling when he wakes up," Loch said cheerfully.

"I'll be right back." Sloane kissed Loch's cheek.

"Galgareth. Go. Be with your family." Rota stretched his shimmering tentacles toward Stoker to take over for her. "I'll be here to take care of mine."

"Stoker is family?" Alexander asked dryly.

"He's like a grumpy stepdad." Ollie hiccupped.

"I'll come with you," Galgareth said, reaching for Sloane's hand. "Let's go."

Sloane took Galgareth's hand and braced himself for the teleportation. They were now in the inner sanctum, and he didn't even have a second to prepare himself for the worst.

Luckily, he didn't need it.

Lynnette and Mara were still in bed with Pandora as if nothing had ever happened. Even the pillows and blankets were all as Sloane remembered. Milo was rubbing Lynnette's feet again, Robert and Lochlain were hovering close, and it was like having déjà vu.

Chase chugging a mug of what looked like beer was new, though.

Urilith rushed over, tackling both Sloane and Galgareth in a giant, tentacle-filled hug. "My darlings! You're all right! What's happened?"

"Stoker!" Sloane wheezed, struggling to breathe through Urilith's grip. "Stoker portaled the whole temple out of your world and into another!"

"Oh! That's what all the shaking was about!"

"What did you do, Mother?" Galgareth sounded equally breathless, no doubt from Urilith's continued crushing embrace.

"Well, when everything started to get all topsy-turvy, I sort of… well." Urilith withdrew, and she actually looked sheepish. "I might have assumed my true goddess form and filled the room a tiny bit."

"She was like a goddess air bag!" Milo exclaimed. "She totally squished us all into the floor, the walls—!"

"Gently!" Urilith interjected. "I wanted to make sure no one was harmed, especially the little ones."

"Thank you." Sloane kissed Urilith's cheek.

"Of course, my dear. How is everyone else? Azaethoth and the others?"

"Everybody is okay except Stoker. The spell took a lot out of him and he collapsed." Sloane shook his head. "Loch and Rota are trying to heal him. None of the old gods or cultists got through, though. We're all okay."

"Ollie?" Chase asked worriedly. "He okay too?"

"Yes, him too. Alexander and Rota are taking care of him. He needs to dry up a bit." Sloane went to the bed to snatch up Pandora. "And you! You, baby girl. You're okay!"

"Da-da!" Pandora had been so absorbed in Mara that she hadn't seemed to take any note of Sloane until she was in his arms. She squealed happily and hugged his neck. "Baby! Dad, Dad, Dad, baby!"

"Thank you for taking care of her," Sloane told Lynnette. "Thank you. All of you."

"Hey, we're family," Lynnette said with a kind smile.

"It's what we do," Milo chimed in. "We're all connected by this force that runs through us, it's all around us…."

"By all the gods, I love you," Lynnette gushed.

"Baby, baby!" Pandora rambled on as she patted Sloane's shoulder insistently. "Baby!"

"Yes, sweetheart. Lynnette has a baby." Sloane kissed her hair, breathing her in. "And you're my baby."

"—are disgusting!" Stoker snarled, his voice traveling down the hall.

"I didn't actually do it!" Loch argued.

Sloane grinned. "Ah, and there's your daddy. Sounds like Stoker is awake now too."

"You are an absolute *imbecile!*" Stoker raged on. "Why would anyone think that was a good idea?"

"Sloane has told me to ask permission first!" Loch defended. "So, I *asked you*—"

"*Imbecile!*"

"Oh!" Urilith moved to intercept Loch and Stoker, wrapping the quarreling pair up in her tentacles for another big hug. "Azaethoth! Jake!"

Stoker and Loch squirmed and gasped, but at least it silenced their arguing.

Pandora wiggled out of Sloane's arms so she could charge over to Loch and then wrap herself around his leg.

"Hello, my spawn," Loch wheezed.

Urilith released Stoker first, and he cleared his throat, straightening out the fresh tie of the suit he had conjured for himself.

"Hey! Stoker!" Sloane smiled warmly. "You gave us quite a scare."

"Please, Mr. Beaumont." Stoker tipped his head. "There was never any reason to be alarmed. I merely exhausted my resources temporarily."

"Shut up." Sloane hugged him. He felt Stoker stiffen but then slowly wrap his arms around him. "Thank you. For saving us all."

Stoker held on tight before letting go, his poised shield slipping away for a moment when their eyes met. His expression was soft and his smile warm, and he looked years younger. "My pleasure, Mr. Beaumont."

Sloane gave him a small shove.

"And what was that for?" Stoker raised his brow.

"Next time you need help moving an entire temple, how about asking for it?"

Stoker's familiar sly smirk fell into place. "I will never make you a promise that I cannot keep. Besides, you were a tad tied up at the time."

"Oh! Sloane, my love!" Loch was finally free from Urilith's hug, and he scooped up Pandora on his way over to embrace him. "I have the most excellent news to share."

"What is it?" Sloane asked.

"The Asra are waking."

"Oh! Wonderful!" Urilith sighed in relief. "I was so worried. I really do still feel just awful. I didn't mean to break our army."

"It's all right, Mother." Loch smiled reassuringly. "The little temple shake seems to have done the trick. At least a dozen of them were awake when I offered Stoker my—"

"*Please*. Don't even say it." Stoker pinched the bridge of his nose.

Sloane tried not to laugh. "Loch, while I'm sure you meant well... I'm not even going to finish that thought."

"Probably for the best," Stoker agreed.

"What exactly happened up there?" Chase asked. "I thought Ollie's big countdown was go time for the battle."

"It was and it wasn't." Sloane replied carefully. "Ollie said we had to be ready to go then or else we would lose. Even if he was wrong about why we needed to be together, he was right about the what."

"What do you mean?"

"If we hadn't been all together and ready to fight the battle for the universe precisely at that time, Daisy would have been able to bring the old gods through to the temple. We wouldn't have been ready. Half of us might not have even been here." Sloane frowned. "Which also makes me wonder.... Why the hell did they come after us here? And how?"

"Daisy has been to that world before," Stoker reminded him. "When we fought Cleus. It's your mother-in-law's temple. Not too difficult to put together that we may have been gathering here. If things are not going well with Ell, it stands to reason they still see you as a threat and decided to come looking for you."

"Me?" Sloane blinked.

"Yes, *Starkiller*. You. Daisy was obviously kind enough to share with them that she knew where that world was."

"And where's this one? What's to stop them from coming here?" Sloane tensed. "Where did you bring us, Stoker?"

"We are in my Hidden World." Stoker crossed his arms. "A dimension I built within the fabric of space in Aeon. A world within a world."

"*What?*" Loch scoffed. "That's impossible."

"And yet, here we are."

Now Sloane knew why the city looked so familiar—Stoker must have modeled his Hidden World after the same part of Archersville where his club, the Velvet Plank, was located.

"So, safe for now, hopefully." Sloane cringed.

"Yes," Stoker assured him. "I've closed down the walls so no one can leave or enter, not even gods, unless they have a magical key that I created. It's for an entrance into this world for us to exclusively use, so that no one can try to follow us if we have to make a fast retreat."

"Well, hopefully, there will be no retreating." Sloane squeezed Loch's arm for comfort. "The plan remains the same as before. The Asra are waking up, so we finally have our army. When they're ready, we can.... *Shit*."

"We can shit?" Chase echoed with a raised brow.

"No! Fred!" Sloane grimaced. "We never found him."

"By all the gods. Shit is right." Lochlain cringed miserably. "He might still be back there. We left him! Fuck, I left him behind *again*—"

"Hey, no! You looked for him! You tried to find him!" Robert attempted to soothe. "If you and Galgareth couldn't figure out where he was, then there's no way they would be able to."

"We don't fucking know that!"

"Hey, hey." Sloane gestured for calm. "We'll figure it out. He may have portaled out, right? There's still a chance that he—"

"I absolutely hate traveling via portal!" a familiar voice cried miserably as a floating glowing blue ball appeared. "I am going to be *sick*!"

Along with the talking ball, Grell was suddenly standing there back in his human form, drawling, "You're a ghost. You can't be sick. You don't have a stomach."

The ball shook with indignant rage. "I am still able to feel the effects, I assure you!"

"Professor Kunst!" Sloane waved at the ball. "Hi! It's nice to see you again!"

Professor Emil Kunst was an expert in Sagittarian lore and history who had sacrificed himself to destroy a totem that would have awoken Salgumel. Before his soul could pass on to Zebulon, he managed to escape the bridge in Xenon and later received a position in the Xenon royal court.

The way Sloane understood it, Kunst had given himself the position without any prior approval, and King Grell hadn't felt like arguing.

"Oh, hello, Sloane!" Kunst sounded like he was smiling. It was hard to be sure, however, since he was just a spirit bound to a ball now. "It is so very good to see you. I hope you and your family have been doing well."

"I popped back in to Xenon to check on my queen and wouldn't you know it?" Grell batted his eyes. "My beloved occult advisor has some exciting revelations for us."

"Yes!" Kunst inhaled sharply. "I tried to reach you when you returned to raise the army, but you were, uh, occupied. Ahem. I have been studying the legends of the Kindress extensively, and seeing as how there is a high chance of going into direct battle with him—"

"We're going to try and avoid that at all costs," Sloane said firmly.

Kunst sighed. "While I understand the desire to not do battle with the Kindress, you should all be prepared for that possibility. A key discovery in my research is that as the god of life and death, the Kindress has no dominion over those who have drawn breath between those realms of existence."

"Like a ghoul," Sloane said immediately. "Fred is a ghoul. He was able to go inside Ell's bubble. I mean, it was still hurting him, but it didn't immediately turn him into a puddle."

"In theory, those who have been resurrected would also be equally resistant."

"Like Ted," Grell said quietly.

Lochlain grimaced. "And me."

"And the Asra?" Chase asked. "They were kinda dead, right?"

"Not quite dead enough. Think of their slumber as *diet dead*."

"Well, Ollie died a little once. Full flavor."

"Ollie?" Kunst said the name like it was an alien word. "Oh! Oleander Logue, of course. The great scholar. His translations of the Death Song of the Kindress were a critical part of my work. I would so love to meet him!"

"I think he's sleepin' one off, chief. Maybe later."

"Ah, that's all right. Ahem." Kunst calmed himself. "What you need to know, especially you, Sloane, is that starlight alone may not be enough to defeat the Kindress. He is a being of pure starlight, after all. While there is certainly a chance that it may be the one thing that can harm him, it is also just as likely that it will do nothing."

"Great." Sloane's stomach tightened.

"The tears are the key," Kunst said firmly. "The tears of not only Great Azaethoth, but also of the Kindress as well."

"*Ell's* tears?"

"Yes. Mr. Logue's translation was very clear that it was not only Great Azaethoth's tears that ended the Kindress's life, but his own tears as well."

"Right, so, let me get right on that. Collecting tears from the two most powerful beings in all of creation." Sloane scoffed. "No problem."

"It is reasonable to believe that the cultists have them," Grell mused. "From Great Azaethoth anyway."

"Wait, what?"

"And how exactly did you come to that conclusion?" Stoker demanded, his eyes narrowed. "Because trust that I have personally looked for the tears and never found them."

"Never got around to popping over to Xenon to look for some, did you?" Grell smirked. "Once upon a time, we had a tiny issue with a god stealing bones from the Asran dead. He was bribing my traitorous subjects with vials of Great Azaethoth's tears. The vials we found were destroyed, but that doesn't mean he didn't have more."

"Gronoch," Sloane said suddenly. "He had them?"

"He did indeed."

"Shit, shit, shit."

"What is it?" Stoker asked. "What's wrong?"

"Don't you see?" Sloane shook his head. "I know you have your own reasons for wanting to murder the crap out of Jeff, but Alexander and Rota are after him because of what he said, that he might have known Gronoch."

"And Gronoch knows where Rota's body is."

"It stands to reason that if Gronoch had access to the tears somehow, maybe some secret stash, that he might have given some to Jeff like he did to the people who were helping him in Xenon. After all, Jeff and Gronoch wanted the same thing."

"It would also explain why the cultists are so keen on contacting the Kindress," Loch said with a frown. "They have the remote control for the chainsaw."

"If the chainsaw doesn't wake up the hammer, they just click the remote."

"In English, please?" Grell asked.

"We never understood why the cultists wanted to use the Kindress to awaken Salgumel," Sloane explained. "It seemed like overkill, like using a chainsaw to get a hold of a hammer. But if Jeff actually has the tears, he probably thinks he can use them to make the Kindress do whatever he wants. I think he wants to wake up Salgumel and continue to use the Kindress to help them take over the world."

"That is very arrogant and very, very stupid."

"That's Jeff." Sloane smiled bitterly.

"But if that's true," Stoker pointed out, "then that means Jeff has the tears and probably with him right now."

"And the fruit," Sloane added.

"Ah! The fruit!" Kunst exclaimed. "That must be destroyed immediately! Even a weak harvest may be enough to sway the Kindress. After all, he has not had such an offering in ages. He might not be able to resist it."

"So far, he's not biting," Alexander declared as he walked in with Ollie in tow, Rota's shimmer clinging to them both. "I was just there before shit here went to hell. He's refusing the offer for now."

Some of the color had returned to Ollie's cheeks, though he still swayed a bit.

Alexander guided him over to the edge of the dais to sit down. Once he seemed sure that Ollie wouldn't tip over, he pulled out a pack of gum from his trench coat. "Here." He offered a piece to Ollie and then took one for himself.

"Feeling okay, Ollie?" Sloane asked gently.

"Super." Ollie groaned. "That Asra was real mad about me getting sick on him."

"Hello, Mr. Logue!" Kunst said, floating toward him. "And may I just say, what a fan I am—"

"Ah! Talking ball!" Ollie screamed. "Dead guy! Freaky dead guy! In the ball!"

"Why, I never!" Kunst jerked back. "I merely wanted to praise you for your translation—"

Alexander eyed Kunst with a sour glare. "Maybe some other time."

"Glad to see you up and around, Oleander," Stoker said. "I was... concerned."

Ollie stared at Stoker. "I'm not calling you dad."

"Pardon?"

"Don't ask." Alexander snorted.

"Can we get back to the task at hand?" Grell interjected. "Army. Battle for the universe. Very bad things afoot."

"Yes." Sloane nodded firmly. "As soon as the Asra are ready to go, we should leave. Any element of surprise we had is probably lost now. Daisy had to have seen them all before Asta pushed her back in the portal. We should move as soon as we can."

"Mother, will you stay here with the squishy mortals and little ones?" Loch asked.

"Of course, sweetie," Urilith replied. "I will make sure everyone is safe."

"Yeah, but hey, this squishy mortal is going too," Chase declared. "Merrick is there right now trying to help the AVPD. I can take over for him with the evac so he can come help you guys out."

"Okay." Sloane thought for a moment. "We know they have the park completely surrounded. We need to draw them away from Ell so we can try to talk to him."

"Plus take a swipe at Jeff and destroy the fruit," Loch said.

"And steal the tears," added Grell.

"Grell, do you think you and the Asra can pull the old gods away? Even getting just a few of them out of the way would be a huge help."

"Gladly."

"I can go with them," Galgareth offered. "We can try to take them to a part of the city that's already been evacuated."

"Perfect." Sloane glanced at Loch. "Loch and I will wait until there's an opening and try to get to Ell. If he's still refusing to take the fruit, maybe he'll be reasonable. Maybe he'll listen to us."

"We'll go with you," Alexander said. "Where Ell is, that's where Jeff is gonna be. We take him out and destroy the fruit, that's half the fuckin' battle won."

"Don't forget about the cultists," Stoker warned. "There's enough of them there to be trouble."

"I'll send some of my Asra to entertain them," Grell said. "They won't be a problem."

"So. That's it." Sloane reached for Loch's hand. "We'll make sure Chase gets into the city safely so he can relieve Merrick to come help us. Grell, Galgareth, and the bulk of the Asra will go in first to try and get the old gods out of the way. The remaining Asra plus Stoker will handle the cultists. Me, Loch, Alexander, and Rota will make a move to get to Ell and Jeff."

"And what about Fred?" Lochlain asked quietly.

Sloane sagged. "We hope that he shows up if and when we need him. That's all we can do right now. We don't have time to go look for him. We have to end this. Once and for all."

The inner sanctum fell silent.

Sloane didn't know what else to say, and he felt awkward with everyone looking to him. He squeezed Loch's hand, adding, "Anyone wants to say anything, now's the time."

"Thank you, Sloane," Lochlain said suddenly.

"What?" Sloane was surprised, and he turned to frown at Lochlain. "For?"

"For everything," Lochlain replied with a sweet smile. He wrapped his arm around Robert, pulling him in close as he continued, "I know the world has been in peril more times than we can count, and you probably feel like you're responsible in some way."

"I mean, yes, a little." Sloane cringed. "More than a little, really."

"But think about all the good you've done." Lochlain beamed. "I only got to marry the man of my dreams because of you. It took dying for me to see what I had right in front of me, oops, but I was able to do that because of you and Azaethoth."

"Yeah!" Chase chimed in with a grin. "Your lil' prayer is what sent me off to magic enforcement where I got to meet Merrick. That was because of you too."

"Oh, hey!" Ollie perked up. "You're the one who told Alexander and Rota about me. We wouldn't be together either if you hadn't done that."

"I... I guess I did." Sloane blushed, and he smiled bashfully. "Thank you. For giving me another way to look at it."

"Thank *you*," Lochlain said.

"You haven't done shit for me," Grell teased, "but I'll take an IOU just so I feel included."

Sloane laughed. "Done!"

"See, my sweet husband? You brought us all together," Loch said with a sweet smile. "By the power of love, friendship—"

"Thank you—"

"—and your ravenous desire for my seed."

Sloane sighed, and he tried to hide a smile.

"On that delightful note," Stoker said, "I think it's time to go."

"Yes," Sloane agreed. "We've had our soup, we have our totems, and we have our army who is now awake. There's not another second to lose." He gave Pandora a big hug, allowing himself to enjoy a family embrace with Loch. He let it linger only for a moment, a new sense of urgency pulling him away sooner than he would have liked.

They'd just been attacked, and their escape hadn't been an easy one. But they had to move.

It was time to go on the offensive.

A small amount of bribery in the form of magically summoned cookies was the price paid to get Pandora to return to Urilith's care without complaint, and Sloane's heart ached as he led the way out of the sanctum. He hated to be leaving her again so soon, but he knew this was what had to be done.

It was for her and everyone else he was leaving behind.

It was for his best friend, Milo, and his dear girlfriend, Lynette, and their beautiful newborn daughter, Mara. It was for Lochlain, a man whom he'd first met with romantic intentions and then ended up solving his murder, and for Lochlain's husband, Robert. It was for Urilith, his goddess mother-in-law, who had found it in her heart to love and forgive Sloane in spite of having slain several of her children. It was for Kunst, the professor whose very life Sloane had also taken as a sacrifice to save the world once before.

In the same ritual that had killed his parents, whose death had been the catalyst for all of this.

It was for those who were running into battle with him, charging through the ranks of Asra toward a portal where death might be waiting on the other side.

For Chase, the snarky cop with a heart of gold.

For Galgareth, a kind and devoted sister.

For Grell, a sarcastic but wise and beloved ruler.

For Asta, Grell's son and equal parts trouble and infectious charm, plus his boyfriend, Jay, back in Xenon, and Ted and Graham too.

For Alexander and Rota, a bitter young man and a gentle god who had first found love under the most horrific circumstances and then found it again with Ollie, equally troubled but eternally kind, who was lingering to say farewell to his lovers even as the portal back to Aeon opened.

For Stoker, the ever-mysterious gangster whose ruthlessly brutal facade hid a surprisingly tender heart that loved the everlasting people he protected here in his Hidden World.

And for Loch—ridiculous, wonderful, always irresistible Loch. His love, his husband, the father of his child, and gorgeous god who had completely changed his world from the moment he first sat down in Sloane's office eating blueberry pie.

It was for him too.

And Ell.

By all the gods, for Ell and Fred too.

Sloane couldn't let himself forget about them, his friends who were hurting and in need. He was worried for them both, but especially for Ell. Sloane made a promise to himself that he would do everything he could to save him.

But if he had to....

He didn't finish the thought, well aware of what was at risk if he couldn't raise his sword. He stood in front of the portal, looking back at the crowd behind him. He saw his parents' faces smiling down at him as he summoned the sword of starlight, and he tried to be confident that he would be able to visit them in Zebulon when all of this was over. For now, it was time—

"Wait, wait, one last thing!" Ollie came barreling over to Sloane. "Here!"

"Ow?" Sloane flinched as Ollie slapped his shoulder. There was a tingle of something magical in his touch. "What's this?"

"It's a second." Ollie smiled. "You'll know what to do."

"Okay!" Sloane nodded. "Thank you, Ollie."

"No problem." Ollie gave a little salute, backing away from the portal. "Have fun storming the park!"

"Uh, I'll try." Sloane grimaced.

Loch reached out with a tentacle to caress Sloane's face. "Are you ready, my sweet mate?"

"Almost." Sloane leaned in to crash his lips against Loch's, kissing him with everything he had and all the love he wished he knew how else to say with the few precious moments they had left. It left him breathless and his heart pounding, and he whispered, "I love you."

"And I love you, always."

"Let's go."

CHAPTER 11.

THE RUSH of a portal had never felt so intense, and Sloane was certain it was because of what was waiting for them on the other side: a battle for the fate of the universe.

His eyes opened, and he could see they were gathered one block down from the southern end of the park where they'd last seen Ell. This area had already been evacuated by the AVPD, so thankfully there were no civilians around to see the giant army of Asra and old gods. He'd hoped the city would be empty by now, but Sloane could still hear the hum of traffic a few blocks away.

Galgareth was in her true goddess form, and Sloane assumed she had left Toby behind at the temple to keep him safe. Loch, too, had changed into his god form, but his vessel was draped over the hood of a car.

"It's fine," Loch said when he noticed Sloane looking. "I'll come back for it later."

If there is a later, Sloane's stressed mind unhelpfully supplied.

Grell and Asta were dividing the Asra, choosing who was going to be in the main assault and who would stay back to help Stoker face the cultists. Galgareth spread out her tentacles to give all of them her blessing of serendipity, and soon they were ready.

Chase was on his phone, waving a quick farewell as he headed off to find Merrick.

"Good luck!" Sloane called out to him.

Chase tipped his hat, and then he was gone, racing off through an alleyway.

"Should we wait for Merrick?" Galgareth asked.

"No," Sloane said. "They could literally be giving Ell the fruit at any second. We need to go now."

"It's time," Grell said, arching his back and letting out a roar.

The sound rippled through the Asra like a wave, their growls and howls joining his in a haunting symphony.

Sloane was sweating, and his hand trembled around his sword of starlight. He climbed up on Loch's back and then scooted down to straddle the base of his neck. He squeezed with his legs to make sure he had a solid seat, taking a deep breath.

"We will be victorious," Loch said firmly. "This great battle will be written in the stars alongside the tale of our mating and our legendary love."

Sloane managed a smile. "You really think so, huh?"

"I know so." Loch turned his head to smile back at Sloane. "I love you, my sweet Starkiller."

"I love you too, Azaethoth."

"To battle!" Grell howled suddenly.

That was all it took. Those two simple words and the Asra took off. They were fast, zooming through the alley and into the park like black bolts of lightning. They were gone in a blink except for the small squad left behind with Stoker.

Galgareth took to the air, soaring above them as they charged over the grass and through the trees and bushes.

Ebbeth was at the far end of the park all by himself, and they went for him first. He screeched in surprise and pain as the Asra overwhelmed him, and Galgareth swooped down to tackle him to the ground.

Zarnorach and a few of the other gods left the crowd to help Ebbeth, though they soon found themselves being overrun by the Asra as well. The Asra were immensely powerful, swarming the gods one by one and forcing them away from the park. Sloane knew most of the gods by name, like Elgrirath the Astute, goddess of regret, Traceth the Steadfast, goddess of compassion and sparkles, and Solothipharos the Jouncing, the god of beards and storytelling.

Revered deities or not, they were the enemy now, and Sloane hoped the Asra could keep them distracted long enough so they could get to Jeff and Ell. As the rest of the old gods came to help Ebbeth and try to fight off the Asra, the mortal and everlasting cultists were left without any godly protection.

"Let's go!" Stoker shouted as he raced forward with the remaining Asra.

"Stoker! Wait!" Sloane called.

Stoker turned just in time to catch the sword of starlight Sloane tossed to him. "Hey! Little warning next time, Mr. Beaumont, if you please."

"Sorry, thought you could handle it." Sloane smiled. "Be safe."

"Trust that I can handle anything you want to give me." Stoker flashed Sloane an appreciative smirk and then took off running again before Sloane could reply.

"Crochet! Your organs!" Loch shouted after him.

Stoker flipped him off.

"You ready, Starkiller?" Alexander asked with a roll of his eyes.

"Yeah, I'm ready," Sloane said quietly. He didn't specify what he was ready for, and thankfully Alexander didn't elaborate on the task at hand. Even with the levity of Stoker's usual teasing and Loch's threats of visceral crafting, dread weighed heavily in his guts.

They both knew what was at stake here and what Sloane might have to do.

"Let's go." Alexander went first, Rota's tentacles wrapping around him like a shield as he marched ahead. "We're going to the edge of the bubble. Jeff wouldn't have gone far from Ell, and those fucks can't get inside."

"No totems, huh?" Sloane asked.

"Nope. Never saw anyone actually try to go inside, but judging by all the new puddles, Jeff and Daisy volun-told a few of their cultists."

Sloane grimaced. "We'll be right behind you. We're gonna try to get in to talk to Ell again. We have to get him to drop that bubble."

"*Talk.*" Alexander scoffed. "Yeah, sure. Have a nice chat. We're gonna go get the tears from Jeff. Let me know when you're ready to kill him."

Alexander, Rota scolded.

Rota, Alexander countered mockingly. *Let's clear a path, huh?*

Yes, sweet boy. Let's.

Alexander stretched his arms out as he entered the park, guiding Rota's tentacles to whip across the ground around him. Any cultist that came at them, mortal or otherwise, was crushed, thrown into the air, or smashed upon landing.

Loch took off into the air, gliding over them as they made their way toward the bubble.

Sloane tried to ignore the staggering amount of bodies left in the wake of Alexander and Rota's destructive path. He shuddered as Loch roared and sent out blasts of his prismatic fire to thin out some of the crowd ahead.

The bubble was getting closer, and there was no sign of the old gods. The plan to distract them away from Ell seemed to be working beautifully, though it also meant only Galgareth and the Asra were fighting their most powerful enemies. Stoker and the Asra with him were cutting through the cultists like butter, and the resistance Alexander and Rota faced was dwindling fast.

Although Sloane was worried for Galgareth, he knew they had to get to Ell.

That's what mattered.

Jeff! Alexander's angry growl cut into Sloane's thoughts.

Sloane looked ahead and saw a cluster of cultists who were refusing to leave the bubble. Jeff was right in the middle of them, and he was holding what looked like a gray strawberry the size of a basketball. Alexander and Rota raced toward him, but Jeff saw them coming.

Instead of fleeing, however, Jeff called for help.

Zarnorach lurched away from the battle with the Asra and Galgareth to cut Alexander and Rota off. Rota materialized to his full gargantuan size, swinging his giant fist at Zarnorach as Alexander directed his tentacles to swipe at the cultists shielding Jeff.

There was a loud howl in the distance, and Loch perked up. "Uncle!"

"Merrick?" Sloane asked. "He's coming?"

"Yes! He is going to help Galgareth!"

Sloane looked over to see Galgareth smashing Elgrirath into a nearby building while holding Ebbeth in a nasty chokehold. The Asra were keeping the other gods at bay for now, but Merrick would certainly be a welcome addition to keep the odds in their favor.

Loch stopped at the edge of the bubble, his great wings flapping as he hovered there, saying, "It is time, my love."

"I am ready," Sloane said more confidently than before. "We can—"

Traceth, a giant tentacled serpent, came out of nowhere, snatching Loch right out of the air and taking him to the ground with a snarl.

"Fuuuu-*uck*!" Sloane managed to hang on until they crashed, and then he went flying across the ground. He hit his head on something, and his skin was scorching like he was burning all over. He sat up with a grunt, and then he gasped sharply.

He was inside the puddle bubble.

Although his skin was stinging like hell, it was not rotting. Feeling very thankful for the totem's magic, Sloane whirled around to look for Loch.

Loch was tangled up with Traceth just a few yards away outside of the bubble, and he shouted, "Go, my love! Go now! Go to Ell!"

"No!" Sloane shook his head furiously, trying to think fast. "Hey! You still have your totem on?"

"Yes?" Loch paused to breathe fire, trying to drive Traceth back. "Why?"

"Drag her in here! Into the puddle bubble! Come on!"

"Oh! What a wonderful idea!" Loch snapped his teeth around Traceth's neck and began to walk backward into the bubble.

"You fool!" Traceth's yelled. "We're moments away from victory! Victory—"

"Dear beloved relative of mine, please allow me to introduce you to the puddle bubble," Loch mumbled through his mouthful of Traceth's flesh. His powerful hind legs dug into the earth, growling with effort as he dragged Traceth back into the bubble.

Loch hissed in obvious discomfort as he stepped inside, no doubt feeling the same burning sensation Sloane was, but Traceth was not so fortunate as to have such mild repercussions.

She melted the instant he touched the bubble, and Loch scrambled out of the way to avoid getting splashed.

"Where was one of these delightful things when we battled Cleus or my ridiculous brothers?" Loch lamented. "It would have made things so much easier!"

"Well, we didn't know Ell was the Kindress and could actually make a big god-killing puddle bubble of death."

"True." Loch nuzzled Sloane's chest. "Are you all right, my dear Starkiller?"

"Yeah, I'm okay." Sloane petted Loch's head. "We gotta hurry."

Inside the bubble was eerily quiet, the magic somehow muting the battle going on right outside. It sounded like a distant hum, and not an insane conflict between old gods and mortals. There were occasional flashes of light that looked like fireworks going off, and the quiet was sporadically pierced by a strange howl.

Sloane saw Ell sitting on the bench where he'd been before.

He was hanging his head, his crown of stars broken and dim, and the bubble around them was definitely getting bigger. Its growth seemed to slow as Sloane approached, and he didn't know if that was a good sign or not.

Either way, he summoned a sword of starlight.

"Ell?" Sloane said. "Hey, it's Sloane."

Ell glanced up at Sloane with a sigh. "You again."

"Yes, me." Sloane smiled, though it was strained. "Do you remember me?"

"Only as the mortal who won't stop bothering me," Ell drawled. "I don't know you."

"You came to my wedding," Sloane insisted. "Do you remember that? You gave me a book, *Starlight Bright*. You—"

"And strawberry-flavored lubricant!" Loch whispered loudly from behind him.

"That too." Sloane cringed. "You were there with Fred! You remember Fred, don't you?"

"Fred?" Ell sounded uncertain, and he lifted his head. "No. I don't... I...." He frowned, staring off into the distance. "I don't think I do."

"Your boyfriend. You were his ghoul doctor? You guys went to Robert and Lochlain's wedding too. We all got drunk at Lynnette's Galmethas party."

"I went to a party?" Ell's nose scrunched.

"Yeah! It was the first time we really got to meet. We'd seen you at the wedding, but uh, we got caught up cleaning up the bees and all that."

"There was a little girl." Ell's eyes widened. "She asked a swarm of bees to aid her in smiting her enemies."

"Yeah! They took her bubbles, and Loch maybe sort of taught her the spell so she could have her tiny revenge." Sloane grinned sheepishly. "No bees at Lynnette's party, thankfully, just us finally getting to hang out with you and Fred. You guys were so cute together, and I could tell right away how much he cared about you—"

"Fred!" Ell suddenly shouted.

"Wait! You remember him?" Sloane asked hopefully.

Ell didn't respond, but he was definitely staring at something.

Someone, Sloane realized as he turned to follow Ell's gaze.

At first, Sloane thought it was a cultist because they were wearing a black cloak. As the hood flew back, Sloane saw that it was Fred. He had no idea how Fred had gotten here or where he'd gotten the cloak from, but it was definitely him.

Fred's body was wildly decomposing and reanimating all at once. He hadn't been around when the totems were passed out, and Sloane watched in horror as Fred fought through what had to be absolute agony in an effort to reach Ell.

"Ell!" Fred groaned as he lurched forward, not slowing down for a second even as parts of his skin sloughed off.

"Fred?" Sloane gasped. "Are you okay? How did you—"

"Later!" Fred grunted sharply, his attention focused on Ell. "Ell, please! Hey, listen to me, baby."

"That's not my name," Ell protested even as he rose to his feet, staring uncertainly at Fred as he approached.

"Yes, it is." Fred gritted his teeth. He was panting heavily as he stood before Ell, saying firmly, "You are Elliam Sturm—"

"Stop it."

"—and I love you."

"Stop it!"

Fred's hands were skeletal and then flesh once more in a breath as he reached for Ell's face. "You're my Ell. My Trip, my hero, my knight in a shining rainbow llama shirt—"

"No!" Ell shuddered away from Fred's touch.

"Please, Ell. *I love you*—"

"No, you don't!" Ell suddenly screamed, the ground trembling. He stared at Fred with a new sense of recognition, and his rage was palpable. "You abandoned me. You turned on me. Like everyone always does. You say you love me, but you were afraid of me. You actually thought—"

"I was wrong!" Fred pleaded. He was obviously in intense pain, coughing through a mouthful of blood as his jaw unhinged and he had to shove it back into place to keep talking. "I'm sorry! Okay? This is just like when Princess Daisy thought Blix poisoned her! Do you remember that? And she tried to have him killed! But then she found out it was really—"

"Lord Dastardly." Ell actually smiled. "It was such a terrible name. It made it so... obvious." His brow scrunched, and he put his hands to his head as if fending off a terrible headache. "I... I don't understand."

Sloane hesitated to say anything, not sure whether he should intervene. It seemed like Ell was coming to his senses, and he looked back at Loch.

Loch shrugged, which looked almost comical when he was a giant tentacle dragon.

Sloane turned back to watch Fred and Ell, deciding to stay silent for now. He thought there was a chance Fred was getting Ell to come to his senses. This could be it.

"You're remembering," Fred said softly. "You remember the show we used to watch. Maybe even the book I gave you? The one when we first met?"

"The book... yes." Ell shivered again, and the puddle bubble shrank drastically. "I do. We watched every episode over and over. We talked about how obvious it was that Lord Dastardly was going to turn out to be evil, and...."

Fred reached again for Ell, his hand staying solid as he touched Ell's cheek. "How unfair it was. Because Blix got shit on constantly, but he deserved a happy ending too."

"Yeah." Ell smiled, and the violet light vanished from his eyes. "I remember...."

"I gave you that book 'cause I had such a big crush on you." Fred smiled too, though he had to drop to one knee as his body was ravaged by the effects of the bubble. "I wanted you like I ain't never wanted anything before. You made me feel fuckin' alive again, and being with you is the best fuckin' thing that's ever happened to me."

"Fred...?" Ell laid his hand over Fred's, and the rapid decomposition stopped.

Sloane held his breath.

Fred's body healed in moments, and there was no further sign of deterioration even though he was still inside the bubble without a totem to protect him. He gasped, a real breath of air, and Sloane was startled to hear it because ghouls didn't actually need to breathe.

"Yeah, baby," Fred said quietly. "It's me. It's me, and I love you."

"I saved a scale," Ell whispered. "I saved the last Vulgoran scale for you."

"Yeah! That's right, baby." Fred's eyes brimmed with tears. "For our wedding. 'Cause I'm gonna marry you."

"Marry me." Ell said it as if he couldn't believe it, and the glow had nearly faded from his eyes. "You really want to marry me?"

"I love you," Fred said passionately. "Ell, I love you more than anything. You have no idea what the fuck I've been through to get to you." He kept petting Ell's cheek. "I took out some of them nutso cultists, stole their shit, and snuck back through their portal with the rest of 'em 'cause I knew they'd be coming back here. To you."

Ell gently touched Fred's face, his expression confused. "You did all that... for me?"

"Yeah, baby. For you."

"I don't understand...." Ell frowned. "If you love me so much, then why am I hurting so badly? It's like there's this *thing* inside of me, this monster, and it's eating everything up. It hurts so much that it's hard to breathe, and then I can't even think clearly. I just get angry. So fucking *angry*, and I want to do such terrible, *terrible* things." He gritted his teeth, on the verge of tears as he demanded, "Why is death and pain all I remember?"

"I don't know, baby." Fred leaned into Ell's touch. "But it's gonna be okay, I swear. I know there's good stuff in you. I know you don't want to hurt nobody, and we're gonna get through this. You're gonna get your happily ever after—"

"You don't know me." Ell withdrew as if Fred's skin scalded him.

"Yes, I fuckin' do!" Fred reached for him again.

Ell smacked Fred's hand away. "You don't know anything about me. I don't deserve some fairy-tale happy ending. You have no idea what I've done, what I *will* do—"

"Ell, please—" Fred's eyes widened as he tried to stand, the hand Ell had touched starting to rot down to the bone.

"No!" Ell grabbed the top of Fred's head, forcing him back to his knees.

"You deserve to be fuckin' happy! You deserve to be fuckin' loved just like I love you!" Fred insisted. "Do you hear me?"

"Oh?" Ell bowed his head and glared, his eyes turning a brilliant violet once more as they burned into Fred's. "I deserve to be alone. I have no further use for you. Not now, not ever again."

"Ell, no—"

Ell roared.

"No!" Sloane bolted toward them, but he was too late.

Fred's body was enveloped in white light, a blinding glare that stung Sloane's eyes and made the ground tremble. Fred shouted as if in terrible pain, but Sloane couldn't see what was happening.

"Stop, Ell!" Sloane shouted, trying to shield his eyes as he charged forward. "Stop this now!"

Fred yelled.

The light faded....

And Fred was gone.

"N-No...." Sloane faltered, losing his grip on the sword as he fell to his knees. The magic vanished in the wake of his anguish, and he had to swallow back a sob.

There was nothing where Fred had been kneeling, not even a puddle.

He'd been completely obliterated without a trace left behind, and Sloane wished he'd intervened sooner, that he'd done something, anything—

"Wait... I...." Ell stared at the empty space where Fred had been and collapsed. His horns shrunk, his glow dimmed, and he clawed at the dirt in front of him, bursting into tears. "No, no... please... please, no! What did I do? Please! No! *Fred*!"

The protective bubble faded away, letting in the roar of the battle still raging around them.

Ell dug at the ground until his fingers were bloody, sobbing miserably. "Fred, no... I love you. I love you so much! Please! I didn't mean to!" He looked at Sloane and Loch with wide eyes and pleaded, "Please help me. I need to fix it! I have to fix this!"

"I'm so sorry," Sloane said earnestly. "We can't. I don't know how, but you—"

"No, no, *no*! *Please*! I didn't mean to—ah!" Ell grabbed at the sides of his head, screaming hysterically, a desperate howl that rose above and surpassed the roar of the battle.

Sloane stepped toward him. "Ell, please listen to me. You have to—"

White light exploded out of Ell's eyes and mouth as he screamed, and the force of it sent Sloane flying backward. His ears rang, the world spun, and he hit the ground with a heavy thud.

Loch's tentacles wrapped around him, warm and safe, and Loch was trying to talk to him because his mouth was moving, but Sloane couldn't hear him. Even the sound of Loch's voice in his head trying to speak to him psychically was garbled, and Sloane's body ached all over.

And Ell….

He was not Ell.

Not anymore.

He was a massive beast with a thick mane of long tentacles spiraling around his massive horns, and his crown of stars was sparking violently as if it was going to explode. His form was lean, practically skeletal, and his skin was a vibrant shade of purple just like his glowing eyes. He stood on twisted legs with strange vines spiraling around his taloned feet.

The plants seemed to be woven in his very flesh and were in a slow but steady cycle of both bloom and decay. It was almost impossible to make out his face for the blinding glow of his gaze, but his jaw was definitely lined with curling tentacles, and his short snout was full of sharp teeth.

This wasn't Ell.

This *thing* was the Kindress.

"My lord!" Jeff called out. "My beautiful lord, please hear me!"

Without the protective bubble keeping them out, the cultists were rushing toward the Kindress with Jeff leading the charge.

"No," Sloane protested weakly. The ringing in his ears had faded enough so he could make out Jeff's voice, and he pushed away from Loch to stumble toward it. "We have to… we have to stop him!"

"My love!" Loch cried. "Wait! You are hurt! You're bleeding!"

"Please!" Sloane fell right over, but he was close enough for Loch to catch him with his tentacles. "We have…. No…." He coughed, staring dumbly at the blood in his hands. "Fuck, there's no time!"

Jeff stood before the Kindress with the fruit in hand. He dropped to his knees, offering it above his head, talking rapidly with a wild grin.

Sloane couldn't make out what he was saying, but he didn't need to.

He already knew what Jeff was asking for.

Galgareth tried to swoop in, but she was snatched out of the air by a wounded Ebbeth. Merrick was there to aid her, but there was no way they'd make it in time. The other opposing old gods formed a line to keep the rest of their forces back, but King Grell broke through them to race over. He tore the cultists apart that were in his way, but it didn't matter.

He wasn't fast enough.

It was too late.

The Kindress took the fruit, looking it over for a moment. He popped it into his mouth with a noisy slurp. The ground shook when he spoke, his booming voice declaring:

"Your boon is granted. Salgumel will awaken."

CHAPTER 12.

SALGUMEL WAS going to wake up.

Sloane thought he was going to be sick. They'd fought the cultists for months and thwarted multiple attempts to destroy the world. He had nearly been killed in the process, had his family threatened, and not to mention the fact that he'd killed several old gods along the way. All of that effort and pain felt wasted now.

This was it.

They'd failed.

Sloane clung to Loch, whispering, "Don't suppose you think you can convince your dad to maybe not destroy the world?"

"I will most certainly try," Loch said firmly. "This isn't over yet, my sweet Starkiller. Now here, quickly, *drink*."

Sloane didn't hesitate to accept Loch's tentacle into his mouth, swallowing down the rush of sweet fluid to heal himself.

The bulk of the remaining cultists had gathered at a wary distance behind Jeff, but they were cheering excitedly. The old gods, both friend and foe, had ceased fighting for the moment, and the Asra appeared to be retreating.

Shit.

Sloane's heart thudded with dread as he tried to find his friends and family out on the battlefield.

Galgareth was standing with Merrick, the pair hard to miss even at this distance. Rota's shimmer was closer, though Sloane couldn't actually see Alexander. There was no sign of Stoker, but he could have been anywhere. Sloane assumed Grell and Asta were leaving with the other Asra, and although he was upset, he couldn't blame them.

They had lost.

The Kindress had left Jeff and was busying himself studying a grove of old oak trees.

Sure, why not?

He'd only just summoned an absolutely insane old god who would most certainly destroy the world in a few minutes. Why wouldn't he want to go hug some trees?

Sloane didn't have long to wonder what the hell the Kindress was actually doing before there was a rush of wind that nearly toppled him over. He could taste the raw magic boiling in the air, the ground trembled, and Sloane clung to Loch to brace himself.

Salgumel the Unfailing was here.

He was as tall as a building, a green behemoth with massive wings and a thick beard of tentacles. His black claws were giant hooks, his eyes were endless pools of galaxies, and he let out a yawn that made the entire park shake.

The cultists dropped to their knees before the mighty god, and Jeff was actively sobbing.

Sloane waited for the world to stop moving and then took a step forward, summoning forth his sword of starlight. He didn't know what he was going to do, but—

"Great Salgumel!" Jeff shouted. "We have waited for you—"

"What year is it?" Salgumel demanded in a booming, hoarse voice.

"It is 2023, my lord," Jeff replied. "It has been far too long since you've blessed us mere mortals with your divine presence. You have no idea what we've gone through to wake you up. We are here and ready to serve you in the new world! We will help cleanse the blasphemers and remake this planet as it rightfully should be, a haven for the righteous followers and our gods!"

"No." Salgumel yawned.

"Pardon... my lord?"

"No." Salgumel sat down and made the ground shake again. He seemed tired, reaching up to scratch the tentacles of his beard as he closed his eyes.

Sloane looked back at Loch in alarm, asking, "What the fuck?"

"I don't know!" Loch hissed in reply. "The fuck is unknown!"

"What do you mean *no*?" Jeff was just as confused as they were. "Don't you hear what I am telling you? We need you, Salgumel! We need you to remake the world! Please! *Please*! Your dreams—"

"Have finally grown peaceful, and I would like to get back to them." Salgumel spared a brief glance over at the other gods. "Great Azaethoth still slumbers, and so shall we. Our time will come again. I have seen it in the dreaming, visions of the world that could be and will be if we are patient, and I will wait until that day comes. Our place is to return to the dreaming, all of us. *Now*."

The gods all shuddered from the force of the command, even Loch.

"My love." Loch grunted. "I'm afraid...."

"What is happening?"

"I have to go...!"

Sloane watched in horror as the other gods vanished one by one, even Galgareth and Merrick. He dropped the sword so he could turn to Loch and grab his leg. "Hey, hey! Stay with me!"

"I'm so sorry, my love," Loch murmured drowsily, his eyes fluttering. "He's calling us back to the dreaming... I... I do not think I can stay. I am so very tired."

"No! Stay awake!" Sloane smacked Loch's chest as hard as he could.

"You must seek out peace within yourself," Salgumel was saying to Jeff. "Even if I did remake the world as you so desire, it would not fill the hole inside of you. I cannot give you back what you've lost. Not even a thousand new worlds could do that."

"But... no!" Jeff stared stupidly, pleading, "Salgumel... no. Please don't go."

"Until Great Azaethoth wakes and walks the world of Aeon once more, we sleep." Salgumel reached down, lightly tapping the top of Jeff's head with one of his claws. "You will find what you seek in your dreams, mortal child."

"Salgumel, no!" Jeff screamed, his voice rising to a hysteric wail as Salgumel faded away in a flurry of shimmering lights. The world trembled a final time, and he was gone. "No! No! *No!*"

"Jeff," Daisy murmured, trying to reach out for him. "We.... We need to—"

"No!" Jeff howled and violently shoved her to the ground. "Get the fuck off me!"

Daisy cried out, staring up at Jeff in shock and cowering.

Loch yawned loudly. "A nap does sound so nice...."

"Loch!" Sloane shook Loch frantically. "I will stab you with my sword, I swear!"

Loch chuckled and his eyes closed. "Heh. Kinky."

"No! Come on! Please!" Sloane hugged Loch's shoulder. "The Kindress is still here! Jeff is still right over there! Please stay. I *need* you."

"Right." Loch groaned lightly and shook his head, baring his teeth. "Yes. You need me. You need me very much. To mate with you."

"Loch! By all the gods—"

"You need me to rock your body with quivering pulsing pleasure and ecstatic explosions of coital bliss—"

"*Azaethoth!*"

"It's keeping me awake!" Loch defended. "Thinking of being with you. Of giving you my hot seed. Please!"

"Okay! Fine!" Sloane wanted to scream. "You can have all the mating you want if you stay awake! I love it! I absolutely love your magical seed and how good it feels filling me up! I just can't get enough of it! I love your giant crazy tentacles and how great they feel fucking me! Now stay awake, godsdamn you!"

Loch groaned and blinked rapidly. "Ah, well. There we go." He grinned. "I do believe that worked. Further proof that our mating will be—"

"Legendary, yes, got it." Sloane sighed in relief. "I love you."

"I love you too." Loch snorted. "I can't believe my father talked to Jeff and didn't even say hello to *me*. How rude."

"Yeah, this definitely didn't turn out the way I thought it was going to."

"Perhaps he needed coffee."

"Maybe."

"Does this mean it's over?"

Sloane spied Jeff stomping toward the Kindress. "Uh, maybe not."

"You!" Jeff pointed angrily at the Kindress. "This is bullshit! You liar! I asked you to awaken Salgumel! I gave you the fruit—"

"The boon was granted," the Kindress replied. He had been tending to one of the old trees whose branches had wilted and cracked from some sort of disease. The limbs were now full of lush green leaves, and it was actively growing beneath the Kindress's touch.

"No! He woke up for five seconds and then fucked off back to Zebulon with the other gods! I have spent years of my fucking life waiting for this moment, and I am not letting you fuck it up because Salgumel couldn't be bothered to wake the fuck up! I command you to—"

"Command me?" The Kindress turned to Jeff, staring down at him as if he were a flea.

"Yes! I *command* you to wake him again! For real this time" Jeff reached into his coat, pulling out a vial of a glowing blue liquid. "Or else."

"The tears!" Sloane gasped. "Jeff doesn't think he can…. Does he?"

"Oh, but I think he does," Loch said, daring to sound gleeful.

Jeff held up the vial, shaking it at the Kindress. "These are the tears of your father, Great Azaethoth! If you don't do as I say, I am going to—"

The Kindress touched Jeff's forehead.

Jeff screamed in pain as his skin melted away, revealing the muscle beneath. From the ground erupted a sapling that quickly grew into a twisted trunk, sprouting right through Jeff's chest. The limbs of the tree moved like snakes, shooting in and out of Jeff's torso and arms. As the tree grew, it lifted Jeff along with it, and he howled in agony as the trunk consumed him.

He tried hurling the vial at the Kindress, but all it did was bounce off harmlessly without breaking and then land over in the grass. The tree grew around and through Jeff's body, and his awful screaming did not stop even when he had been completely consumed. The tree shot up until it was as large as the other trees in the grove, and only after several agonizing moments did Jeff's muffled wails of pain finally cease.

The Kindress smiled.

"Holy shit." Sloane cringed.

"The vial," Loch whispered.

"What?" Sloane was still trying to get over the shock of what he'd just seen.

"It's over there on the ground. Next to the Jeff tree!"

Sloane scanned the grass and saw a glimpse of something shiny. "Shit."

"Shit is right," Stoker agreed as he approached. His jacket and tie were gone, and his vest was unbuttoned. He was covered in blood, but it didn't appear to be his own. "It seems that our plans have been derailed."

"We have to get that vial," Alexander chimed in as he approached, appearing equally worn from battle. "Look! The cultists are losing their shit right now. They're about to run any fuckin' second since they lost Je-fahfah and their godly backup."

"We lost most of ours too!" Sloane grimaced.

"Not all," Rota's voice said.

"Rota?" Sloane looked up, surprised to see Rota's familiar shimmering outline hovering over Alexander. "I thought Salgumel called all the old gods back to the dreaming!"

"I was not affected," Rota replied. "Perhaps a body is required to be called. Plus, I am bonded to Alexander."

"How did Azaethoth manage to stay?" Alexander asked.

"Ah!" Loch beamed. "Because of my love for Sloane and our—"

"There. That's it. That's the only reason." Sloane patted Loch's shoulder. "Don't need to share anything else."

Alexander raised his brows, but said, "We should move now."

"And do what?" Sloane demanded. "Jeff is gone. The old gods are gone. Yes, the Kindress is over there doing some weird shit with those trees, but he's just—"

"I can hear you," the Kindress said.

Sloane froze.

"While your efforts have been absolutely adorable, I'm afraid it will be for nothing." The Kindress petted the trunk of the tree that used to be Jeff. "I've seen enough of this world, and there are no more pitiful boons to accept. There is no reason to let it linger."

The puddle bubble returned in full force, even bigger than before, and the trees the Kindress had been caring for moments ago turned black and crumpled into ash. The grass browned, and the bushes withered, and the very air turned stale.

The cultists screamed, several of them trapped in the bubble and immediately reduced to puddles. Sloane didn't see Daisy among those trying to flee and assumed she was one of the new puddles. The bubble continued to grow, and it caught up to those fleeing in seconds. It was soon consuming the streets and buildings around the park. At this rate, it was going to take the city in minutes.

Sloane cringed as his skin burned, and he glanced at his hands to make sure the totem was still working. When he saw that it was, he ran toward the Kindress. "Stop this! Now!"

The Kindress didn't answer.

Loch was right behind him, roaring, "Kindress! Hear me! I am Azaethoth the Lesser, brother of—"

"No." The Kindress raised his hand.

Loch was thrown back as if a train had crashed into him. He skidded across the dried-out ground as he tried to catch himself, sending up a cloud of dirt as he scrambled for traction.

"Loch!" Sloane shouted.

"Ow!" Loch snarled in annoyance. A wound opened up in his shoulder, fetid and black, but it slowly began to close back up. "Oh, no more Mr. Nice God. It is time for you to taste my godly wrath!" Loch took to the air to breathe down a blast of prismatic fire, the flames hot enough to melt the earth into molten rock.

The Kindress shrugged it off like a cool breeze.

Sloane gripped the sword with both hands as he raised it over his head, shouting, "Alexander! Rota! The vial! We have to try!"

"On it!" Alexander surged ahead, Rota's tentacles clawing at the ground as they ran.

A distant howl caught Sloane's attention, and he looked back to see the Asra racing to join them. King Grell and Asta were leading the pack, and Grell broke off to catch up to Sloane and fall into step beside him.

"Miss me?" Grell teased.

"Where the fuck have you been?" Sloane barked.

"Circling around the bloody park to attack Salgumel from behind, that's what!" Grell snorted. "Except he wasn't there by the time we got there seeing as how he decided to go back to his little nap nap. Was hoping your little plan to talk Ell down would save us the thrill of another glorious battle."

Sloane cringed, allowing himself a brief ache at his failure and the weight of its cost. Fred was dead, Ell was effectively now too, and for the sake of the universe and everyone he loved, he would have to do the one thing he didn't want to do.

He was going to have to kill the Kindress.

"Yeah, that didn't pan out." Sloane inhaled sharply. "That's not Ell now. That's the *Kindress*!"

"And what's the plan now, then? Do we try a tea party? Braid each other's hair?"

"No!" Sloane pointed. "Vial! Tears! Sword!"

"That's more like it!" Grell flashed his teeth. "Come on, Starkiller! We'll get you there!"

The Asra flanked Sloane and pulled in front of him, all of them racing toward the Kindress and the vial of tears. Loch was flying overhead and raining down prismatic fire while gracefully dodging the Kindress's blasts of magic.

They were like pulses, nearly invisible except for a violet shimmer, and they were devastating. Sloane watched a group of Asra take a direct hit and practically explode, and he made sure to keep his shield up high just in case.

Grell shouted something, and Asta darted back to help the Asra who had fallen, and he continued to lead the charge right toward the Kindress. He dodged the Kindress's next attack with a nimble flip, replying by launching a massive ball of fire from his mouth.

The Kindress knocked it away with a wave of his hand. The fire careened over and struck a car out on the street, promptly reducing it to a fiery blaze of twisted metal.

Grell persisted, letting loose another raging ball of fire as he continued to press forward alongside Loch's raging fire.

Although none of the attacks were doing any obvious harm, the Kindress was affected enough to take a few steps back. Perhaps he was just annoyed.

Sloane followed Grell, desperate to close the distance between him and the vial. The Kindress was only a few yards away, but it might as well have been a mile with how efficiently he was deflecting their assault. Still, Sloane continued onward, and when he thought he was close enough, he hurled the sword at the Kindress, aiming right for his chest.

The thunk of the blade piercing the Kindress's chest was satisfying, but....

The Kindress didn't do much except stumble back a step, laugh, and *absorb* the sword. The weapon melted into raw starlight that then seeped into the Kindress's skin, and he smiled. "Is that all?"

Well, *shit*.

That did not bode well for Sloane's chances of slaying the Kindress, but perhaps a blade soaked in the tears of Great Azaethoth would fare better.

Now they had to get to them.

Grell aggressively pushed closer, and Sloane stayed with him, the vial of tears only a few feet away now. He considered trying to sprint up and grab them, but the Kindress's relentless waves of magic made him think otherwise.

The Kindress seemed to know they were after the vial, and he focused his destruction on anyone who got too close.

But wait, there!

Sloane saw a shimmering tentacle dart forward and snatch up the vial before quickly retreating.

Rota!

Loch saw him too, concentrating more fire at the Kindress and forcing him to turn his head. It was just long enough for Rota's tentacle to drag the vial back into Alexander's hands, and Alexander used Rota's magic to teleport him across the park right to Sloane. "Here!"

Sloane quickly summoned another sword of starlight. He used his teeth to pop the cork of the vial, his brain only questioning such wisdom or the lack thereof until after he'd already done it. Carefully, he tipped the vial up and poured the liquid inside over the sword.

The blade glowed even brighter now, and it was eerily heavier than it was before. Sloane quickly closed the vial and then stuffed it in his jacket pocket. He took a deep breath and seized the pommel with both hands.

It was time.

"Go!" Alexander snapped. "We'll cover you!"

"We're with you!" Grell howled.

Loch roared from above, and Sloane knew it was now or never.

He bolted forward, lifting the sword up high as he charged at the Kindress. His heart was pounding in his throat, his fingers were tingling, and he was running so fast that he barely felt his feet touching the ground.

Alexander and Rota sprinted ahead, and Rota's tentacles created a fantastic shield that blocked the Kindress's magical blasts.

The Kindress seemed annoyed that he couldn't break Rota's shield, and he increased his efforts, hurling another wave of magic that made the ground erupt in its wake. Alexander hissed, but he and Rota didn't falter, and the shield remained. They turned away from Sloane, keeping the Kindress's attention but maintaining the shield's massive size to protect Sloane as well.

Grell and the other Asra flanked the Kindress on the other side, firing fearsome blasts and calling on torrents of fierce magic, but the Kindress forced them all back with a huge wave of his awesome power. His attention was focused on Rota and Alexander now, and the Asra seemed to be nothing but pesky flies.

The Kindress growled and doubled his efforts, actively using his arms to propel more fierce blasts toward Rota and Alexander. He appeared to be set on breaking through Rota's shield, but Rota and Alexander's combined efforts refused to falter.

Alexander's nose was bleeding, but he didn't stop.

Alexander, Rota warned silently.

Shut up, shut up! Almost there! Fuckin' almost! Alexander argued back frantically.

Sloane pushed in between the edge of Rota's shield and the attacking Asra, certain that the Kindress was about to whirl around at any moment and strike him down. He desperately whispered a prayer as he swung back the sword of starlight. He was there, he was right behind the Kindress, and he thrust the sword into his back with everything he had.

Starlight on starlight created an explosion of sparks that blinded Sloane and nearly knocked him back, but he didn't stop. He refused to let go and drove the blade through the Kindress until he was stopped by the hilt. He sobbed from the waves of pain racking his body as he fought to maintain the blade's integrity. His hands were on fire, his arms were aching, and it was hard to breathe.

But he'd done it.

He'd killed the Kindress.

It was over....

The blade was backing out.

Wait, *no*, what was happening?

Sloane blinked, trying to focus his vision as he watched the blade moving in reverse and forcing him to backpedal.

The Kindress turned around calmly, a single finger pressed to his chest where the blade had sliced through. The Kindress had literally used one finger to push the sword out, and the wound was already closed as he said, "And what exactly did you think that was going to do?"

Sloane laughed stupidly.

Oh *fuck*.

He took a few careful steps back, the sword vanishing away as he scrambled to think of something clever to say. Nothing would come to him as the only thought rattling around in his head was the urge to run away very, very fast.

"Sloane?" Alexander called out hesitantly.

"New plan! New plan! New plan!" Sloane quickly threw up a new shield as he fled, but it wasn't enough to protect him from the Kindress's next attack. A wave of magic struck Sloane and he went flying. He bounced for several yards before coming to an unpleasant stop in a cluster of dead bushes. He couldn't even breathe because of the way his body seized up in pain, finally exhaling in a miserable scream.

He thought he heard Loch calling for him, but he couldn't speak. Everything hurt so much, he could taste blood, and his hands were numb. He tried to pull himself out of the bushes, but he fell, face planting right into the dirt.

"Hey! I got you!" a familiar voice said, strong hands reaching down to help Sloane up.

Sloane grunted in pain. "What the...." He looked up with gasp. "Ollie?"

"Hi!" Ollie waved.

"But you aren't wearing a totem! Wait, wait, what the fuck are you doing here?"

"So, I am immune. Which is cool. But super weird." Ollie grinned nervously. "Look, I see what I have to do now! I figured it out!" He helped Sloane stand. "It's gonna sound so very whack, but you have to listen to me."

"What?" Sloane demanded. "Tell me!"

"You know that second I gave you? You have to—"

"Ollie? Ollie!" Alexander shouted frantically as he and Rota hurried toward them, retreating from the Kindress. "No! Are you fucking stupid? You have to get out of here right now!"

It is not safe for you! Rota said firmly. *You need to portal yourself back to safety at once!*

"It's okay!" Ollie yelled back. "I'm starsighting so hard right now and—"

The Kindress snarled, and the ground shook as he hurled another blast of magic....

Right at Ollie.

Sloane couldn't react fast enough, his hands clawing at empty air as he tried to pull Ollie out of the way. "No!"

Someone shouted in pain.

It was Alexander.

Alexander had left the protection of Rota's shield and shoved himself in the way of the Kindress's blast, taking the full brunt of it to save Ollie.

"Alexander!" Ollie screamed as he lunged forward to catch Alexander as he fell.

Alexander wheezed, his body limp as Ollie helped him to the ground. The front of his chest and left side was open, his exposed skin turning black as the rot ate its way down to muscle and bone.

"What have you done, you bastard?" Rota roared, his voice booming with the same fury as the Kindress's. "How could you?"

"I will not stop," the Kindress replied solemnly. "Not even for you, my child."

"Alexander, no, no, no!" Ollie clung to Alexander, trying to press his hands over the giant gaping wound. Even with the totem, the rot was spreading fast. "This wasn't supposed to happen. I didn't see this!"

Alexander smiled weakly, dropping a hand over Ollie's. "Ollie, it's okay."

"It is the opposite of okay! You have a hole in your fucking chest that could hold a fucking melon or something else melon-sized! That is not okay!" Ollie cried angrily. "Come on!"

Alexander closed his eyes. "I love you, Ollie." He smiled again. "Love you, Rota." He peeked over at Sloane. "Fuck you, Starkiller."

Sloane offered a strained smile. "Fuck you too, Alexander. You're a real piece of work."

"Damn right." Alexander coughed, bright blood splashing over his lips. "Shit. Rota... I... the bond...." *It's breaking. You're gonna be free.*

Rota was fighting to keep up the shield of his tentacles to protect them all, barking passionately, "You listen to me, sweet boy! You absolutely do not have my permission to die! Do you hear me? After everything we have been through, this is not how this ends! It is not your time to go!"

"Go." Ollie echoed and his eyes glassed over. "Right! The thing!" He reached out to Sloane. "You! You have to go! Do the thing! Go do the thing right now! Don't forget about the second! You'll know what to do with it! And oh, oh, when to do it! You'll see!"

"What thing? What second?" Sloane asked urgently. "What am I supposed to do?"

"Go!" Ollie grabbed the front of Sloane's shirt and pushed him hard. "Now!"

"But what—" Sloane teetered, falling back and expecting to land on his butt.

Instead, he was falling through nothing. The swirling wind and darkness were indicative of a portal, but Sloane had no idea what he was supposed to be doing or where he was going. He grunted as he landed on hard, cold ground and found himself staring up at a glowing lavender ceiling.

Xenon, he realized.

He was back in Xenon.

"Sloane?" Ted asked, staring down at him with wide eyes. "Is that you?"

"Yeah. Hi." Sloane waved weakly. "It's me."

"What the fuck are you doing here?"

"That… is a very good question."

CHAPTER 13.

"WHAT THE fuck happened?" Ted demanded. "Where's Grell?"

Sloane groaned as he sat up. "Back in the park. Fighting the Kindress."

"You mean Ell—"

"No, I mean the Kindress." Sloane frowned deeply. "I know this is going to be hard to hear, but he is not Ell. Not now. He…. He killed Fred."

"What?" Ted gasped.

"He killed Fred, he took the fruit, and woke up Salgumel—"

"Holy shit balls! What the fuck—"

"No, no! It's okay!" Sloane grimaced. "I mean, no, it's not, but Salgumel refused to remake the world of whatever for Jeff! He went back to the dreaming, took all the other gods with him except Loch and Rota. They're back there fighting too. Alexander got hurt; he might not make it. I don't know about Grell and Asta, so don't even ask me. The Kindress's bubble is gonna take out the whole city in a matter of minutes, and it's just gonna keep going if we don't stop him."

Ted stiffened. "You mean kill him."

Sloane closed his eyes. "Yes."

"Then what the fuck are you doing here?" Ted scoffed bitterly. He rolled his eyes, scoffing, "Why aren't you back there stabbing him with your stupid sword? Because if you fuckin' think—"

"I tried." Sloane shook his head.

"What do you mean, you *tried*?"

"We got a hold of some tears of Great Azaethoth that Jeff had, I coated the blade with them and stabbed the Kindress, but he was mildly annoyed at best." Sloane grunted as he stood. "It didn't work."

"The fuck." Ted's brow scrunched. "So, what, Grell sent you here to look for more tears or something?"

"Ollie sent me. He said I'm supposed to do something. He told me he'd given me a second of time and that I'd know what to do with it." Sloane's thoughts raced. "I think maybe he meant giving it to you?"

"*Me?*"

"Yeah, you." Sloane dragged his fingers through his hair. "Why else would he send me here to you? Now I just have to figure out what we do with a second of fucking time."

Ted's expression was grave. "Take it and go fuck yourself with it. I'm not helping you hurt my brother."

"Ted! Listen to me!" Sloane pleaded. "He is not your brother right now! Okay? He murdered his boyfriend right in front of us, and he's trying to kill everyone in the entire city! Anyone and everyone we've ever known in Archersville is dying right now! It's not going to stop! He's going to kill everyone and everything on the whole damn planet! Do you understand me?"

"Fuck you!" Ted shouted, his jaw quivering. "I fuckin' hear you! I just… I…." His eyes brimmed with tears. "He's my baby brother. He's my fuckin' family. I thought he was gonna be okay and now you're telling me he just went fucking nuts and now he's gonna kill everybody?"

"He *is* killing everyone," Sloane corrected. "There are thousands dying right now, and more will follow if we don't do something!"

"What the fuck am I supposed to do?" Ted snapped. "You just said your stupid little sword and Great Dude's tears didn't do shit! I don't think being able to talk to fucking dead people is really that helpful right now!"

"There has to be a reason why Ollie sent me here!" Sloane took a deep breath, trying to calm down and lower his voice. "It's you. It has to be."

"I don't fucking know!" Ted stalked toward a large well-stocked bar, still shaking his head. He fixed himself a drink, pouring a dark brown liquor straight into a glass. "What's the deal now? With the tears? Kunst was sayin' somethin' about this shit earlier."

"Right." Sloane nodded. "According to his research into Ollie's translation, it's not just Great Azaethoth's tears that kill the Kindress. It's his own."

"So, Ell's tears." Ted snorted. "And where exactly do you think we can get those?"

"Well...." Sloane hesitated, remembering the strange void he'd seen Ell in when they'd attempted the location spell.

Ell had been crying so hard that there was a pool of tears....

"There was a place," Sloane said suddenly. "We tried to track down Ell before—"

"Oh, so now he's Ell again?" Ted drained the glass with a roll of his eyes.

"Please just listen!" Sloane gritted his teeth. "I saw Ell in a pool of his own tears, but I couldn't see where he was. It was just this big dark void. It was...." He closed his eyes as he fought to recall any detail at all.

Darkness, more darkness, and....

"A cemetery," Ted said.

"What?"

Ted looked shaken, and his hand trembled as he quickly refilled his glass. "I can... I can see, like... an echo. Of a ghost. Real old one. On you. It must be from where you tried to reach out to Ell and somehow you touched the fuckin' cemetery where he was at. Or maybe it touched you."

"I'm being... haunted?"

"No. Like I said, it's just a fuckin' echo. It's like a ghostly smudge. It's real weak. I never would have noticed it if you hadn't said somethin' about needing me." Ted slurped at the liquor. "After Ell ran away from our parents, we didn't talk much. I knew he was strugglin', but he just wouldn't let me help him. He kept telling me it was better this way or some shit...." He coughed to hide his tears. "But he told me once about this cemetery near one of the shelters he used to live at. Said he'd go there sometimes to think or just hang out 'cause it felt safe."

Sloane grimaced, all too aware why a cemetery would feel safe to someone whose touch to the living was deadly.

"Fuck, it's been so long since he told me about that damn place." Ted rubbed his forehead. "We searched the whole fucking city and never thought once to go there. I'm a fuckin' idiot—"

"Hey, hey!" Sloane cut in. "You can beat yourself up about having a shitty memory later! Where is this cemetery? Is it in Archersville?"

"Yeah." Ted polished off his drink. "Let's fuckin' go."

Sloane waited expectantly.

"Are you gonna do the thing?" Ted asked.

"What thing?"

"A portal thing?"

"I can't portal!"

"Well, fuck. I can't either!" Ted groaned. He raised his voice, shouting, "Hey, Kunst!"

"How is he gonna hear—"

"Trust me. He just knows."

Kunst did indeed appear, his glowing ball practically vibrating as he exclaimed, "Hello, Your Highness! How can I be of... oh! Sloane!" He sounded surprised. "What are you doing here? What has happened?"

"Big puddle bubble killing everyone in the city and Great Azaethoth's tears plus a sword of a starlight do not a dead Kindress make," Sloane replied grimly. "Ted thinks he knows where to find some of Ell's tears, and we need to get there fast."

"Oh!" Kunst gasped. "Yes! It is as I theorized from Ollie's translation! Both sets of tears are required to end his life!"

"Can we please just fucking go?" Ted grumbled. "Oakwood Cemetery in Archersville. Chop-chop."

"Oh, oh yes! Of course!" Kunst wiggled, and then a small portal opened. "Let us go!"

Sloane wasn't going to question the technical details of how Kunst could still cast magic even though he was nothing but a soul attached to a ball, choosing instead to jump through the portal. The whoosh was brief, and then he was standing in a cemetery.

It was old judging by the state of the headstones and the size of the trees clustered about, though it was well manicured with tidy narrow paths leading around the various sections. He realized they weren't that far from the park, and he could see how Ell had ended up there.

That also meant the puddle bubble would be here soon, so they needed to move fast.

Sloane looked for where the trees were the thickest and headed there.

That should be the Sagittarian section.

If Ell had gone anywhere for sanctuary from his thoughts, Sloane reasoned it would be there.

"—stubborn little shit!" Ted was griping as he popped in behind Sloane.

"Potty mouth!" a tiny voice snapped.

"I am so very sorry!" Kunst fussed. "I didn't even see him!"

Sloane turned around to see what was the matter and almost laughed when he saw Ted trying to pry a very determined Graham from around his neck.

"He moves silently!" Kunst continued to complain. "It's the soft little paws!"

"Just… go find tears or whatever!" Ted snapped, still unable to break Graham's apparently iron grip.

"Oh! Yes, of course, Your Highness." Kunst floated over to hover beside Sloane. "Shall we?"

"Let's go." Sloane nodded and hurried ahead toward the trees.

"You're not leaving me behind!" Graham was arguing. "I'm coming too!"

"But it's not safe!" Ted protested.

"So? I'm already dead!"

"Well… you… you might get *more* dead!"

"That's *dumb*!"

"Now, you listen here, young man…!"

Ted's voice faded as Sloane charged forward, his hand raised for a perception spell. He was looking for anything that might be out of the ordinary, perhaps some sort of godly glimmer or a strong magical aura.

"There!" Kunst gasped.

There was a puddle of silver fluid beside one of the largest trees. It looked like liquid mercury, and it had yet to be absorbed into the grass. It sat right on top as if it were oil in a nonstick pan.

Sloane summoned his starlight to create a capsule so he could scoop the silver liquid up, and he grunted as the capsule broke. He tried again, focusing more power to contain it.

"Here, Sloane." Kunst pressed against Sloane's shoulder.

Sloane gasped as a surge of magic rushed into him and strengthened the capsule. It held, and he was able to put it in his pocket. "Thank you, Professor."

"Of course, dear boy." Kunst sounded like he was smiling. "Here we are again, heh. Trying to save the world."

"Feels like a lot more than just our world is at stake this time. The whole *universe*."

"Yes, well, I do believe we will triumph," Kunst said firmly.

"Yeah?"

"Of course!" Kunst's orb flickered. "Why else did Great Azaethoth place a sword of starlight in your hand? He gave you the power you needed to finish this, and I have faith that you will."

"Thank you." Sloane took a deep breath.

A scream drew his attention, and he whirled around to see the puddle bubble closing in on the cemetery.

"Shit!" Sloane hissed. "Professor! Go get Ted and Graham out of here! *Now!*"

"Oh my! Yes, yes, of course!"

Sloane ran into the bubble and toward the park, noting the eerie silence. It was immediately unsettling, and he ran faster. There were no horns blaring, no dogs barking, nothing.

Loch! Sloane tried to focus his thoughts. *Can you hear me?*

My love! Loch replied inside Sloane's head. *Where are you?*

I'm here! I need you!

No sooner did the thought leave Sloane's mind than Loch appeared, diving out of thin air and landing in front of him. "My sweet Starkiller! My mate!"

"I've got Ell's tears!" Sloane climbed up on Loch's back. "The bubble is almost outside the city!" He frowned at Loch's many wounds. "Are you okay to fly?"

"Yes, my love. But be ready! We may only have one shot at this. The Kindress has been relentless. The Asra have all but fallen, and I'm afraid it's only been myself, Rota, and Stoker fighting." Loch took off into the air, his great wings propelling him at incredible speed. He grunted with each flap, no doubt in pain, but he sounded sure as he said, "But we will be victorious!"

"By all the gods, I hope so." Sloane squeezed Loch's neck with his thighs as he summoned his sword. He reached into his pocket to first grab the vial of Great Azaethoth's remaining tears. Then he got the capsule of Ell's.

No, of the *Kindress's*.

He broke the starlight holding the powerful liquid very carefully. As he drizzled it on the blade, it mixed with Great Azaethoth's tears and created a purple glow.

The sword was vibrating from the strength of such powerful magic, and Sloane took a deep breath to help steady his grip. "I'm ready!"

"I love you, Sloane Beaumont."

"I love you too, Azaethoth the Lesser."

Loch brought them to the park in an instant, and the scene below was chaotic.

Alexander and Ollie were huddled behind the bulk of Rota's shimmering form while Rota continued to attack the Kindress. Stoker was helping Grell and Asta portal out the wounded Asra while the few left alive were still fighting.

Loch flew up high, and from this new vantage point Sloane could see the puddle bubble was now past the city limits. He hoped Ted and the others had been able to get out, not to mention all the other citizens Chase and the AVPD had been trying to evacuate, but he didn't have time to spare them much more than a passing thought.

He had to kill the Kindress.

"Let's go!" Sloane shouted.

Loch dove.

Sloane clung to Loch as the air whipped all around them, holding the sword above his head. Loch was diving so fast that the wind felt like it might tear the sword right out of Sloane's hand, but he only held it tighter.

This was it.

The Kindress had his back to them as he battled Rota's relentless strikes. He continued to deflect the Asra's efforts as well, and he looked bored even under the assault of so many opponents. His ability to attack and defend simultaneously was effortless, and his gaze often drifted off to the city streets or one of the nearby withered trees.

Sloane didn't care where the Kindress looked as long as he didn't look up.

Don't look up, don't look up, don't look up, just don't look fucking up, Sloane thought desperately as Loch's rapid descent brought them closer. In only a few moments, they would be in range and Sloane could end this.

He had to.

It was for the people who had died in battle and everyone who might if he didn't stop the Kindress now like his friends and family waiting for him in another world and those here still fighting, and it was also for himself—for the scared boy he once was whose tearful prayer had disrupted an ancient cycle and who could have never imagined the devastating repercussions.

There, right there! They were right there about to close in, Sloane gritting his teeth as he prepared to swing. Loch turned at the last moment, allowing Sloane to have a clear shot at the Kindress's exposed back, and then Sloane's arm came down.

The Kindress sidestepped the blow.

Fuck!

Sloane missed!

The Kindress grabbed Loch's tail, yanking him right out of the air and grounding him with a ferocious blast of magic.

Sloane fell off as Loch tumbled, and he half-expected to impale himself with his own sword. He was able to keep a hold of it without any injury, groaning as he dragged himself to his knees. A flash of searing pain drew a scream from his lips as the Kindress grabbed his face, forcing him to look up and meet his glowing violet gaze.

"How curious," the Kindress mused. "Who are you, little Starkiller?"

"I am Sloane Beaumont," Sloane griped hoarsely, "son of Daniel and Pandora.... Oh, fuck it!" He went to thrust the sword, but....

He saw himself in the reflection of a large mirror, one he thought looked familiar, but it was gone too quickly for him to recognize where he'd seen it before.

Wait.

Something was wrong.

The sword faded from his hands, all of the magical tears lost with it. He looked down, gasping when he realized his body was rapidly decomposing. He was fading into little specks of nothing because the Kindress's other hand had plunged into his chest.

He was dying. That's what this new pain was, his soul leaving the fetid husk that used to be his body and would soon be a fucking puddle.

No, no, no, this couldn't be—

Sloane opened his eyes.

He was riding Loch through the air, diving through the air as they had been a few moments ago. He didn't understand what was happening at first, but then he gasped when Loch turned to give him a clear shot at striking the Kindress.

He'd seen the future, a vision of what was going to happen, but....

Don't forget about the second, Ollie had told him. *You'll know when to use it.*

Sloane swung, missed again, and he struggled to exclaim anything coherent. His brain wouldn't work, all he got out was, "Loch! Tail! Tail!"

"Huh?" Loch grunted.

Sloane's warning came too late, and Loch went to the ground again when the Kindress grabbed his tail. Sloane was able to catch himself this time because he knew the fall was coming, and he bounced up to his feet to face the Kindress head-on.

He saw the Kindress reaching out to grab his face, but Sloane knew the Kindress's other hand would be coming. He wasn't going to be fast enough to evade both attacks, but there....

The second.

Sloane felt it like an itch that needed to be scratched, a strange magic he didn't understand nor did he know how to unlock. He growled when the Kindress's fingers latched on to his face and he screamed in pain once more, narrowing his eyes defiantly.

Now, now, *now!*

"How curious," the Kindress mused. "Who—"

That precious second was all Sloane needed to twist away from the Kindress's deadly strike, and then he thrust the sword forward into the Kindress's chest.

The Kindress froze and stared at the blade in shock. "... are...?"

Sloane screamed as he drove the sword deep, gritting his teeth and snarling as he fought against the wild burning pain seizing his hands. He pushed and pushed, closing his eyes as he forced the blade in up to the hilt.

The Kindress gasped, clawing weakly at the blade. "No... no...! What have you...?"

Sloane let go of the blade and staggered backward, watching as the sword melted into a luminous metallic violet liquid.

The liquid spread over the Kindress's body until he was completely covered, gushing up into his gaping mouth. He gurgled miserably, clutching at his throat as the liquid kept pouring and splashing all around him. It was like a waterfall now, rushing into his mouth and spilling out his nose as he fought to breathe through it.

Sloane fell to his knees and closed his eyes.

It was done.

He didn't need to see anymore, though he could hear the Kindress thrashing and choking as he drowned.

Sloane flinched when he heard a *thump*, and only then did he look at the Kindress again.

The bubble was gone, though the damage left behind remained, and the Kindress lay in a bed of freshly bloomed flowers, the one spot of life in the now desolate park. He was not moving, and the glittering liquid had evaporated away like vapor.

Loch limped toward Sloane and then nuzzled his shoulder. "My sweet mate... I love you."

"I love you too," Sloane said quietly, reaching up to stroke his cheek.

"Is it over now? Please say it is."

"Yes. I think it really is."

The cultists and gods were gone, although there were still untold numbers of civilian casualties despite the best efforts to evacuate the city. The Asra were tending to their wounded while Grell and Asta shrouded the Asran dead, no doubt preparing to take them back to Xenon.

Rota's giant form was impossible to miss, cradling Alexander while Ollie clung to them both.

Chase was there too, although Sloane wasn't sure when he'd arrived, his hat in his hands as he looked on at the trio with a somber smile.

Stoker stood a few yards off in a fresh suit, his head held high. He smiled when he caught Sloane looking his way and then bowed politely.

"Galgareth. Merrick." Sloane squeezed Loch's shoulder. "Are they okay?"

"I cannot hear my uncle yet for the dreaming still holds him close, but Galgareth is...." Loch cocked his head. "Going to use the vacant hollows of our foul enemies' bones as bulbs for a Lite Brite. Hmm, I wonder what that means?"

"It means you two are totally related," Sloane teased.

"Of course we are," Loch said flatly. "Was there ever a doubt?"

Sloane was going to clarify, but then he saw Ted walking toward the Kindress's body. He tensed. "Oh no."

"I think you mean, oh yes, because the Kindress is dead," Loch drawled.

"But that means Ell is too."

"Oh." Loch frowned. "Right."

Kunst was hovering a few yards back with Graham riding on top of him. He floated over to greet Sloane and Loch, saying somberly, "Hello, Sloane. Azaethoth. Congratulations are in order."

"Doesn't really feel like it, does it?" Sloane said as he watched Ted stop in front of the Kindress's body.

"We did save the universe," Loch said, trying to be cheerful, but even his usual jovial attitude was dim.

"I know." Sloane sighed. "Still feel like shit anyway."

"I tried to convince His Highness to stay in Xenon once we escaped from the cemetery," Kunst fussed, "but he insisted on returning—"

"Ted threatened to shove him in the toilet and duct tape the lid shut," Graham said. "They both used a lot of very bad words."

"Obviously, I refused to bring anyone back here until we knew it was safe!" Kunst huffed.

Ted dropped to his knees beside the Kindress, reaching for his hand.

"Your Highness!" Kunst shrieked. "You must not touch him!"

"What?" Ted demanded with angry tears in his eyes.

"We have no idea if it's safe!"

Ted looked ready to scream or sob, perhaps both. He wiped at his eyes, croaking, "That's some bullshit."

Grell hesitantly approached, and he offered out his paw with the totem bracelet. "Here, my queen. This will protect you."

"Thanks," Ted mumbled. He unclipped the chain, but then he clearly struggled to fasten it around his own wrist.

Grell did it with a nod of his head.

Ted checked the fit before slowly reaching out to take the Kindress's hand. He made a face, as if mad at himself for hesitating, and he held the Kindress's hand against his cheek. His expression now read only pain, and he sobbed, breaking down completely and collapsing on top of the Kindress's chest.

Sloane knew Ted's pain better than most, and he could see himself as a child crying over his parents just as Ted now cried for the Kindress. He turned to embrace Loch, sniffing through a few tears of his own as Loch's strong wings wrapped around him.

He knew they needed to check on Alexander and the Asra to see if there was anything else they could do to help. He wanted to get back to the Hidden World as soon as possible so they could share the news of their victory and he could hold his child in his arms.

But this, holding Loch and breathing him in, was what Sloane needed right now.

A strange surge of magic made Sloane shiver unexpectedly, and he lifted his head to see what the source was.

Something was happening.

Magic was in the air, ancient and vast, and it stole Sloane's breath away. The air was lit with soft sparkles of starlight falling like snow, glowing with a violet radiance and a unique power Sloane recognized immediately.

"Great Azaethoth." Sloane breathed out a soft sigh.

The magical sparkles clung to everything—the dried grass, the withered trees, even Sloane and Loch and all the others, including the dead. It was soon a thick blanket like a blizzard of freshly fallen purple snow.

Sloane stepped forward, breaking away from Loch's hold as he was entranced by the spellbinding sight. "By all the gods… just look at it."

"Yes, my love," Loch whispered. "I see."

Loch lowered his head to rest on Sloane's shoulder, and Sloane could see the starlight glittering along Loch's scales. He reached up to pet Loch's snout, watching the magic continue to drift down from the stars above.

It was beautiful, and Sloane could have never prepared himself for what happened next.

The park surged back to life, every tree and bush revitalized in an instant. The fallen Asra were on their feet, and a heavily protesting Alexander appeared to be flying by the way Rota was swinging him around. Sloane could hear people shouting off in the distance and a barrage of horns honking, and he realized that everyone who had fallen was alive once more.

Well, except the cultists.

Jeff also still appeared to be a Jeff Tree.

And the Kindress….

Ted looked around wildly, watching the mass resurrection in awe and growing rage. He looked up at the sky, barking, "Hey! Great Asshole! You fuckin' missed one!"

"Ted, my beloved—" Grell gently tried to intervene.

"No!" Ted raged, swatting Grell away. "It's fuckin' bullshit! I... I'm...." He buried his face in the Kindress's chest as he sobbed. "Oh, I'm so fuckin' sorry. I should have done more. I should have been there. Fuck, I should have done a thousand fuckin' things differently. I should have told you every damn day how fuckin' special you were and how much I loved you. You're my little brother.... I don't give a fuck what nobody says. You always will be."

A curious light shone from the Kindress's chest. At first it was a mere flicker, but it soon grew into a brilliant zigzag that looked like lightning dancing over his skin. It took Sloane a few moments to realize that it was, in fact, the many paths of Ted's tears.

"What the fuck is going on?" Sloane asked worriedly.

Loch glanced skyward. "I do not know, but I hope my great-great-great-grandfather knows what he's doing."

Ted shielded his eyes from the brilliant light as it consumed the Kindress's entire body. There was a quick flash, and then the light was gone, as was any trace of Great Azaethoth's magical presence.

The Kindress was a strange gray color now, as if he was made of stone.

Ted touched the Kindress's arm and immediately recoiled. "The fuck? He's... he's a statue?"

The pattern of Ted's tears remained, a gilded network of lines and small splashes, and Ted flinched as one of them cracked. There was a faint hint of movement *inside* the Kindress's body, and Ted immediately punched its chest.

The gray skin shattered, revealing that the body was now nothing more than a hollow husk, and Ted scrambled to pull the pieces out of his way. His eyes widened as he looked inside, and he suddenly shouted, "Ell!"

"Ted...?"

CHAPTER 14.

"TED...? Is that you?" Ell murmured drowsily as Ted pulled him out of the husk. The shattered pieces turned to fine dust, and soon the entire shell disintegrated into nothing.

"It's me! It's fuckin' me!" Ted scooped Ell into his arms and crushed him against his chest. "Fuck, you're alive! You're okay!"

Ell appeared dazed, dirty, and he still had a pair of small caprine horns peeking out from his hair. "What happened...?" He blinked rapidly. "It's all kinda fuzzy."

"It doesn't matter," Ted insisted. "Everything is gonna be okay."

Sloane's heart soared, and his eyes grew hot. "Great Azaethoth is truly great."

"That he is," Loch agreed warmly.

"What would be real great is a stiff drink and waking up my man from his godly nap," Chase said with a tip of his hat. "We got some saving the world type celebrating to do."

"Hey, wait, wait!" Ell exclaimed. "Ted! You're not supposed to be touching me! I could hurt you!"

"Nah, I got this little bracelet thing on," Ted said. "We're good!"

"You mean this bracelet?" Grell was in his human form, holding up the totem bracelet with a very concerned scowl.

"Huh." Ted glanced at his wrist. "Shit, I must have broke it when I was bustin' Ell out of this crusty thing."

"What does this mean?" Ell asked worriedly. "I... I'm not supposed to...." Fingers trembling, he raised his hand to touch Ted's cheek.

Nothing happened.

"Hey, baby bro." Ted beamed, laying his hand over Ell's. "Ain't that some shit?"

"It would seem your little wings have been clipped," Grell said solemnly. "Can you perform any magic?"

"I don't know." Ell grunted as Ted pulled him up to his feet. He hesitantly held out his hand and a small ball of fire appeared. He dismissed the flames, his eyes big with confusion. "I… I don't understand. I can still do magic, but…." He looked down.

Flowers were actively blooming around Ell's feet as they had before, but they didn't die this time. They bloomed beautifully, and more continued to sprout up.

"Maybe this is Great Azaethoth's version of an apology," Sloane said. "The cycle has finally been broken. You're free now to actually live your life without having to worry about hurting anyone."

"It was Ted," Ell whispered. "I could hear him crying. Crying for me. And I didn't understand why he was so upset… but it was because he loves me so much. Because I am really worth loving. Me, *Elliam*, am worth loving. Like how Fred loves me…." He gasped. "*Fred!*"

Sloane cringed, quickly looking around the park for any sign of their fallen friend.

The only dead left were the cultists, but it didn't make sense that everyone else would have been resurrected, and not Ell's boyfriend.

Ell whimpered miserably, turning to sob into Ted's chest. "No… no, no, no. I did it, didn't I? He's gone!"

"I'm sorry," Ted murmured as he wrapped his big arms around Ell. His eyes filled with tears, shaking his head. "I'm so fucking sorry."

Grell approached them, looking to Ted for permission before he squeezed Ted's shoulder. "The gods work in mysterious ways. There must be a reason."

"Yeah," Ell spat bitterly. "To punish me."

"No!" Ted argued. "It's not your fault."

Bells jingled softly in Sloane's ear, prompting him to look around.

He didn't know where the sound came from, and no one else seemed to notice it except for him. His eyes fell on the area where Fred had died, and he raised his hands for a perception spell. He didn't know exactly what he was looking for, but maybe some sort of clue to understand why Fred hadn't been brought back.

And there….

He saw it.

"Hey, Grell!" Sloane said urgently.

"Yes, Starkiller?" Grell drawled. "Having a bit of a moment here. Don't you have a family of your own to go gush over?"

"There was a portal," Sloane snapped. "Look! I don't think Fred is dead."

"What?" Ell looked up with a tearful frown.

"I don't think you killed him." Sloane pointed to the spot. "Grell, can you track that portal? It's faint, but maybe not too faint for the King of the Asra?"

Grell appeared dubious, but he studied the area Sloane had indicated. His brow raised in surprise, and he said, "Huh. So there is."

"Can you find it?"

"Naturally. Be back in a jiff." Grell blew a kiss to Ted and then vanished.

"I don't understand." Ell wiped at his eyes. "I didn't kill Fred…?"

"There's a chance," Sloane soothed. "A really big one, okay?" He took a deep breath. "Trust in the gods."

"Heh. Considering I am one, that's kinda weird." Ell managed a sad little smile. "Thank you, Sloane."

"Me?" Sloane blinked.

"I guess it's messed up to thank you for stabbing me, but still. Thank you for stopping me." Ell approached Sloane, flowers blooming in his wake. He reached for Sloane's hand as if to shake it, but changed his mind and went for a hug instead.

Sloane smiled, hugging Ell back tight.

"You still have your totem on, yes?" Loch whispered loudly.

"Loch! He's fine now." Sloane rolled his eyes.

"I think I have reason to be concerned."

"It's all right." Ell smiled. "I just hope… I hope I can help fix things."

"Got any bright ideas for how we're gonna explain all this to the fine people of Archersville?" Chase asked dryly. "Because it's usually Merry who thinks up this stuff, and I'm not exactly sure when he's gonna wake up from his new nap." He frowned. "He *is* gonna wake up, right?"

"Yes," Loch assured him. "Galgareth is already awake and will be bringing my dear uncle very soon. I do not believe there is godly coffee, but she is doing her best. I've also let Mother know of our victory. He paused as if listening to something. "She has confirmed there is no godly coffee."

"Well, I'll get him some regular ol' human coffee and hope that does the trick. I'm pretty sure we're gonna be dealing with an absolute ass load of mass panic since everybody died and then came back to life. Not to mention the old gods partying all over the damn city."

"The mayor and the police chief will probably come up with something to cover it all up like they did last time." Sloane grimaced. "No offense, but I'm glad it's you guys, and not me."

"Thanks." Chase laughed. "I'll be sure to let you know if we have to come arrest you for using an unlicensed magical weapon in public."

"Great." Sloane snorted.

"Don't worry," Stoker teased. "I'll loan you my personal attorney."

"Thank you. That's very thoughtful of you." Sloane leaned into Loch's side, closing his eyes as he listened to the renewed hum of the city.

"Can we go the fuck home now?" Alexander grumbled loudly.

"Of course, my sweet boy." Rota was still cradling him like a baby and refusing to let go.

"I'll order Chinese food and make you a piña colada," Ollie promised, stroking Alexander's hair.

"Yeah, and what are you gonna be drinking?" Alexander snorted.

"Water." Ollie shuddered. "So much water."

Chase glanced over to a small crowd of people that was forming near the edge of the park, no doubt drawn by the giant tentacle dragon and shimmering beast standing right there. "Just a thought, maybe you guys should, uh, take the celebrating somewhere else? Or maybe not be giant monsters right now?"

"Fine." Loch groaned. "I will go fetch my mortal vessel." With a pout, he disappeared.

"That probably applies to kitty cat people too," Chase tutted as Asta came strolling up to them with Kunst and Graham in tow.

"What? I mean, I could be very human and very naked if you think that would be less distracting." Asta flashed a toothy grin. "How about it, ginger daddy?"

"Probably not, kiddo."

"The day is won!" Kunst said with a happy bounce, nearly knocking Graham off from where he was still riding on top of him. "We have been victorious! Oh! I must return to Xenon at once to prepare!"

"Prepare what?" Asta asked.

"There is to be a grand feast to celebrate our triumph here today!" Kunst insisted.

"Are you the royal party planner now too?"

"I am going to take young master Graham home with me and begin the planning right away." Kunst scoffed. He gave a little nod of his ball toward Sloane. "Take care of yourself, Sloane. Thank you. For all of your valiant efforts."

"Thank you, Kunst," Sloane replied. "For everything."

"Are you coming, Your Highness?" Kunst asked Asta.

"No, your party sounds lame." Asta smirked. "You can take the other Asra back, but I'm gonna go get naked with my hot boyfriend and touch his—"

"Your *Highness*!"

"Innocent ears!" Graham complained. "Ew!"

"Sorry, kitten." Asta chuckled. "You guys have fun. See you during the next universe-ending crisis, so hopefully, like never again." He winked at Sloane. "Tell Azaethoth I stole his garlic bread. I really didn't, but it'll drive him fuckin' nuts."

"Will do." Sloane chuckled. "Goodbye, Asta! Bye, Graham!" He waved. "Bye, professor!"

Asta opened a portal and dove through, Kunst and Graham following along with the rest of the awakened Asra trailing behind.

Chase shook his head, laughing to himself. "That prince is really somethin', ain't he?"

"He sure is." Sloane raked his fingers through his hair. He looked to Ollie, Alexander, and Rota. "You guys heading out too?"

"Yeah." Alexander freed himself from Rota's iron embrace, adjusting his jacket only to have Ollie grab him in a big hug. He sighed as if annoyed, but he was smiling. "Think we've all been heroic enough today."

"Agreed." Rota made himself invisible, but Sloane could still see a hint of his smile, as if he simply couldn't hold it in.

Loch suddenly appeared next to Sloane just as the trio left, once again in his mortal body. He gave Sloane a firm kiss that tasted wonderfully sweet and minty, and Sloane didn't even care when Loch grabbed his ass.

The distant wail of a siren interrupted their kiss, and Loch said, "I swear I didn't do it."

"Do what?" Sloane asked suspiciously.

"Exactly."

"Best of luck to you all," Stoker said curtly. "That's my cue to exit. I have a large temple in my Hidden World to attend to, and I'm not much for entertaining the authorities."

"Fuck you too, Stoker." Chase smirked.

Stoker bowed, his eyes finding Sloane's as he stood. "Mr. Beaumont. Enjoy yourself. You've earned it."

"Thanks, Stoker." Sloane smiled warmly. "So have you. Take it easy, all right?"

"Will do." Stoker eyed Loch. "Azaethoth."

"Jake." Loch held his head high.

"Have the day you deserve." Stoker winked and with that, he was gone.

"Have the day you deserve," Loch mocked, scoffing in disbelief. "I really do not like him."

"I know." Sloane patted Loch's shoulder.

"Like, *at all*."

"I know, baby."

Galgareth and a very sleepy-looking Merrick popped in, both of them back in their human vessels. "Hi, guys!" she said, waving excitedly. "Sorry about the nap, but hey! We're back!"

"I rise, but I am not able to shine at my full capacity currently," Merrick grumbled.

Chase tackled Merrick in a passionate kiss while Loch and Sloane hurried to embrace Galgareth. It was a wild tangle of tentacles and arms for a few moments, and Merrick couldn't stop yawning. So caught up in their greetings, Sloane almost didn't notice Grell returning.

Or that he had not come alone.

Fred!

Fred was alive and scowling, barking, "What the fuck is going on? Where's Ell?"

"He's right over there, you ridiculous decomposing sack of viscera and anger issues." Grell pointed at where Ted and Ell were standing together. "See?"

Fred had eyes for no other once he found Ell, sprinting over and sweeping Ell up into his arms. "Ell!"

"Freddy!" Ell cried, instantly bursting into a frantic sob as he hugged Fred's neck. "Oh, Freddy. Oh, baby. I'm sorry. I'm sorry! I'm so, so sorry!"

Fred kissed him.

Ted cleared his throat, politely taking a few steps away so they could enjoy their reunion. He walked up to Grell and laid a sweet kiss on his lips.

Grell seemed surprised, asking, "Oh, does this mean I'm forgiven now?"

"Not yet." Ted grinned. "But I got some ideas on how you're gonna kiss my ass real good and make it up to me."

"I will be happy to put my mouth anywhere you'd like, my queen."

"Where was Fred?" Sloane asked. "Another world?"

"Yes." Grell nodded. "Seems like even as the Kindress, Elliam couldn't stand to hurt his bulging lover." He glanced around the park. "Where is my charming spawn?"

"He headed back to Xenon to see Jay," Sloane replied with a chuckle. "Kunst and Graham went back too, took the rest of the Asra with them. Stoker's already left too."

"Damn. I was hoping to ask who his tailor was."

"Maybe next time." Ted wrapped his arm around Grell's shoulders. "I think it's about time for us to head back, but uh… how does Xenon feel about people who used to be gods but are only a tiny bit godly now?" He looked back to where Ell and Fred were still making out.

"I think perhaps we can make a small exception." Grell smiled. "He is family, after all."

Ell and Fred had finally come up for air, and Ell burst into tears, clearly overwhelmed by a wave of emotions. He collapsed against Fred's chest, sobbing, "I'm sorry! I'm so, so damn *sorry!*" He tried to hide his face as he cried, his shoulders shaking with every wail. "I, I thought I'd killed you… I, I hurt so many people…."

"Hey, hey," Fred soothed. "Listen to me, okay?"

"I'm just so, so fucking sorry!" Ell whirled around to face the others, staring at them all with wide, tear-filled eyes. "Sloane. Loch. Everybody." His face was red and blotchy from crying so hard. "*Please.* I'm sorry. I-I understand if you can't forgive me. I-I don't think I can ever forgive myself, but please, *please* just know I wish I could take it all back."

"Ell, baby, listen to me." Fred turned Ell back to look at him. "I love you. I forgive you. I never doubted you for a fuckin' second. I knew this shit was gonna work out."

"How could you have possibly known that?" Ell peeked up at him, sniffing miserably.

"Because I love you." Fred pressed a firm kiss to his lips. "You're not the Kindress, not no more. You never were, not to me. You're Ell, and you're always gonna be Ell. Even when I was scared, I knew it was still you in there."

"But—"

"No buts. No nothin'." Fred cradled the side of his face, saying softly, "Even in the dark clutches of the Baron's darkness, your beauty shone through brighter than a thousand unicorns, and your love sparkled more brilliantly than all the goblins' gold."

Ell sniffled. "In hindsight, you know, *dark clutches of darkness* is a really bad line."

"Yeah." Fred smiled. "But you're fuckin' perfect."

"Me? Heh. No… but you sure are." Ell managed a little smile in reply, and he laid his head on Fred's chest. "I love you, Freddie."

"Love you too, Ell."

"If you please," Merrick said, rubbing at his eyes. "I hate to ruin the touching moment, but I think it may be best for anyone who is from another world to head there shortly. The AVPD will be here soon, and I do not yet have a plan for what we are going to tell them."

"We'll figure it out, Merry." Chase rubbed Merrick's back. "Maybe after we get you some coffee, huh?"

"Yes, *please.*"

"We'll stay back and get this shit figured out," Chase promised. "You guys go on and get the hell out of here. Go kiss that baby girl of yours."

"We're on it." Sloane smiled. "So, Loch, shall we—"

Ell knocked the wind out of his lungs with another crushing hug. "Thank you, Sloane."

"No problem!" Sloane squeaked. "Ahem, yeah, sure. Happy to help, Ell." He smiled. "You guys enjoy your feast, okay?"

"I would invite you, but meh." Grell shrugged. "No gods allowed and all that."

"We should all get together for Dhankes!" Ell exclaimed. "Here in the city somewhere!"

"Seriously?" Ted chuckled lightly. "You wanna do that? You don't think maybe you've had enough of fuckin' parties and shit considering what happened at the last one?"

"Just because I maybe tried to destroy the universe one time…." Ell cringed. "Too soon?"

"Just a tiny bit." Fred kissed the top of Ell's head.

"We'll figure out something," Sloane said. "I would love to celebrate Dhankes with all of you. You're family."

"But we will not have an orgy," Loch added firmly. "Sloane is very anti-orgy."

"Yes, I am." Sloane hugged Loch's arm. "Let's get outta here."

They all said their final farewells, although Ell insisted on coming back in for another hug. He really seemed to enjoy hugs, but it could have also just been the novelty of being able to touch people without hurting them. Grell, Ted, Ell, and Fred left for Xenon while Chase and Merrick headed over to deal with the crowd and assist the AVPD with trying to restore some semblance of order.

Sloane, Loch, and Galgareth headed back to the temple in Stoker's Hidden World, and Sloane was promptly tackled by a very excited Pandora. He held her close, sighing in relief as he peppered her hair with kisses. He didn't even care when her arms turned into tentacles and hugged his neck too tight.

There had been too many moments when he honestly didn't know if he was coming back to her.

"You're back! You're really okay!" Milo pounced next, tearfully gushing all over Sloane. "We were so damn worried, dude! It felt like it was taking a million years—"

"It was a pretty intense battle." Sloane grinned. "But everybody is okay!"

"Fred?" Lochlain asked urgently.

"Yes! Ell didn't actually kill him. He shot him off to another world, and he's currently on his way to Xenon with Ell, King Grell, and Asta."

"Oh! A god in Xenon." Urilith gasped. "That's sure to stir up some trouble."

"I think they can handle it." Sloane chuckled lightly, pressing his cheek against Pandora's forehead. "I'm just so glad it's over."

"Da-dad," Pandora mumbled. "Dad, Dad."

"That's right, baby girl. Dad's here."

Loch wrapped his tentacles around Sloane and Pandora both, sighing contentedly. "And I'm here too, of course. That's really what matters most, you know." He winked.

Sloane laughed.

"Galgareth gave us the condensed version of what happened when she swung by to get Toby," Lynnette said, looking up from where she was nursing Mara. "Did Ell really pop out of a big shell like a terror dog in *Ghostbusters*?"

"Yup. Totally did." Sloane nodded. "And his touch doesn't hurt anyone now. Great Azaethoth must have taken it away. I don't really understand how, but… it's done. The cycle is broken. Ell is just Ell again."

"It's really over," Robert murmured. "I still… I can't quite believe it. And the cultists are all gone? Really gone?"

"Any of 'em that were left in Archersville at least," Sloane said. "I think once word gets out about what happened today, maybe they'll think twice about messing around with waking the old gods."

"Let us hope so," Urilith said solemnly.

"Does this mean we can go home?" Lynnette asked. "Not that I mind being waited on hand and foot in a beautiful godly temple, but I would *love* a hot shower."

"I will so wash your back," Milo promised.

"That's very sweet, but you're gonna be busy taking care of our daughter," Lynnette teased.

"Whatever you want, baby." Milo was practically floating as he headed back to Lynnette's side for a sweet kiss. "And my other baby." He kissed the top of Mara's head. "So, uh, how do we get home?"

"I can take care of that," Loch promised. "Whenever you're ready."

"Now would be great," Lynnette said. "Worrying about the world ending is pretty exhausting, and that shower is calling my name. I'll see you all at Dhankes! You're all invited, of course."

"Ell definitely wanted us to have a big party for Dhankes," Sloane said. "He's invited too. Fred naturally. That crazy cat king and Jay and Asta can come as long as Asta wears clothes. Alexander and Rota too."

"Wait, who's hosting this party?" Lochlain laughed. "I thought Robert and I were going to do it this year. You literally just gave birth hours ago—"

"And since I already gave birth, I am free to host a party now."

"Just nod and say yes ma'am," Milo advised Lochlain with a wink. "It makes life much simpler."

"Yes, ma'am." Lochlain nodded dutifully.

"I would be honored to bake my Dhankes cake for the celebration," Urilith gushed.

"We would be honored to have you." Lynnette beamed. "So! Everybody! Me and Milo's place! Dhankes! Don't be late!"

"We'll be there," Sloane promised,

They all waved farewell as Loch transported Milo, Lynnette, and Mara away. Pandora was very upset to see Mara go, and Sloane tried to tell her that they would see her again very soon. After exchanging more goodbyes, Robert and Lochlain decided they were ready to head home as well. Galgareth and Urilith came back with Sloane, Loch, and Pandora, and Sloane had never been so happy to be back home.

Plus, he was absolutely starving.

Urilith was happy to create a magnificent feast for them, and they all sat down together to eat. Sloane cleared his plate and went right back for seconds. Pandora enjoyed mashed sweet potatoes and some small bites of chicken, though once she was full, she decided to put the sweet potatoes in her hair. The conversation was happy, light, and they mostly talked about their plans to celebrate Dhankes together.

It was hard to believe they'd been fighting to save the universe just a few hours ago.

Being here among his family and enjoying a delicious meal felt surreal, but Sloane was happy. The nagging guilt that had been eating at him since he'd first found out it was his prayer that awoke Tollmathan was gone, replaced by the deep satisfaction that he'd finally made things right.

His loved ones were safe, they were alive, and they were likely enjoying their own celebrations right now.

Lynnette and Milo were no doubt loving their first evening at home with Mara, and Sloane could imagine Milo keeping Mara occupied so Lynnette could get that hot shower she'd been craving. They would probably put Mara down for bed and then fall asleep on the couch watching sci-fi movies.

Robert and Lochlain would be having wine as they got settled into their living room, perhaps sharing a tray of cheese and crackers. They might talk some, they might not, and Sloane liked to picture them just holding each other and enjoying the closeness.

Alexander was probably three sheets to the wind on piña coladas by now, and Rota and Ollie would cook a great dinner for them to eat and help soak up some of the booze. Sloane didn't know why, but he thought they'd probably climb to the roof of Ollie's apartment building to look up at the stars together.

Chase and Merrick were probably the least likely to be celebrating since they were working to contain the chaos of Archersville's citizens having died via puddle bubble only to be miraculously resurrected. They had a long night ahead of them, but Chase would definitely sneak them some donuts to share.

The feast Professor Kunst had organized for the kingdom of Xenon was probably a grand and extravagant event, and Grell struck Sloane as someone who did like a big party. Not so much Ted or even Ell and Fred, but he hoped they were having a great time, and not having to worry too much about letting a slightly godly person into their world.

Asta was most likely still shacked up with Jay and avoiding the feast, if Sloane had to guess, though he was confident the pair would sneak in later. They'd avoid Grell and Ted, steal some food, and then hurry back to their room to go again.

It was hard to say what Stoker was up to. Sloane liked to think of him sitting somewhere cozy in front of a big fireplace. He'd have a good scotch or a nice whisky on hand, sipping it slowly while he played with Madame Sprinkles. Alone, yes, but Sloane decided Stoker probably liked it that way.

Everything was finally as it should be, and Sloane's heart felt overwhelmingly full.

His stomach was too, and he couldn't quite finish his third plate despite his best efforts.

Pandora was happy to take Sloane's sweet potatoes to add to her hair.

Urilith insisted on giving her a bath after that, leaving Sloane and Loch to clean up the kitchen and the table. Galgareth helped them finish with a quick snap of her fingers, and by then it was already after midnight.

A freshly bathed Pandora toddled around the living room with Loch's old rattle, happily banging it on every solid surface she could reach—which was pretty much everything with her tentacles wiggling around. Sloane watched her from the couch, feeling more like a beached whale than a brave Starkiller.

He was tired, overly full, and he swore he felt a tingle in his hands as if he was still holding the sword of starlight.

Loch took his hand as he sat beside him, bringing it to his lips for a soft kiss. His tentacles curled around Sloane and drew him in close. He was watching Pandora too, smiling happily. "We did it, my beautiful mate."

"Yeah, we did." Sloane snuggled in tight. "Hmm. What are we going to do now that we don't have to worry about your dad waking up and ending the world?"

"We enjoy our life with our beautiful spawn. We watch her grow, we cherish every sweet moment, and when you're ready, you can finally ascend to Zebulon as a god at my side where we will spend the rest of eternity together amongst the stars."

"That sounds wonderful."

"It will be."

"Will I get tentacles?"

"Perhaps." Loch chuckled. "We will have to wait and see."

Sloane yawned, "I hope I get tentacles."

"You can have some right now if you'd like."

"How about tomorrow?" Sloane laughed quietly. "Saving the universe is exhausting."

"Do you wish to go to bed, my sweet husband?"

"Not yet." Sloane smiled, watching Pandora tinkering around with the rattle and a stack of blocks. "I wanna stay out here with Panda a bit longer."

"As you wish, my love."

Sloane enjoyed Pandora's playtime until his eyes were too heavy to keep open and he dozed off in Loch's arms. He could still hear Pandora's cooing and giggling as she stacked the blocks and then toppled them over. Urilith and Loch chatted some while Galgareth played with Pandora, and Sloane finally drifted into a deep sleep.

He became vaguely aware of being carried to bed, but he didn't wake up completely. He knew it was Loch tucking him into bed, and he smiled when he felt Loch kiss his brow. He sensed Loch walking away, maybe to put Pandora to bed too, but Sloane realized he wasn't alone.

A hand touched his shoulder, and he was sure he had to be dreaming because it felt like a woman's or a young man's hand, and it couldn't be Galgareth because he could hear her talking to Loch out in the living room. The hand was weirdly familiar, and he fought against the lull of sleep to open his eyes to see who it was.

Sloane, my beautiful boy.

"What…?" Sloane croaked quietly, blinking his eyes open to see a faint figure sitting on the edge of the bed beside him. There was a second figure standing next to it, and his eyes filled with tears. He knew who they were immediately. "Mom? Dad?"

We're here, Sloane. His dad smiled at him.

We love you so much. His mother touched his cheek. *We're so proud of you.*

"I miss you," Sloane whispered. "I miss you so, so much."

Miss you too, his dad said. *We'll all be together again one day. But don't you be in any hurry, okay? Maybe take a break from heroics for a little while.*

"Heh, okay. I will." Sloane smiled, trying to swallow back a sob. "I promise, I will."

Enjoy your husband and that beautiful little girl, his mother soothed. *Enjoy your life, son. We love you.*

"Love you." Sloane sniffed. "I love you both so much."

Their images faded in a shower of green sparkles, and Sloane knew this visit had been a gift from Great Azaethoth. He could taste the ancient magic in the air just as surely as he knew he'd smelled his mother's perfume.

Loch walked in then, and he seemed surprised to see Sloane awake. "My love? Are you all right?"

"I'm good." Sloane wiped at his eyes.

"What's wrong?" Loch crawled into bed and then pulled Sloane into his arms. "Tell me, my sweet husband. Whatever it is, I shall amend it immediately with intestinal crafts if need be."

"No, really. I'm great." Sloane smiled. "I'm just so happy. Life doesn't really get any better than this."

"I'm inclined to agree, though I think I can come up with a few ways to improve it." Loch winked.

"Let me guess." Sloane chuckled. "None of them involve clothes, do they?"

"No, they do not." Loch kissed him sweetly. "I love you."

"I love you too." Sloane hesitated, eyeing Loch for a moment. "Wait. That's it?"

"What?"

"You're not going to try and talk me into having ravenous tentacle sex?"

"You're tired, my sweet husband. It'll be better if you rest first, and then I can ravage you in the morning." Loch grinned. "You'll need your full strength when I properly thank you for saving the universe."

"I can't wait."

CHAPTER 15.

LOCH SHOWED Sloane his gratitude four times that next morning and then several more throughout the day and into the night.

Saving the universe was quite the turn-on, apparently.

The mayor of Archersville announced that the old gods were apparitions summoned by a criminal cult, and they had used illegal spells to erase citizens' memories. There was no way to cover up the battle at the hospital, especially since it was going to take weeks if not months to repair the damage. There had been countless witnesses, not to mention the multiple cell phone videos that had gone viral, and the public was skeptical about the mayor's declarations.

No one remembered the puddle bubble, much less dying and being resurrected, but the repercussions of having the entire city wiped out in mere minutes was great. There had been thousands of car wrecks, construction accidents, a bad sewage spill, and more. The mayor insisted the chaos was the result of the criminal cult's spell, but many citizens had their own ideas about what happened.

Some Lucians claimed that the apparitions were sent as a punishment from the Lord of Light, others believed it was a government experiment gone wrong, and a few actually boasted to have seen the infamous Smoane Momont fighting the gods with a glowing sword. Interest in the Sagittarian religion continued to soar, and new theories developed that the old gods might finally be returning to Aeon.

Chase and Merrick later said that the mayor hadn't been interested in the truth so much as he wanted a story he could sell to the public to keep them calm. It was beneficial, at least, in that Sloane and the others didn't have to worry about any possible charges, though Sloane did hate the dishonesty. The people of Archersville agreed, and there were several protests that nearly turned into riots. A few even took place in the very park where Sloane had killed the Kindress.

Sloane ignored the news as much as he could and hoped the disorder would die down soon.

Life was pretty uneventful at home other than the occasional fire, and Sloane was eager for things to get back to normal—well, at least as normal as his life was anyway.

Today he would be going with old god husband and demi-goddess daughter over to his best friend's house to celebrate Dhankes with several rogue witches, a ghoul, Asran royalty, two mortals with starsight, and several other old gods, including one who had very recently tried to destroy all of existence.

Just another day in the life of Sloane Beaumont, Starkiller and private investigator.

He woke up from a deep sleep with a smile and a yawn, feeling Loch's tentacles lightly massaging his shoulders. "Mm, good morning."

"Good morning, my gorgeous husband." Loch was on his side facing Sloane, and he kissed Sloane's brow. "How did you sleep?"

"Wonderfully." Sloane gasped as a tentacle slid up his thigh. "A-and you?"

"I rested some. I also spent many hours planning out what I wanted to do to your supple, succulent mortal flesh."

"How is that resting?" Sloane laughed.

"It's quite relaxing, I'll have you know." Loch grinned and licked his lips. "But I can certainly think of other activities that are much more satisfying."

The hunger with which he looked at Sloane never ceased to amaze him, and his cock was thickening up fast. He shivered as Loch's tentacles slipped between his legs, and goose bumps prickled along his skin. The anticipation was deliciously thick, and he was dying for Loch to make a move.

Kiss him. Grab him. Do something, anything, to break the tension.

"Loch—" Sloane started to speak.

Loch was on him with a growl, kissing him hard and wrapping him up in his tentacles. Loch's kisses always tasted of mint, and Sloane loved how the flavor filled his mouth. The tentacles were writhing around him, curling around his arms and legs, teasing his nipples, his hole, and his cock, and he couldn't contain his moans.

Sloane couldn't think of a better way to wake up.

He let Loch spread him wide, pinning his arms to the mattress and parting his legs so he could slide between them. Already one of Loch's slitted tentacles was pushing inside of Sloane, Loch's magic easing the way, and Sloane shouted as Loch zeroed right in on his prostate.

"Shit! Loch!" Sloane's hips jerked, and he fought to breathe through the tremendous pressure.

Loch was hitting every single sweet little nerve deep inside of Sloane, and the resulting rush made Sloane's head spin. His balls were tight, his dick throbbingly hard, and he couldn't believe he was already so full. He suddenly felt on edge, as if Loch had been teasing him for hours, and he couldn't keep still, frantically grinding on the tentacle thrusting into him.

"My mate," Loch groaned. "You feel so perfect. You always feel so perfect... mmm, my husband. My beautiful husband."

"I love you. I love you so much!" Sloane whimpered as Loch's tentacle twisted, and he cried out at the new depth of sensation. Loch's weight on top of him was grounding, especially when he was being carried away with pleasure. His pulse was pounding in his loins, all around his stretched hole stuffed by Loch's tentacle, and he screamed as he came.

It happened so suddenly that he briefly feared it would be over before he could even enjoy it, but Loch kept it going with more feverish slams. Just as the ecstasy was dipping, his second slitted tentacle wriggled in alongside the first. The sharp increase in pressure tore a scream from Sloane's throat, and his orgasm was instantly surging, cresting along new heights as he came again.

Sloane wanted to beg for mercy, but he couldn't form a single word. All he could do was moan as Loch fucked him wide open with both tentacles, snaking down his body to claim his come with long licks and heated kisses. Loch drank every drop that he found, and even when the mess was clean, he kept lapping along Sloane's cock in search of more.

The two tentacles curled together as they pounded into Sloane's body, stretching him wide and pushing him right back to the edge. Sloane could feel the coils shivering, slick and pulsing as they fucked him, and he knew he was going to come again. Having all of his senses overwhelmed by this insane bliss was almost too much, and he sobbed as he surrendered to it a third time.

Loch groaned, both of his tentacles firing off thick loads, and he sucked Sloane's cock into his mouth to take his come straight from the source.

"Loch!" Sloane cried out, staring down at Loch's head buried between his legs.

Loch rarely used any part of his human vessel for any intimate acts except for kissing, and seeing him down there and feeling his hot mouth, his firm tongue, was a wonderful treat. Sloane rocked up, watching his cock vanish past Loch's lips, and he let out a spectacular whimper.

"Wow...." Sloane couldn't stop smiling. "You're so incredible."

Loch pulled off with a greedy little lick, looking quite proud of himself. "I know."

"Mmm. That was awesome." Sloane kept staring at that smug little smile on Loch's face. "Oh, you're not done yet, are you?"

"No, sweet husband. I am not."

Sloane gasped as he was suddenly pulled up and flipped over on his hands and knees, positioned easily by the barrage of tentacles holding him. The twin slitted tentacles that had been inside of him pulled out, and Loch now kneeled behind him, rubbing Sloane's hips.

Loch slid his hands down, now cupping Sloane's ass and using his tentacles to spread his legs. "I do so love seeing you like this... so wet, so open... so very mine."

"Yeah?" Sloane groaned, Loch's fingers now probing his wet asshole. His body was already trying to clench back up, but Loch kept him open, sliding in and out with ease. "Ah, gods... yeah... I can feel it."

"I want to wake you up like this every day so I can bask in the beauty of your claimed body, to see how I've made you mine." Loch's fingers moved away, and the thick head of the tentacock took its place, pushing in and making them both shudder and groan.

"No complaints here," Sloane managed to pant. "Fuck, not a one." Even though they'd been intimate quite a lot recently, the tentacock's girth still made him ache. Loch was holding his hips and easing him back on it, and Sloane could feel it stretching him wide, groaning from the incredible throb it created.

Loch went all the way to the fat knot, sliding out and slowly back in, whispering, "Oh, if only you could see it... how your body always wants to open up for me, pulling me right into you... it's beautiful."

"I love you," Sloane whispered breathlessly. He arched his hips and pushed back until he hit the knot, groaning deliriously, "By all the gods, I love you."

"I love you too, my gorgeous Starkiller." Loch snapped forward, thrusting the tentacock deep and hard.

"Ah, fuck!" Sloane clawed at the sheets, grunting and sobbing as Loch fucked him. Loch was so damn big that every thrust felt like it was going to break him, and Sloane bowed his head down, having no choice except to offer up everything he had in worship to his beautiful god. The ache now took his breath away, and he gritted his teeth as he fought to relax and breathe through it.

The pleasure was creating flashes of stars right before his eyes, and he loved how greedily Loch was grabbing his hips and ass, latching on tight as he fucked him ruthlessly. Sloane was left dizzy by it, and his head dropped, no longer able to keep up with being an active participant. It was taking all that he had not to pass right out, and he sobbed when the knot began slipping in.

There was a hint of pain, something deep and sharp, but the bliss that followed smothered it out. Sloane didn't think this could get any more intense, though it was clear Loch had other ideas. His slitted tentacles latched on to Sloane's cock and balls, sucking and pulsing, and then Loch shoved his knot all the way in.

"Fuck!" Sloane cried, the force of the slam pushing his body flat against the bed. "Loch!"

Loch moved with him and never lost rhythm, his tentacock slamming away at Sloane's tight hole. The knot got bigger, so now the depths of his thrusting was limited, but he didn't stop. He kissed and sucked along Sloane's shoulder and neck, still rutting away with impossible strength, groaning, "No, say it... say my name, my love."

"Aza...." Sloane tried weakly, crying as the knot swelled inside of him, pushing into every delicate nerve he had. There was a jerk, a hot pulse of muscle, and a glorious surge of heat flooded his hole, and he screamed, "Azaethoth!"

"Yes, my love. Say it!" Loch growled as he pumped his thick load deep inside of Sloane.

"Azaethoth! Yes! Fuck." Sloane was nearly hysterical, and his excitement reached an incredible apex as he came several times in rapid succession. He was coming so hard that his head hurt, and he went limp against the bed, Loch's tentacock still pumping as the ache faded into pure bliss.

Loch could keep this sweet moment of orgasmic bliss going for several minutes, offering eternal ecstasy as only a god could, and he wrapped Sloane up in his arms when it finally faded. "Mm, my love. My sweet mate. My beautiful, beautiful Starkiller."

"Mmph." Sloane gave a small grunt in reply, certain he couldn't move even if the apartment caught fire. His entire body was thrumming with pleasure, buzzing wonderfully and totally exhausted. While he waited for his brain to come back online, he managed to get a hold of one of Loch's hands and kiss it.

Loch laid beside him, petting his back with long loving strokes of his tentacles, cradling him close with a very loud and very satisfied sounding sigh. "Now, *that* is how we should start off every morning."

Sloane was able to laugh, though it was more of a long huff than a proper chuckle. "Uh... huh."

"Did I ruin you, my gorgeous husband?"

"In the best possible way." Sloane flopped his head over so he was able to look up at Loch. He was sweating, flushed, and honestly ready to go right back to sleep.

"Excellent."

Sloane was able to laugh then, and he beckoned Loch down for a kiss. "Mmm. We need to get up."

"We do?"

"Yes. Need food. Need to get Panda up. Breakfast. Make something for the feast tonight. Maybe a shower first, though."

"Ah, very well. I will join you for the shower to make sure you are properly and deeply cleaned, and then I will make breakfast for you and our beautiful spawn."

"Sounds good."

Loch helped herd Sloane into the shower and was in the process of coaxing out another orgasm when they heard Pandora fussing. Loch left Sloane to finish bathing with a promise to help *finish* later, and Sloane enjoyed the rest of his shower in quiet solitude.

More pleasing than the deep satisfaction of being thoroughly ravaged by an immortal was the knowledge that this really was going to be how he spent the rest of his life. He would wake up every day with the god he loved and get to raise their beautiful daughter together. The threat of endless world-ending crises was finally over, and he could focus on more mundane problems.

Like how to make his mother's sausage balls for the Dhankes feast tonight.

Sloane didn't have a lot from his childhood, but one of his most treasured possessions was his mother's old cookbook. He'd never used it much, but he had often read her handwritten notes on how she adjusted the recipes, and there was a section in the back with blank pages where she'd written a few of her own. It was there he'd found the recipe for the sausage balls.

Sloane remembered her making these for Dhankes when he was a kid, and making them seemed easy enough. It was basically combining everything in a big bowl, rolling spoonfuls into balls, and then baking them. He could handle that, plus he had a very adorable and enthusiastic little helper.

Pandora morphed her hands into tentacles to help mix the ingredients while Loch turned up his nose at the use of processed cheese. Sloane refused to let him change the ingredients, but he did appreciate his help getting the trays of balls into the oven to bake. Being able to clean up the mess in the kitchen with a snap of magic was nice too.

Sloane tucked the sausage balls into two Tupperware containers, grabbed two bottles of wine, and decided they were ready. They headed out to the car, and Loch got Pandora into her car seat in the back.

It was no surprise that the straps were already a bit tight for her and had to be adjusted.

"She's gonna be ready to start kindergarten before she's a year old," Sloane said with an amazed sigh. "Not really sure how we're gonna explain that to the school."

"Forgery. Obviously."

Sloane chuckled as he started the car. "Well, we may need to wait until she's a bit older anyway. Can't have her slapping the other kids with tentacles. Might raise some questions."

"Our daughter would never!"

"No?"

Loch paused, thinking it over as he got settled in the passenger seat. "Only if the other child very much deserved the slapping."

"No slapping other children, Panda." Sloane handed the Tupperwares of sausage balls over to Loch to hold once he was settled. "Here."

"I don't see why we have to share the tiny balls of sausage and processed cheese," Loch complained. "We could have brought a box of crackers instead."

"It's Dhankes," Sloane scolded.

"They are terrible. We should have left them at home."

"Terrible, huh?" Sloane chuckled. "Is that why you ate ten of them?"

"Yes."

"You just don't want anyone else to eat them."

"It is tradition to leave out offerings for the gods on this night. You should give me the sausage balls as my offering."

"I'll think about it."

Sloane didn't miss Loch's tentacles sneaking a few more sausage balls on the drive over to Milo and Lynnette's house. He had to park on the street when they arrived because Fred's truck and Chase's car were already in the driveaway. He turned to Loch, shocked to see both Tupperwares were gone.

"Loch?"

"Yes, my sweet love?" Loch replied.

Sloane narrowed his eyes suspiciously. "Where are they?

"Where are what?"

"The sausage balls."

Loch gasped. "I would not pilfer from my own beloved mate! Your terrible sausage balls are perfectly safe! Why, they are right…." He frowned down at his empty lap. "Huh."

Pandora belched.

Sloane and Loch both turned at the same time to stare at Pandora who was safely buckled into her car seat with two empty Tupperwares in her lap. Her face and tentacles were shiny with grease, and she was grinning from ear to ear.

"*Sausage!*" she cheered gleefully.

"Panda!" Sloane sighed, but he couldn't help but laugh. "Like father, like daughter."

"She really will make an excellent thief," Loch said with a proud smile. "That was quite impressive, wouldn't you say? Already a master of stealth!"

"Yeah, real great, except now we don't have anything for the feast."

"I have it on good authority that there is a grocery store with tolerable blueberry pie in the vicinity."

Sloane laughed. "I think it'll be okay."

"Nonsense!" Loch kissed Sloane's cheek. "My husband wants an offering for the feast, and that is what he will have."

"Loch, wait—"

Loch winked as he vanished.

"Daddy go poof!" Pandora declared. "Pooof!"

"Yup. That he did." Sloane rolled his eyes. "Come on, baby girl. Hopefully Daddy won't get himself banned from another store."

"Bannn."

"That's right, baby."

Sloane got out of the car and then freed Pandora from her car seat. He got some wipes out of her diaper bag to clean her up with before carrying her to the front door. Other than smelling distinctly of sausage, she was presentable for the celebration, and he cuddled her while waiting for someone to answer the door.

He didn't get to hold her for long, though, because it was Urilith who opened it, and she immediately snatched Pandora away to smother her with kisses. Sloane was next, but Urilith waited until Sloane had come inside and shut the door before she wrapped him up with her tentacles.

"Hello, my darlings!" Urilith gushed. "Oh! Where is my dear son?"

"Getting a pie." Sloane snorted. "A little someone ate our dish for the feast on the way over here."

Urilith grinned and cooed at Pandora, "Aw, was that you?"

"Sausage!" Pandora declared. "Sausage, sausage, sausage!"

"I'll take that as a yes."

Urilith led Sloane into the bustling kitchen where Lynnette was tending to several pots and pans on the stove with Chase beside her following her every order while Milo ran back and forth to grab more ingredients for them from the pantry. Merrick was looking on from the small breakfast table with a fond smile, Galgareth seated across from him and offering her advice for various spices.

Robert and Lochlain were hovering nearby, and Lochlain was doing his best to steal a taste of everything but was met with the fierce smack of a wooden spoon courtesy of Lynnette. Fred was propped against the doorway that led into the living room with Ell tucked under his arm, and Ted and Grell were arguing over what to watch on TV with Asta and Jay. Ollie was trying to mediate while Kunst offered his own movie picks and Graham pleaded for cartoons. Alexander appeared to have a headache, and the shimmer of Rota's tentacles was visible as they rubbed his shoulders.

For a few moments, Sloane could hardly speak.

It was pretty amazing to have all of his friends and family together under one roof.

He was surprised by the heat that sprung up behind his eyes, and his chest tightened from the wealth of love he felt. He took a deep breath to steady himself and then cheerfully called out, "Hey, everybody! Happy Dhankes!"

Sloane was promptly swamped in greetings, and he had to make a full lap to say hello to everyone. Robert and Lochlain gave big hugs, Galgareth gave an even bigger one, Merrick shook his hand, and Lynnette insisted on smooching both of his cheeks. Chase offered a friendly nod as he was dicing fresh vegetables for the next dish, and then Milo dragged Sloane into a crushing embrace that made Sloane's back pop.

"Hey, hey!" Sloane laughed. "Easy there!"

"Sorry! I'm just so excited!" Milo exclaimed. "This is amazing, right?"

"It's definitely something," Sloane agreed.

"Just think where we were last Halloween, right? How much has changed in just a damn year? Oh! Last *Dhankes*, I mean." Milo grinned sheepishly. "Sorry, still learning."

"You're doing great, buddy. Everything is really freakin' great. Hey, where's Mara?"

"Napping! You know, for now." Milo laughed, and then he looked like he might cry. "I really miss sleeping."

"Welcome to the wild world of parenting."

It hadn't escaped Sloane's attention that Ell seemed to be trying to hide behind Fred, and Sloane approached slowly.

"Hey, Sloane," Fred grunted, clasping Sloane's hand and giving it a hearty shake. "Happy Dhankes."

"Happy Dhankes." Sloane smiled warmly. "Happy Dhankes to you too, Ell."

"R-Right. Happy Dhankes." Ell's smile was shy, though he did take a hesitant step forward to shake Sloane's hand. "I'm sorry. Still getting used to all the touching. And the people. And the whole maybe, oops, I accidentally sort of on purpose tried to end the universe thing." He cringed.

"Hey, it's all right," Sloane said firmly. "Really. I'm sorry about, you know, the whole stabbing you with a sword of starlight thing."

"No, no, I'm really glad you did." Ell laughed nervously. "I mean, everything worked out, right? I don't remember much about what happened, but thank you. For said stabbing."

"I'd say anytime, but I really don't think any of us ever want to do that again," Sloane teased.

"Gods, no." Ell's eyes widened in horror. "No, no, no—"

"Ell, Ell, it's okay. I'm kidding."

"Oh. Right."

Loch suddenly appeared behind Sloane with a stack of boxed pies, declaring, "The staff at that grocery store were most unhelpful!"

"What did you do?" Sloane asked with a sigh.

"All I wanted was to try one of their barely passable pies, and they told me I had to pay for them first." Loch huffed. "They kept saying it was stealing, and I told them, *no*, this isn't stealing, grabbing a display of pies and then leaving would...." He trailed off, staring at Fred. "Why, Fred! You're alive."

"Yup." Fred smiled.

"Wait, what?" Sloane blinked, turning to look at Fred again. He didn't want to put up a perception spell to see for himself because that would have been rude, but he asked, "Really? Like alive *alive*?"

"Sure am. Flesh and blood and bones. The whole nine." Fred kissed Ell's cheek.

"But... how?" Sloane sputtered.

"So, the whole touching people and bringing death is gone, but the bit with bringing life to dead stuff, not so much?" Ell blushed. "I'd always been able to make ghouls alive again with enough healing, but I didn't want to do that with Fred. I mean, if I did, we wouldn't be able to, uh, do... stuff." His blush deepened. "Anyway! So, I'd been holding off, but then we realized it didn't matter now since—"

"Fred! This means your penis is fully functioning now!" Loch gasped excitedly.

"Yes, it sure fuckin' is." Fred grinned.

"Oh gods." Ell hid his face, laughing. "Yes, it functions very, very well."

"Go put down your stolen pies," Sloane scolded, shooing Loch over toward the counter. "But seriously, I'm really happy. For both of you."

"Thank you, Sloane," Ell said sweetly. "For everything."

"You're welcome, Ell."

Loch had to make his own rounds to say hi to everybody in the kitchen, but then he rejoined Sloane so they could head into the living room. Ollie had somehow wrangled control of the remote and put on a cartoon about a talking cat in boots, and that was being tolerated—though not without some colorful commentary.

"So, he's got the boots and the little fuckin' hat," Ted said slowly, "but his balls are what? Just hanging out? Swingin' around in the air while he does flips and shit?"

"Sort of like that Donald fellow who refuses to wear pants," Grell noted. "You just have to use your imagination. His little kitty balls are definitely swinging."

"I refuse to believe that this is the kind of discourse Giovanni Francesco Straparola had in mind when discussing an adaptation of his work," Kunst declared. "We could instead be focusing on the literary elements of—"

"Wait, did you say something about a strap-on?" Asta teased. "I didn't know you got down like that, *Cunst*. Good for you."

Jay tried not to laugh.

"By all the gods." Kunst groaned. "*Straparola* is what I said, and you know very well that is not how you say my name!"

"Shhh! I like this part!" Graham fussed. "You guys are making it weird!"

"Sassy lil' thing, isn't he?" Grell chuckled.

"He gets it from you," Ted drawled, winking playfully.

"Hey, guys!" Sloane waved. "How's it going?"

"Ah!" Ted got up from the couch to give Sloane a hug. "Hey, Sloane!"

The slap of Ted's hand was enough to knock the wind out of Sloane's lungs. "Oof, hey, Ted."

King Grell was kind enough to only shake Sloane's and Loch's hands, and Asta flipped them off. Jay hugged Sloane before Asta dragged him back to the recliner they were cuddling on, and Ollie gave fist bumps.

Alexander, who still appeared quite miserable, mouthed, "Help me."

Rota smacked Alexander's shoulder, saying, "It is very nice to see you both. Happy Dhankes."

"Happy Dhankes, guys!" Sloane grinned. "How was the party in Xenon?"

"Lame!" Asta called out.

"Ignore him. It was fabulous." Grell smirked. "Other than the tiny bit of a fuss the court had for bringing Ell, but really, it was fine."

"Tiny fuss?" Kunst's voice was shrill. "By tiny fuss, he means it was nearly a catastrophe that I personally averted by finding—"

"He found an old crusty piece of paper that said only *living* gods were barred from coming to Xenon," Ted cut in. "Ell's only, like, half a living god now since he died and everybody in Xenon totally saw his soul pass through the bridge. It was this whole big thing, but then we partied our asses off."

Sloane swore Kunst was pouting, and he said, "Well, it's awesome that the professor was able to do that! His knowledge is seriously impressive." He smiled when Kunst appeared to perk up at the praise. "I'm glad everything worked out."

"And then some," Ted agreed. "Was nice to finally get the big party I wanted for our wedding. Oh, and I got to introduce the world of Xenon to Jägerbombs." He smiled over at Ell. "And had everybody there I wanted too."

"Hey!" Lynnette called from the kitchen, barking like a drill sergeant. "It's time to start setting the table! Gods, Asra, mortals, everybody! Got a ton of food here to serve! Let's go!"

Back into the kitchen they went, and everyone helped take a dish or two into the dining room. Sloane couldn't explain how, but the table was impossibly long with chairs for all of the guests to sit. It had to be a trick of some kind because Sloane knew the dining room hadn't been large enough to hold such a big table, and he suspected Loch had something to do with it by the way he smiled.

There were soups, stews, chilis, a savory squash lasagna, and more. Just about everyone had brought something for the feast, and Sloane swore the amount of food magically doubled in between trips to the kitchen. Loch was getting Pandora set up in her highchair while Lynnette, clearly exhausted, was already sitting down with Mara cradled in her arms. Everyone was filing in to take their seats when there was a knock at the door.

"Oh! I'll get it!" Sloane was the closest as he'd just come back into the kitchen for more napkins, already anticipating Pandora was going to destroy that lasagna. He opened the door, staring in shock at the person who was waiting there. "Stoker? Hi!"

"Hello, Mr. Beaumont." Stoker smiled. "Sorry to bother you. I promise I won't keep you long." He held out a small cake box.

"What's this?" Sloane accepted the box with a laugh. "Please don't tell me this is a prank and it's full of glitter."

"No. Just a small token of my appreciation for saving the universe."

Sloane was skeptical and lifted the lid just enough to confirm it was indeed a cake with a creamy frosting. "Wow. Okay. Well, thank you. That's nice of you. It smells great." He took a step back and waved Stoker in. "Hey, why don't you join us? We're sitting down right now to eat."

"Thank you, but no." Stoker smirked. "But please do me one small favor. Wait until after Azaethoth has eaten that cake to tell him I made it. I'd like him to think I may have poisoned it."

Sloane snorted. "I'll see what I can do. Wait, you made this?"

"Yes. Pumpkin cake with cream cheese frosting."

"Wow, gangster and a baker. You are just full of surprises." Sloane laughed. "Are you sure you don't want to come in?"

"And risk being interrogated by Detectives Chase and Merrick while I'm trying to enjoy my meal?" Stoker chuckled. "No thanks. Be sure to tell everyone hello for me." He tipped his head. "Happy Dhankes, Mr. Beaumont."

"Happy Dhankes, Stoker." Sloane watched him walk away before shutting the door. He turned to head back down the hall, nearly smacking right into Loch. "Oh! Hey! Sorry about that."

"Is everything all right?" Loch eyed the box. "What's that?"

"It's a cake from Stoker," Sloane replied. "He wanted to wish us a happy Dhankes. Isn't that nice?"

"It's probably poisoned." Loch sniffed at the box warily.

"He told me to tell you he made it so you'd think it was." Sloane chuckled.

"Hmmph. Well, we're about to eat, but Lynnette wanted to take a photo." Loch looped his arm with Sloane's to lead him back into the dining room. "Come along, my sweet mate. You may deposit that baked abomination into the trash."

Sloane brought the cake with them despite Loch's protests, quickly taking his seat when he saw that everyone had been waiting on him to get the picture. Lynnette had given her phone to Rota who was at the end of the table with Alexander and Ollie.

Rota raised the phone up high to make sure he got everyone in the photo, saying, "All right! Is everyone ready?"

"Ready!" Sloane called out, grinning as Loch squeezed his hand. "Here we go! Big smiles! In three, two, one…."
Click.

SLOANE SAW the picture later once the first round of feasting was over and asked Lynnette to send him a copy. He was already planning to have it printed and hang it right up in his living room next to the photo of him with his parents they'd taken at a Dhankes many years ago.

They lit candles for the dead, put out offerings for the gods, the wine flowed, and Sloane later caught Loch eating the cake Stoker had brought. Loch claimed it was horrible, and yet he went back for a second piece when he thought Sloane wasn't looking.

Chase and Merrick were the first to leave. It was getting late, and they had another long day ahead of them tomorrow at the precinct. Grell and Ted were next, and they took Graham and Kunst with them. Jay and Asta lingered for a bit longer, but then they were suddenly very eager to return to Xenon because there was something important happening in a video game.

Galgareth had to get Toby home but promised to visit again soon. Urilith decided she was going to stay for a few days and help take care of Mara to give Milo and Lynnette some time to catch up on sleep. They headed for bed the second Urilith took charge of her.

Robert and Lochlain left then, and while Robert wished everyone a happy Dhankes, Lochlain reminded Loch that they'd yet to go on a heist together. Loch promised to remedy that soon and mentioned that there were several very shiny exhibits coming to town in the next few months.

Surprisingly, Alexander, Rota, and Ollie were among the last to leave. Rota and Ell had gotten caught up in an exciting conversation about old worlds they both knew. Though their memories were heavily fragmented, they were able to piece together several places that could be potential hiding places Gronoch may have used to stash Rota's body. When Alexander did finally leave with Rota and Ollie, he was smiling.

Fred and Ell headed out after that, but not before Ell gave Sloane one last giant hug and thanked him again for everything. Sloane walked them out, tired but happy as he dragged himself back to the living room to check on Pandora.

She had fallen asleep in Urilith's arms with Mara cuddled up right beside her. Urilith assured him that she was fine to watch her for a bit longer since Loch was busy doing gods knew what in the kitchen.

Probably stealing more cake.

Sloane drifted over toward the back door where Lynnette had placed an altar for everyone to light their candles. So caught up in the reverie, he realized he had nearly forgotten to light one for his parents.

"Though souls stir in the slumber of stars, breathless but bright...."

"Surrender forgotten flesh and dream once more," Loch finished for him, coming from behind to hug his waist.

The candle's flame ignited, and Sloane smiled, whispering, "Happy Dhankes, Mom and Dad." He watched the flame flicker, and he hoped that meant they'd heard him.

"Are you all right, my sweet husband?"

"I'm good." Sloane nodded. "Mm, tired. And thinking about the last time I was lighting a candle for my parents. It was in my office right before I met you. I was so angry that I hadn't been able to solve their murder yet. I was still afraid of blowing myself up with my magic then, and I felt so helpless." He smiled. "And then you came crashing into my life in a dead man's body—"

"*Formerly* dead man."

"Yes, formerly dead man. And wow...." Sloane's smile grew. "Here we are. Happily married with a great family, solved some crazy cases, saved the world a few times, and then the universe."

"I told you we would be legendary." Loch leaned forward to nuzzle Sloane's cheek. He turned him around for a proper kiss, letting the press of their lips linger as his tentacles curled around Sloane's hips.

"I love you, Azaethoth the Lesser," Sloane whispered. "Brother of Tollmathan, Gronoch, Xhorlas, and Galgareth. Son of Salgumel, he who was spawned by Baub, the child of Zunnerath and Halandrach, they who were born of Etheril and Xarapharos, descended directly from Great Azaethoth himself."

"And I love you, Sloane Beaumont, husband of Azaethoth the Lesser, father of Pandora Azaethoth the Lesser Junior Beaumont, son of Pandora and Daniel Beaumont."

"Forever?"

"And always."

Keep reading for an excerpt from
By the Red Moonlight
by Amanda Meuwissen!

CHAPTER 1

On All Hallow's Eve when the sky glows bright
Life and death in your hands by the red moonlight
A decision made to affect all others
The city's doom or salvation shall be on your shoulders

AND TO think, once upon a time, Bash loved Halloween.

"Are you sure you don't want a drink?" Deanna asked, often trying to distract him when Halloween came around—get him drunk, get him into a bar fight, get him laid if she could. It never worked.

Bashir "Bash" Bain was a Seer, but his prophecies were rarely as specific as he would have liked. He didn't know on which Halloween he would have this supposed decision to make. Red moonlight might only be a metaphor, but while Bash was anxious every Halloween ever since he'd gone into a trance and spoken those words—words he alone had heard and that he remembered well, though he didn't understand them—anytime the moon was red or even mildly orange on Halloween night, like tonight, he wondered if this would be the year.

"Thanks anyway. I'd rather keep working." Bash drummed his fingers along the edge of the car door, the passing lights highlighting his reflection in the window and the hues of his brown skin and wavy chestnut hair, as Deanna, his Second and surrogate sister, drove him through the city.

A clever decoration or costume would catch his eye on occasion. Centrus City took Halloween seriously. Even City Hall got away with fake spiderwebs at its corners, though come morning that would likely be accompanied by toilet paper.

"Let's finish the pickup," Bash said, "then join Siobhan on patrol. You know how the riffraff gets uppity on Halloween."

"Us shifters, you mean?" Deanna asked from beside him. "Or the humans in costume?"

"Exactly."

She chuckled, shaking out her bobbed black hair.

Shifters were a small subset of the population but powerful and influential in almost every major city. Most were run by wolves, like Bash, some by one of the many great cat packs, like Deanna's black panther lineage from Asia, others by wererats or scaled shifters. Bash was Alpha of Centrus City, but his inner circle wasn't made up of only one race. He welcomed everyone, wolves and cats and scales alike.

Other packs in other cities didn't appreciate how that scoffed at tradition, but Bash didn't care. Mixed company was better and made his pack stronger. It also kept the infighting down, which made it easier to ensure the supernatural remained under the radar to the average human who had no idea what went bump in the night far more frequently than only on Halloween.

Besides shifters, natural-born magic users, and intermittent encounters with vampires, there were a few other rare breeds that could crop up among the supernatural or humans alike. One of which was Seers, people with a gift for seeing into the future. Some saw visions, some spouted riddles, some both. A few were driven mad by their powers. Most had little control and didn't even remember what they prophesized.

That was Bash. He seldom remembered his prophecies, never saw anything clearly, and most of the riddles he spoke were lost if no one else was around to hear. The rarest of Seers had full control over their abilities and exploited them however they could, like Bash's mother when she'd been alive, but she'd died before he turned ten.

There were only two of Bash's prophecies that he remembered plainly: the one about Halloween and his first, when he was thirteen with his father and twin brother, Bari, who hadn't inherited the same abilities.

> *Fury begets fury and blood runs thin*
> *The son to take over for more than only him*
> *Father overshadowed for the shadow he once cast*
> *Your kingdom will be greater when your reign is in the past.*

Everything about Baraka Bain's attitude toward his children had changed after that. He was always a bastard, quick with his claws or a harsh word, even when their mother was alive, but his abuses grew unbearable. Baraka assumed Bari would be the one to kill him, since Bash always fell in line, while Bari was the outspoken one against their pack's occasional criminal dealings.

"Why does so much we do have to be illegal?" Bari would say. "Why do we have to hurt anyone? Living in the shadows doesn't mean we have to be villains."

So Baraka sent Bari to live with a sister city's pack.

Too bad for him he'd guessed the wrong twin.

Subservient as Bash had always been, he was eventually pushed too far without his brother around to share the load, and instead of avoiding the prophecy, Baraka had unknowingly caused it—even if it was a decade later.

Bash had the Halloween prophecy while standing over his father's dead body. Another decade later, he still wasn't sure what it meant, but it had haunted him ever since.

"I can see Siobhan waiting on us," Deanna said as they pulled up to the Rogues Gallery tattoo parlor.

It was one of their many fronts for money laundering and having ears on the ground, but Siobhan was a good artist. Deanna, too, when she wasn't chauffeuring Bash around. The neighborhood wasn't even the dicey kind but had a popular flower shop across the street and a bakery on the corner.

Officially, Siobhan was Bash's Warden, keeper of the peace between races, but everyone needed a cover job, and running the shop was hers. She had the week's spoils waiting. Bash didn't usually participate in pickups, but Halloween was a special night.

Deanna insisted on staying at Bash's side as his most trusted enforcer and Second of the pack—in place of Bari, since Bari didn't live in Centrus. He'd stayed away even after their father died, preferring to not get involved in anything shady. Bash respected that and never pushed. He wasn't like his father; his pack didn't hurt people unless that person earned it, but like most packs in most cities, the criminal side of their business had been set up long before Bash took over as Alpha, necessary in many cases to keep things running smoothly.

And truth be told, Bash liked a little cloak-and-dagger.

Sliding out of the car, Bash carried a natural grace that one might associate only with him being a wolf, but other shifters knew to be wary of that sort of calculated motion. He was a predator through and through, not one to be hunted, and he kept a keen eye on his surroundings with only a brief glance at the red-moon sky.

Tonight was a blood moon, during the most important negotiations of Bash's reign—working out a marriage arrangement with the Alpha of Brookdale, Jeffrey "Jay" Russell, to Bash himself, joining their packs together. It was the only option left that didn't involve bloodshed, considering how at odds Bash's father had been with the surrounding cities. Jay was the only Alpha willing to believe Bash could be different. Centrus and Brookdale combined would be too powerful for opportunistic takeovers.

It was a good deal, even if it was one of the few times when Bash would bow to tradition. He only had tonight off from talks because he'd requested it. Jay was a good sort, a good Alpha from what Bash could tell, but nothing could change that Bash had no interest in marriage other than duty. At least after the wedding and consummation, they could run their cities separately, but Bash was having a hard time getting that point across—as well as an allowance for other men and women in his bed—because Jay kept trying to woo him.

"Siobhan." Bash nodded when he and Deanna entered the shop. "How'd that interview go tonight?"

The shop was narrow but deep inside, with several stations for busy days and photos along the walls highlighting their artwork. They'd lost a couple artists recently and saw enough traffic that there was a Help Wanted sign in the window. They'd only take on another shifter, but Bash liked to see who else might frequent their door.

"A shame, actually." Siobhan hefted the bag of cash for Deanna to inspect.

She was a lizard, trim and slight compared to Deanna's taller, curvier build, with pixie-cut platinum hair and an impressive collection of tattoos, even up her neck to her jawline. Her honey-colored eyes were surreal enough that some might think she wore contacts, just like with Deanna's tint of violet.

"Best artist we've had come through," Siobhan continued. "Cute too. Young. Redhead. Has a record even, just out of prison in Glenwood and looking for a fresh start. Right up our alley. If only he wasn't human."

"Lambert, was it?" Bash asked.

"That's him."

"This his?" Bash noted the portfolio on the counter.

"Yeah, he left a copy. I said I'd show the boss. Maybe we can find him something elsewhere. A good turn for an ex-con and all."

"How altruistic," Bash said, but his smirk faded as he began to peruse the work. It wasn't what he expected and seemed... familiar.

"What can I say? He had an infectious personality," Siobhan said. "I liked him."

There were few actual tattoos in the portfolio, meaning this was a newbie, an artist who'd only recently taken up the trade of skin as his canvas. But what he did have was breathtaking, some photo realistic, some fantastical, some more traditional tattoos. The sketches that caught Bash's eye were intricate collages that would make impressive sleeves or full-body art, most rather grim too—death and macabre imagery of twisted bone and gore.

There was one.... Bash would swear it was like the corded flesh of one of his own worst scars. Another reminded him of his father's open rib cage after he'd killed him. But the last gave him the most pause—a beautiful woman with a third eye staring hauntingly back at him.

"Nothing special about the guy other than his skills and sunny disposition," Siobhan said. "Wouldn't guess he'd be cheerful given the art, though, right? Must have kept his head down in the clink."

"He say what he was in for?" Deanna asked, leaning against the counter.

"Falsifying evidence to get some scumbag put away for killing his son."

"*His* son?" Deanna questioned.

"Nah, Scumbag's son."

"Was Scumbag guilty?"

"Lambert thought so. Wife and daughter of the bastard did too. They used to send Lambert care packages as a thanks for trying. So, like I said, pity he's human. He might have magic in him, but it was hard to tell. Maybe Nell could look into it."

"Yes...." Bash closed the book. Involving a human in their work, unless they knew of their world and were touched by magic, would be too dangerous, but something nagged at him. He often felt this way on Halloween, but it was more than that. "Anything amiss tonight?"

"Not a peep."

"Mmm."

"Want me to load up the cash?" Deanna asked, hoisting the bag over her shoulder. "Maybe finish the other stops early? Still time to get a drink, Boss. Or ten."

"Did you close up the back yet?" Bash ignored Deanna's suggestion and moved around the counter.

"Not yet," Siobhan said slowly, catching on to his tone. "Why?"

"Been through there recently?"

"Something wrong?" Deanna pressed.

"I don't know. Just a feeling." Bash moved at a slow pace, eyes on the door. "Deanna, load the car. Meet me in the alley. Siobhan, lock the door behind me, then the front, and go start your patrols."

"You sure?" The hesitation was clear in Siobhan's voice.

"You know I don't like your 'feelings,'" Deanna said with a hint of a rumble in her voice.

"Just do it."

Continuing at a brisker pace until he reached the back of the shop, Bash stepped out into the alley with a soft click of the door behind him.

Blood. Not visible, but he could smell it. A lot of it. Impossible to detect inside the parlor, because it always carried a faint scent of blood due to the needle work, but outside, Bash had no doubts. Those who knew about him being a Seer knew his hunches were never wrong.

A man sprinted toward him and was stopped cold when Bash shot out an arm to catch him by the throat.

No, not a man.

A *vampire*.

The hiss and growl and snap of fangs made it difficult to hold the creature at bay, especially since he was strong—incredibly strong. Bash could barely contain him, which should not have been a challenge as an Alpha against a newborn, but that's what this vampire had to be, because Bash recognized him, and he hadn't been a vampire a few hours ago. The sire had to be powerful to create a fledgling this strong on its first night turned.

"A shame we couldn't offer you that job, Mr. Lambert," Bash said evenly. Poor man never even made it out of the neighborhood after his interview.

Lambert—*Ethan* Lambert, Bash recalled—snapped again with a click of fangs. A shame indeed, but this had to be Ethan. Bash would have known anyone else lurking about these streets, shifter or human, and the young vampire had natural red hair and a handsome face beneath the raging hunger, just how Siobhan had described him.

Shifter eyes glowed with power when they gave in to their true forms, but a vampire's changed entirely. They shone yellow when fed, amber when hungry, and red when feral. Ethan's eyes matched the moon above. What little control he might have had if he wasn't a newborn was buried in the back of his mind by the overwhelming need to feed.

"The hell?" Deanna bellowed from the mouth of the alley, throwing back her shoulders and letting her fangs and claws extend, her skin darkening to a deep indigo-black, fur sprouting rapidly across her skin. She was ready to tear the vampire to pieces as soon as Bash threw him her way, which was what Bash planned to do....

When he caught the glow of the scarlet moon above Ethan's head.

Somewhere deep within the red of Ethan's eyes was green. Bash couldn't see it, but he knew, like a vision of the man Ethan had once been, beautiful and smiling and utterly enchanting.

With a howl, Bash slammed Ethan's head down into the pavement once, twice, three times before he stilled.

"What did you do that for?" Deanna growled. "Rip his damn head off!"

"No," Bash said, the claws of the hand that had seized Ethan the only part of him changed, and now that too shifted back. He bent beside Ethan, whose fangs were still visible with his lips parted, but his eyes were closed, chest still since he no longer needed to breathe. "We're bringing him back to the den. I have questions."

"What?" Deanna balked, all towering force even as she shifted human, save the glow of her burning violet eyes. "That's a vampire, Bash! A parasite!"

"I'm aware, and we are taking him back with us. Now pick him up."

"Fat chance!"

"Deanna, I am your—"

"Fuck you, big shot Alpha! When you're being an idiot, you're just Bash, and you can't go bringing some fanger home when negotiations with Russell are heating up. If you ever thought a Halloween was the night, this is the one. Kill the guy and be done with it."

That was the easy answer, but if it was easy, why bother with a prophecy? When had a vampire even entered Bash's city? And what did it want? It couldn't be a coincidence that Ethan had been turned and left on Bash's doorstep.

Vampires were vermin, an infestation to be rid of if even one was discovered in pack territory. As they aged, they became far stronger than shifters, which was why they had to be eradicated before they spread, or they might take over. They were messy and foolish and too easily made feral, just like their wild newborns. Better to kill them on sight, always. Bash couldn't even remember the last time a vampire had been spotted in Centrus City.

But if the prophecy meant for Bash to kill Ethan, why have his art so entrancing? Why have his eyes cut through Bash like bullets? Why have every part of Bash's instincts screaming at him that killing was not the answer? There were too many connecting pieces for him to take the easy route like his father would have in his place.

"Pick him up. If I'm right, my future betrothed never needs to know."

"Yeah," Deanna scoffed despite bending to do as ordered, "and if you're wrong, we're all screwed."

K.L. "KAT" HIERS is an embalmer, restorative artist, and queer writer. Licensed in both funeral directing and funeral service, they worked in the death industry for nearly a decade. Their first love was always telling stories, and they have been writing for over twenty years, penning their very first book at just eight years old. Publishers generally do not accept manuscripts in Hello Kitty notebooks, however, but they never gave up.

Following the success of their first novel, *Cold Hard Cash*, they now enjoy writing professionally, focusing on spinning tales of sultry passion, exotic worlds, and emotional journeys. They love attending horror movie conventions and indulging in cosplay of their favorite characters. They live in Zebulon, NC, with their family, including their children, some of whom have paws and a few that only pretend to because they think it's cute.

Website: http://www.klhiers.com

Follow me on BookBub

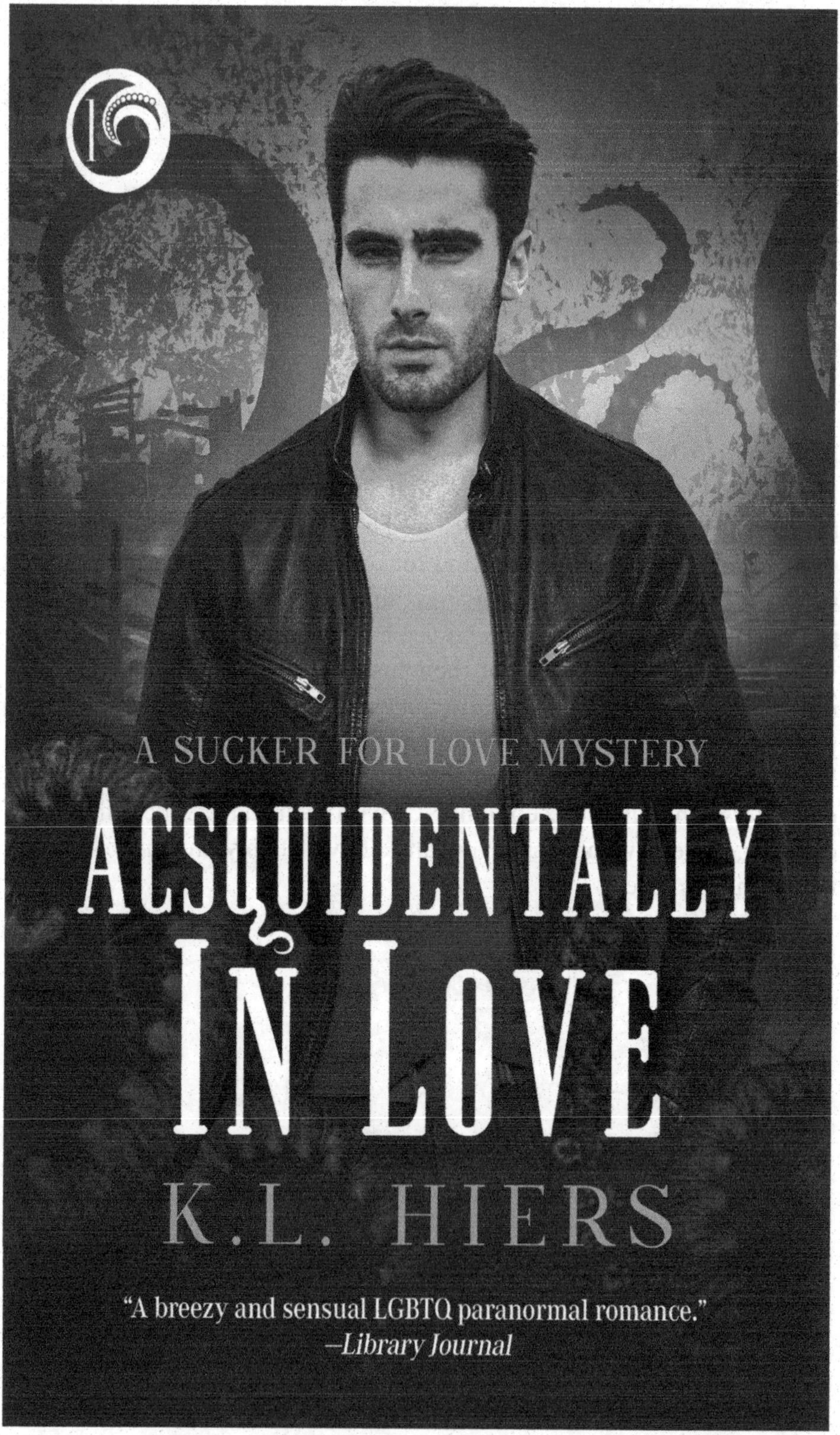
A SUCKER FOR LOVE MYSTERY
ACSQUIDENTALLY
IN LOVE
K.L. HIERS
"A breezy and sensual LGBTQ paranormal romance."
—Library Journal

A Sucker For Love Mystery

Nothing brings two men—or one man and an ancient god—together like revenge.

Private investigator Sloane sacrificed his career in law enforcement in pursuit of his parents' murderer. Like them, he is a follower of long-forgotten gods, practicing their magic and offering them his prayers… not that he's ever gotten a response.

Until now.

Azaethoth the Lesser might be the patron of thieves and tricksters, but he takes care of his followers. He's come to earth to avenge the killing of one of his favorites, and maybe charm the pants off the cute detective Fate has placed in his path. If he has his way, they'll do much more than bring a killer to justice. In fact, he's sure he's found the man he'll spend his immortal life with.

Sloane's resolve is crumbling under Azaethoth's surprising sweetness, and the tentacles he sometimes glimpses escaping the god's mortal form set his imagination alight. But their investigation gets stranger and deadlier with every turn. To survive, they'll need a little faith… and a lot of mystical firepower.

www.dreamspinnerpress.com

A SUCKER FOR LOVE MYSTERY

KRAKEN MY HEART

K.L. HIERS

"A breezy and sensual LGBTQ paranormal romance."
—*Library Journal*, *"Acsquidentally in Love"*

A Sucker For Love Mystery

It's just Ted's luck that he meets the love of his life while covered in the blood of a murder victim.

Funeral worker Ted Sturm has a foul mouth, a big heart, and a knack for communicating with the dead. Unfortunately the dead don't make very good friends, and Ted's only living pal, his roommate, just rescued a strange cat who's determined to make his life even more miserable. This cat is more than he seems, and soon Ted finds himself in an alternate dimension… and on top of a dead body.

When Ted is accused of murder, his only ally in a strange world full of powerful magical beings calling for his head is King Grell, a sarcastic, randy, catlike immortal with impressive abilities… and anatomy. The two soon find themselves at the center of a cosmic conspiracy and surrounded by dangerous enemies. But with Ted's special skills and Grell's magic, they have a chance to get to the bottom of the mystery and save Ted. There's just one problem: Ted's got to resist Grell's aggressive advances… and he isn't sure he wants to.

www.dreamspinnerpress.com

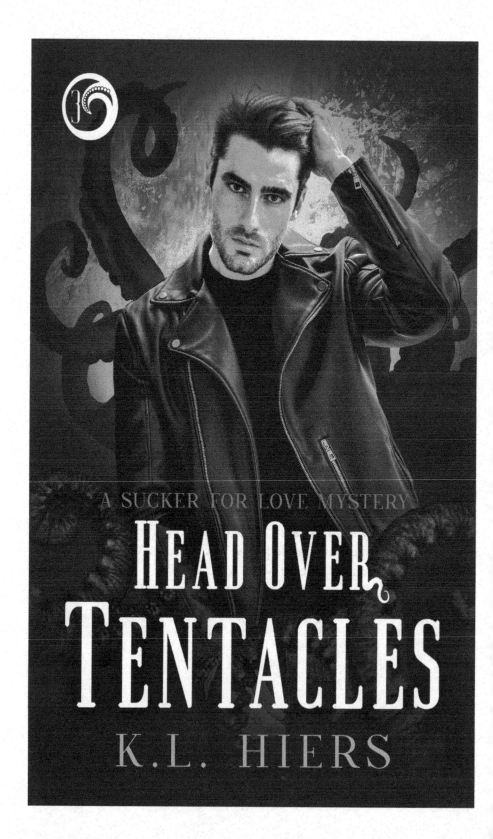

A SUCKER FOR LOVE MYSTERY

HEAD OVER
TENTACLES

K.L. HIERS

A Sucker For Love Mystery

Private investigator Sloane Beaumont should be enjoying his recent engagement to eldritch god Azaethoth the Lesser, AKA Loch. Unfortunately, he doesn't have time for a pre-honeymoon period.

The trouble starts with a deceptively simple missing persons case. That leads to the discovery of mass kidnappings, nefarious secret experiments, and the revelation that another ancient god is trying to bring about the end of the world by twisting humans into an evil army.

Just another day at the office.

Sloane does his best to juggle wedding planning, stopping his fiancé from turning the mailman inside out, and meeting his future godly in-laws while working the case, but they're also being hunted by a strange young man with incredible abilities. With the wedding date looming closer, Sloane and Loch must combine their powers to discover the truth—because it's not just their own happy-ever-after at stake, but the fate of the world….

www.dreamspinnerpress.com

A SUCKER FOR LOVE MYSTERY

NAUTILUS THAN
PERFECT

K.L. HIERS

A Sucker For Love Mystery

Detective Elwood Q. Chase has ninety-nine problems, and the unexpected revelation that his partner is a god is only one of them.

Chase has been in love with Benjamin Merrick for years and has resigned himself to a life of unrequited pining. But when they run afoul of a strange cult, Merrick's secret identity as Gordoth the Untouched slips out… and so do Chase's feelings. The timing can't be helped, but now Merrick thinks Chase only cares about him because he's a god.

Even more unfortunately, it turns out the cultists want to perform a ritual to end the world. Chase's mission to convince Merrick his feelings predate any divine revelations takes a back seat to a case tangled with murder and lies, but Chase doesn't give up. Once he finds out there's a chance Merrick feels the same way, he digs in his heels. Suddenly he's trying to court a god and save the world at the same time. What could possibly go wrong?

www.dreamspinnerpress.com

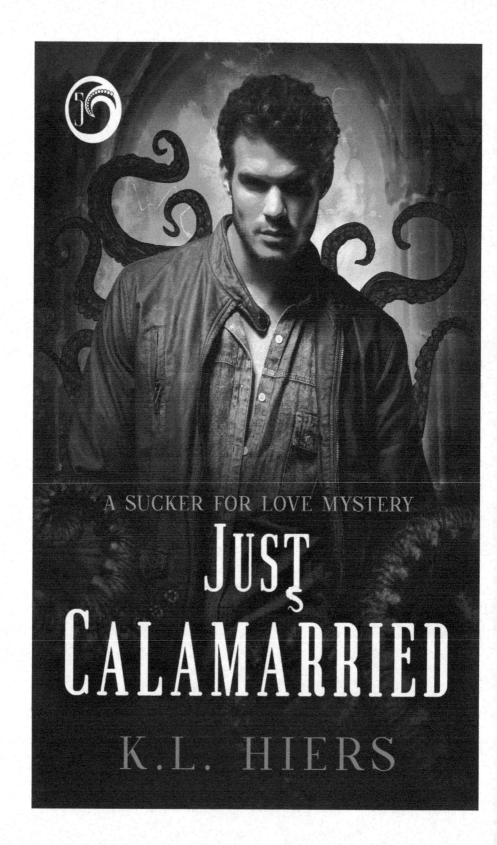

A SUCKER FOR LOVE MYSTERY

JUST
CALAMARRIED

K.L. HIERS

A Sucker For Love Mystery

Newlyweds Sloane and Loch are eagerly expecting their first child, though for Sloane that excitement is tempered by pregnancy side effects. Carrying a god's baby would be enough to deal with, especially with the whole accelerated gestation thing, but it's not like Sloane can take maternity leave. He works for himself as a private investigator. Which leads him to his next case.

At least this strange new mystery distracts him from the stress of constant puking.

When two priests are murdered within hours of each other, a woman named Daphne hires Sloane and Loch to track down the prime suspect— her brother—before the police do. Between untangling a conspiracy of lies and greed, going toe-to-toe with a gangster, and stealing a cat, they hardly have time to decorate a nursery....

www.dreamspinnerpress.com